Match the Hatch

HORSE DOCTOR ADVENTURES

ELIZABETH WOOLSEY

HORSE DOCTOR PRESS

Also By

The Travels of Dr. Rebecca Harper Series

Book 1 A Matter of Time

Book 2 Troubled Waters

Book 3 Lauren's Story

Book 4 Past and Present

Catch and Release Series

Book 1 Catch and Release (Horse Doctor Adventures)

Book 2 Catch and Keep (Horse Doctor Adventures)

Book 3 Match the Hatch (Horse Doctor Adventures)

Small Town Secrets (Horse Doctor Adventures)

A Man's Worth (Horse Doctor Adventures)

Jack's War (Letters to home from an American WWII Navigator)

Parkside Veterinary Clinic (I Want to be a Vet)

Horse Doctor (An American Vet's Life Down under)

You know where I say this book is a work of fiction
and all the characters are made up?
I lied.
Read it and see if you can find yourself.
This one's for you.

But Jensen Centenera,
this book is especially for you.

Chapter 1

I felt my phone vibrating. It was daylight, and I was still in bed. Who would call me? *Oh, my head. Hello. My name is Maggie Kincaid, and I am a once-a-year alcoholic.* I blame my family. The rehearsal dinner was a grog-fest in the true Australian tradition. Before I returned to my cabin, my children all high-fived one another on a successful "piss-up." Yep, it was the traditional alcoholic-fueled orgy that my Australian-born kids expected.

I reached for the phone and dropped it twice before I answered it. I didn't have my reading glasses, and considering my condition, I wasn't sure the glasses would help, anyway. "Hello? Not sure who you are, but it'd better be good."

"It's your soon-to-be husband. Where are the rings, darlin'?"

"In the safe, where you put them. Collie, what are you doing up so early?"

"Are you serious? You realize I'm cooking breakfast for about thirty people?"

"Where's Mrs. Gillard?" Mrs. Gillard was Colin Chandler's housekeeper and the kitchen goddess that made my life worth living. "Breakfast isn't until nine. I wish you would reconsider and let me come."

"Not a chance, and Mrs. G. won't be here for another hour. You aren't allowed over here until the ceremony. I'm not risking the traditional wedding luck by seeing you before the event."

"I think you're being ridiculous, but I'm not dying on that hill. I'll be fishing if I can clear my brain and lose the hangover while you're entertaining the guests. Stay away from the river if you insist on testing my limits, Collie."

"You aren't allowed on my... oops, I mean our property until after the wedding. Just get your Princess Diana wedding dress out of the mothballs and stay home."

I laughed, thinking about my wedding-dress procurement from an Op-Shop, short for opportunity shop, in Australia earlier this year. Op-Shop was another Australian term I preferred over the American secondhand store moniker. The shop owner assured me it was just like Princess Diana's dress.

Thankfully, she was so wrong. It was beautiful and modern. I had to pay more than I had budgeted. Then I remembered the Australian dollar was only seventy-eight cents on the US dollar, bringing it back into my budget. The price was from seventy-nine to seventy-five dollars, depending on the veil. Screw the veil.

The shocker was that my daughter approved. From seven years of age, she announced she was adopted—no fashionista could be related to such a poor dresser. Now, as an adult with children of her own, she still endeavored to advise me on current fashion trends—fail.

"Okay, I won't come over." Behind my log cabin is a national forest with trails and a beautiful lake. "Can you have Luke bring Digger over so I can go to Saddleback Lake to get my fix?" Digger was the horse that clinched my acceptance of Colin's wedding proposal—good-looking, talented, and old-lady-broke-to-death. He was the horse of my dreams. Colin had given him to me when I helped Colin's grandson emerge from a long period during which he didn't speak after watching his mother when she was violently killed in a drug deal gone wrong. Wedding or not—Digger was mine.

"Uh, no. Not gonna happen, darlin'. Magpie, you're testing my limits. You're sadly mistaken if you think this day is for the bride alone. You agreed to the schedule."

My children and grandchildren were already staying with Colin and Luke, my soon-to-be grandson by marriage. My sister, brother, and their spouses were here next door with me in my cabin.

"If Christy isn't feeling well, you can entertain her, but breakfast is at nine, and I expect you to make sure the rest of your family is over here."

The plan was for the bride and groom to be separated until the ceremony at three. Colin would entertain the guests before the wedding. He thought I would need hours to prepare, but my daughter Colleen and my sister Christy would help me. I knew it would be a thirty-minute job.

"Back to the main reason for the call. I can't find the rings. I checked the safe, but they aren't there."

"Not a clue, beautiful boy. The rings are your department. If Luke brought Digger over, I might remember where they are, but..."

"Darlin', Digger will give your grandchildren rides today."

"You win. Check the top drawer of my dresser." I realized Digger might encourage my grandchildren to become interested in riding. How did I fail? Not one of my children was interested in equestrian sports. I'd need to count on the "generational-skip" concept that my parents often discussed.

I rarely fly-fished in Australia, so I could understand them not following me in my other obsession. Like most parents, I worried about not passing on my values. I failed to teach them many things. So far, they've been upstanding and contributing citizens—one arrest for drunk and disorderly behavior aside. They were kind kids, and I was proud of them and loved the grandchildren.

"Maggie, I can't believe our wedding is today. Knowing everything that happened to you since we met, will you please stay at home and do as I ask? I'm simply asking, not demanding. I know where that would go. Please?"

"Well, when you put it that way... How are Lauren and Dr. Harper doing?"

"The Kennedys are still asleep. Jeff's helping me in the kitchen. Darlin', I hate to go, but—" Colin paused, and I could hear drawers opening and closing. "Damn, see you at the altar. Don't be late." I heard him yell for Luke. I knew Luke would know where Colin had placed the rings. He was so keen to have us married.

"Found them?"

"Not yet, but I have a few hours."

"Hey, can you believe the chances of meeting my classmate's daughter in Australia? If Becky were alive, she'd be so proud of Lauren. I'm so pleased she coaxed her father and stepmom into joining us for the wedding. Collie, I love you."

Jeff Harper was my lecturer in vet school. He taught reproduction. He married Becky, my roommate, during our first years of vet school. Lauren was Jeff's daughter from his first marriage, which ended when Becky was killed in a rock slide. Lauren was married to Jim Kennedy, who was also a vet. Meeting Lauren when I did my last relief job for my old vet clinic in Australia was so unexpected.

"I love you too, darlin'. See you later. Oh, no more alcohol until tonight."

"Gelding Collie. Don't try to boss me yet."

"Just a suggestion. Hmm, I need to trim my nails."

Colin and I had cautionary words to signal when one or the other of us went too far for what we referred to as negotiations. Mine was "gelding," which could be a noun denoting a castrated horse or the verb that meant the act of castration. My cue was the verb form—the act of castration.

He decided his cautionary word was not a word, but a single finger pointed upward. Knowing I couldn't see his finger, that was an 'audible.' "Later, beautiful boy. I'm considering my options. The nail trimmers are in the top drawer of my cabinet." Best to keep him guessing. *Please God, one year, but then again, I'll gratefully accept ten more.*

My sister knocked at my bedroom door. "Maggie, a man is at the door. He says he needs to speak to you. I've made coffee. Come on down."

"Coming." Who the hell would be at my door at six-thirty in the morning? *Whoa, even standing up is making me nauseous.*

I threw on a robe and staggered down the stairs to my great room. Standing at the door was a man in a boy scout-like uniform. He looked disheveled and distressed. He was rotund and appeared as a man who'd been up all night. I could see the agony on his face.

"May I help you?"

Chapter 2

"I'm so sorry to bother you. We're searching for a young teenager who's missing in the forest. We'd like to explore your property."

What was going on? I was somewhere between concerned and annoyed. *It's my wedding day, for God's sake.* Then again, a child might be lost in the woods. I couldn't ignore it.

"How long has he been missing? Of course, you can search anywhere you wish. Have you looked in my barn? I can open the garage. What's your organization? I don't recognize the uniform."

I put on some shoes and headed to the barn. Christy stood at the door and said she'd keep the coffee hot, while I allowed this man to search my property. I knew Digger was over at Colin's, so the barn should be empty.

"My name is Andy Chalmers. Our organization is called The Second Chance. We're from the city, and we give at-risk kids experiences we hope will divert them from a life of crime."

He didn't appear to be much of a role model, but maybe I was too critical. Who would have thought I could be a role model for Colin's grandson when I arrived a year ago?

There was no evidence of anyone entering either the barn or garage. I explained I was getting married today, so I wouldn't be available. I suggested that Mr. Chalmers call the sheriff's office to report the missing boy. It was still late spring, and the nights could be cold. Mr. Chalmers retreated into the woods. I called Colin about the encounter. He said he would send a few ranch hands to assist with the search.

Christy and I had a rare chance to be alone, so we took our coffee to my room upstairs. She and her husband, Miles, arrived from the Bay Area yesterday. Her leukemia was in remission. Still, we were aware it could resurface. She wasted no time on niceties—she never had before her illness. "So, Baby Sister. You and the old geezer. Who'd a thunk it?"

"Yeah, not me." I smiled, thinking about how this romance had progressed from a 'not in a million years' to a wedding today. "How's his health?" Christy sat smugly, sipping her coffee.

"Better than yours, but it's a lottery. Hopefully, Collie will outlive me, but you never know." I was eleven years his junior, but his aging genes, or lack thereof, as I like to think of it, were superior to mine.

"Collie told me you're taken care of until you die. Would you ever consider remarrying if you know what happened?"

"Jesus, Christy, I never considered remarriage after the accent, any-way." I had referred to my Australian ex as 'the accent,' since our divorce many years earlier. "Collie's a skilled card player, and he waited until I was vulnerable and made his play. Never play for money with this man. You'll be left dead broke. The worst part is that he was so nice about it while he skewered my heart."

"Yeah. I'm putty in his presence. So, no regrets?" Christy sipped her coffee.

I smiled and shook my head. I glanced out past my creek and toward the forest. "Gee, I sure hope they find the boy. I wonder what's going on with this group of kids and this organization." I doubted if Colin knew about them.

I headed downstairs to the kitchen to refill Christie's cup as my sister-in-law emerged from her bedroom. I held out a cup, and Lonnie shook her head as she entered the bathroom. She whispered, "I need another hour. Oh, happy wedding day."

I shook my head, knowing that Lonnie's current state was self-inflicted, as was mine. Lonnie and I had exceeded our limits last night. On the way from Colin's house to mine, we promised never to do it again. *What happens when you go against a pinky promise? Is there a pinky-promise fairy who makes life hell for you?*

From the other side of the bathroom door, I whispered, "Hydration is the key to salvation," and returned to my room to find Christy asleep. I covered her as I moved over to the window to scan the valley and forest beyond my creek.

I hoped they would find the boy. I observed Gabe Turner and Whit Williams, two of Colin's ranch hands, emerge from Colin's property, cross my creek, and ride their horses into the forest. Colin hired the men for their security skills and ability to manage the property and stock. Gabe and his wife, Betty Lou, had saved my life earlier in the year when my former real-estate agent held me at gunpoint.

I returned to my computer, which was full of many emails with well-wishes from Australia and around the world after we went public with our wedding plans. There had to be ten new ones since I had last checked my inbox. I knew almost all the senders and would reply to them all.

One stood out this morning. I didn't recognize the address. The heading said, "Good luck." The message read, "You'll need it. You're a fool. You will soon regret this. Ask me how I know." I would not reply to that one. The address was cchc@gmail.com. *What the hell?*

Chapter 3

I stared at the email, after which I hit the delete button. I knew that marrying a famous person would bring adversity. Despite his age and rare public appearances, Colin Chandler was still a public figure. Colin had admirers who would be envious of me. While I'd become "almost famous" from my books and adventures, my life was relatively private. My email address was not. *Recalculating route.*

I'll get a new email address, and let my agent deal with this mail from now on, but even my agent, who was based in Australia, was clueless that I'd resurfaced. I'd taken a break from writing and my author's social world, following the debacle with Charlie McLeod's fall from grace and eventual death. I'd inform my agent when the festivities were over later in the week. Colin and I had postponed the honeymoon until July. We'd celebrate with our wedding guests for the next three days. We planned to helicopter Lauren and her family on a fly-fishing trip to Colin's favorite remote river.

Colin would concentrate on Lauren, Jim Kennedy, and Lauren's father, Dr. Harper. I would entertain the rest. Luke and Jim Kennedy appeared to be glued to the hip. They met while we were at my old vet clinic in Australia earlier this year.

I planned to shower before the wedding. I dressed in jeans and a sweater. My family members stirred and emerged from their rooms. They were all heading to Colin's for breakfast, but they shared coffee with me before they left. I rehearsed my vows and speech for the party after the wedding. My anxiety took over. Christy was no help. She observed my hungover face and declared there was no way to fix the damage from the previous night's debauchery.

Christy went to Colin's with her husband, Miles. I was by myself until my brother and sister-in-law, Bill and Lonnie, eventually joined me. Despite a headache, Bill and Lonnie went to Colin's for breakfast. This left me alone to ponder the last few hours of my single life—twenty years between drinks—so to speak.

I glanced out the windows in the great room. I watched to see if I could detect anything amiss, which might show the boy had come this way. The chances were infinitesimal, but if I didn't look, I might miss an opportunity to help locate the boy. I risked a few minutes from my planned wedding preparations and walked down to the creek. The ranch hands had constructed a new bridge over the little brook. The snowmelt made the stream almost a river, and the overpass became extremely handy.

As I walked over the bridge, I heard Lauren Kennedy call out. "May I join you?"

"Sure." I waved her over and was glad for her company. She was a taller version of her deceased mother. I had yet to observe her fly-casting skills, but I knew that tomorrow, she and I would have some time together to fish in Colin's remote river. "How was your room?" We wanted to make sure everyone was comfortable. "Is there anything we can do to make you all welcome? Of course, until this afternoon, I'm in purgatory, but once the ceremony is over, I'll be happy to do what it takes to make you want to come back. Is Collie taking your dad for a ride in his Gator to see the river?"

"Don't stress. They're bonded. I hope my mom isn't abandoned." Many guests arrived last night. Lauren's stepmom, Sherry Harper, and my office manager had discussed Lauren's time in Australia.

My secretary, Jodie, had arrived in the middle of the afternoon by helicopter. Colin had arranged for Doug Cameron to fly her and her husband over from the airport. Jodie and Lauren reacquainted themselves with the clinic gossip and outcome of a few cases. A few of my friends would still arrive this morning.

I asked Lauren how she slept and wanted to know if she'd fished yet. "Did you go down to the river?"

"You mean fish heaven? Sure did." Lauren peered down into the water. "Hey, this creek has fish, too."

"Yes, a few smaller ones. Bill and Miles deepened some pools to make it a happier home for them in this little creek. It's probably illegal, but more trout are here this year than they were last year."

We walked over the bridge and took a trail into the woods. The forest service didn't maintain the trails in this area, but Colin planned to have the ranch hands do some repairs and upgrades after the wedding. I forgot to ask Lauren if she knew about the boy.

"Yeah, Colin told me. Maggie, did you watch the television series *Comstock* when you were young?"

"Of course. All America watched it." I smiled, thinking about sitting with my sister and brother watching television when we were young. "You were too young, but I know Becky did. We used the theme song as a signal to each other. One of us would hum it when we saw a cute cowboy. It never failed to make us laugh. If Becky hummed the tune, I would laugh, and she would wink. We never got further than a few bars before we were hysterically giggling. Gee, I miss her." I stared off into the woods as tears formed. Curiously, Lauren didn't seem emotionally affected by memories of her mother. She simply smiled and appeared utterly happy.

I led the way through the forest. "I would love to find the poor kid before the wedding. I saw Gabe and Whit head over here on horseback. Have you met any of the ranch hands? If anyone could find the youngster, they could. They are more familiar with the area than anyone else is. I'll take you to Saddleback Lake to show you some nice fishing holes. Before you return to Nevada."

"That would be great. Do you think my father could get back there? He still hikes around his property. When my little sister left for college, Dad and Mom finally moved closer to the Smokies."

"Your brother and sister are from Sherry, aren't they?"

"Yep. You would never know we aren't all full brother and sisters. It's never discussed, and my mom or aunt is pretty much my mom, as far as I'm concerned."

"I'm glad you're so happy with your life. Becky would've been so proud to have you as a daughter. When I fall off the perch, I'd want my kids to enjoy their lives."

We walked on and, suddenly, I heard some yelling from around a bend. "Come here, you little shit, or I'm going to shoot you. You won't make it out alive if you give me any more problems."

Lauren and I ran to the source of the argument and discovered the man who had approached my house, looking for the missing boy. Andy Chalmers held the boy by his shirt as he frog-marched him back toward the lake.

We stepped out from behind a large boulder. "Mr. Chalmers, we meet again." Andy Chalmers was a deer in the headlights. The boy, who appeared to be maybe Luke's age, was dirty and frightened.

"Good news. This isn't the boy I was searching for earlier. He's already back in camp by the lake. We're just role-playing. We have a play this evening, and we're studying our parts."

"Huh?" It sure sounded like someone was in danger. I stared at the boy, who would not look at me. "Are you alright, son?"

The boy didn't answer. Andy Chalmers shook the boy and told him to speak.

He mumbled without glancing in my direction. "I'm fine."

I doubted it. Something was going on. I heard horses approaching and was relieved to see Gabe and Whit come around the corner.

"Morning, Maggie. Seems like they found the lad."

I smiled and nodded, but Lauren and I thought otherwise. Lauren walked toward the boy and placed her hand on his shoulder. She saw a small laceration behind his ear. "Is that blood?"

Andy Chalmers was quick to respond. "He caught it on a tree limb while zip lining. We have so many adventures with the boys. Keeps them off the streets for a few weeks and helps break the cycle."

"Oh, of course. I guess the boys have all had their vaccines?" Lauren was onto it.

Whit and Gabe were suspicious as well. I observed them glance at each other and understood what they were thinking. "Our boss needs to get home to prepare for this afternoon, so how about we guide you back to your camp? You're kinda far from your base."

"Thanks, Whit. You're so right. I have hair, makeup, and nails to do. I have only three hours, but it will probably take me twenty minutes. The rest of my family will take longer. I'd better get home." I turned toward Andy Chalmers. "Good luck with your little endeavor."

"Idle hands are the devil's workshop, ma'am." Mr. Chalmers turned the reluctant boy toward the trail.

"Gentlemen, I have a date at the altar." I smiled at Gabe, and I was convinced he would explore this camp.

Lauren and I left the three men and the boy and returned to my cabin. Lauren headed back to Colin's. She mentioned her dad would go for a drive with Colin and might try a quick cast or two. "You know, they may be late for your wedding. We have a history of wedding mayhem." The glint in her eye made me wonder about her wedding. I would ask later.

I considered our last hour in the woods. "You know, Lauren. I don't see a reason to worry anyone about what we saw—at least for today."

"Yeah. No need." Lauren turned toward Colin's ranch to rejoin the festivities.

Chapter 4

"Only three hours, Maggot, and you expect me to perform a miracle?" Christy gazed at my face, turned to my daughter, smiled, and winked.

"Do I smell alcohol?" I knew Colin planned to serve a champagne breakfast. It surprised me that Christy was drinking, considering her recent battle with leukemia. "Whatever floats your boat, I guess." I knew Colleen would not hold back. Colleen was my second bridesmaid. Colin instructed the bride's entourage to dress at my cabin.

"Mum, I could get used to that man."

"Yeah, me too." Christy walked down the stairs to fetch her make-up kit. "Have you got any spackle in the house?" This made me laugh.

"I need to eat something. Unlike you guys, I didn't have a five-star breakfast."

"Mum, if you expect to fit into that dress, I'd advise a carrot and a piece of celery."

"Okay, you two. Enough of the teasing. Today's my big day, and I need some support."

"Uh, I don't think they make iron trusses anymore."

"I'm making a peanut butter sandwich. Anyone want anything to eat? The next order of business is a shower. You two can powwow and prepare for the slagging at the reception." I dreaded the roasting, or, as my Australian family called it, slagging, which I would receive later in the day.

"Mum, slagging would put it mildly. My bros are on it. I said I would defer to them for once."

Christy walked back into my bedroom as I went into the bathroom. "Hey, I hear your mailbox going off on your computer. Do you want me to see what it is?"

I remembered the nasty email and didn't want to alarm anyone, but if murdered, I wanted a witness. "Sure." When I returned, my sister and daughter were staring at the computer.

"I think you'd better look at this." They appeared shocked. I came to the side of the bed where they sat, holding my laptop. A video showed someone decapitating a chicken, which repeated on a loop.

"What the?" It was from the same Gmail account, and the subject was "Your Fate." We almost didn't detect the small attachment. It was a picture of my mailbox, where my driveway met the road.

Christy wanted to know whether it was a joke. I could see nothing to identify the sender. "I'm sure it is. A pretty sick joke, though. Hey, this is my wedding day." I turned off the computer and laughed. I wasn't certain I fooled anyone, but that was beyond the pale. Colin and I would discuss it later. "Do you mind keeping it to yourselves? I don't want to ruin Collie's big day."

"Do you think it's for real?"

"Who knows? I won't let it spoil our wedding day. That's for sure."

"Mum, I reinstate my plea to move back home. These people are all crazy, and they all have guns."

"I'll think about it." I looked up at the ceiling and laughed. "Nope. Shall we start on the war paint?"

My phone rang while I dried my hair. "Can you see who it is?"

Christy glanced at the phone. "It's a silent number. Want me to answer it?"

I couldn't think of whom I knew with a silent number. "No, I'm sure it's a telemarketer." But I wasn't sure.

"Mum, what was your wedding to Dad like? How come you don't have any pictures?"

"It was nice and a wonderful day. I was so in love and excited." I would never tell my kids the truth. It was anything but that. The last time I saw my ex was when the last grandchild was born, and I was invited to see the baby. Colleen had secretly arranged for us to come at the same time. My ex had not changed. He was charming, appeared to care for everyone, and wanted us to get together more often. He even asked to take me to dinner. *Uh, no thanks.*

I protected the kids from his infidelity and the other issues that plagued our marriage. Colleen was Daddy's girl. Colleen had no reason to hate her father. The boys appeared to see through his antics, but Colleen was still his defender.

My other family members returned from Colin's house to prepare for the wedding. While I insisted their wedding attire be casual, they had other plans. Miles and Bill had a quick fish, and each had caught trout. They recounted an informative discussion with Jodie, who told them stories about our lives in Australia. They mentioned that Dr. Harper also fished. He and Colin were expert fly-casters, and Bill and Miles received a lesson in casting.

One of the ranch hands was scheduled to drive over to pick up everyone, except for Bill and me, while a second car would retrieve us just before the ceremony. The boys wasted no time. Colin had stocked this fridge with beer and wine.

There were no official bridesmaids' dresses. Colleen and Christy each had new outfits, but nothing matched. "You all can change your minds and wear jeans, you know."

"Magster, we take our directions from your soon-to-be-better half. Get over any notion that you have a say in the day's activities." Bill was in his element. It was the first time he had a role in a wedding. Their daughter had a quiet, civil ceremony. He was so pleased to be asked to walk me down the aisle to give me away.

Lonnie was concerned about the amount of alcohol Bill had consumed. "You realize they expect you to walk in a straight line, honey?"

"Mag Wheel will keep me straight." I was now worried. It was a small gathering of our family and friends, but if Bill fell during the ceremony, I would kill him.

Chapter 5

Get me to the chapel on time. Well, that didn't happen. It was a comedy of errors, but it was more like a dog's breakfast. Of course, I was the star, and besides the grandkids, I may have been the only sober person there. Sadly, that was my first impression.

Whit Williams drove up in one of the ranch SUVs to collect my family. That left Bill and me. Bill slurred his words. Even Christy imbibed despite her doctor's orders to drink in moderation, if at all. My family ignored my pleas for restraint.

Bill and I sat in my cabin for thirty minutes without the second vehicle arriving to transport the bride. The ceremony was scheduled to start at three, and it was now three-twenty. My phone calls to Colin and Luke went unanswered. Luke would be sober and, as an adolescent, would surely have his phone. Bill continued to drink. I was apoplectic. I attempted to walk over to Colin's through the woods and gate. The gate was locked. I could always walk down to my creek, follow it to the river, and walk up to the wedding venue, but that would take forever and ruin my dress. There was no way Bill would make it.

I considered my options. I recalled my car was in the garage. I pulled Bill up off the couch and headed down to my car. Thankfully, I always left my keys in the ignition—apparently, not always. I reached under the seat and searched all around—no keys.

Finally, Gabe drove up in Colin's favorite truck and, without an explanation, simply said, "Sorry."

I was too mad to say anything. Gabe helped Bill into the front seat, and I crammed myself and the dress into the back seat. *Oh, Lord, please let the rest of the day go as planned.*

Nope—well, not my plan.

I arrived at the wedding venue and was escorted to an area where no one could see me. Christy came over with the bouquet and told me off for being such a sourpuss. Everyone was having a great time, and even the kids were playing dodgeball with the floral decorations. A string quartet was playing music from the Four Seasons—what the?

Bill was weaving, and Christy didn't appear much better. I heard the cadence for the start of the wedding march. "Okay, big bro, let's march." As I stepped out to face the newly created podium, I noticed the boys dressed in suits reminiscent of the Four Seasons 1950s outfits, which made me giggle. Luke was smiling and nodding. The rest, including Colin, were swaying.

"Here Comes the Bride" paused while the tune changed to "Big Girls Don't Cry," sung by Colin, his two boys, and Luke.

Bill, who was still barely standing, suddenly appeared to sober up and said, "Let's do this." Colin and his sons also seemed to be sober. Sam Hampstead walked out from behind the boys to assume his place as the minister. He smiled as I approached the podium.

Sam slurred, "Welcome to the thelebration of the joining of theeths two old geezers. I mean Colin and Maggie. Or thould I have that'd, Maggie and Colin?" I was still down the aisle with Bill, who appeared worried but sober. Bill squeezed my hand.

Sam swayed. "So, let's get thith party started. I know this is a Four Theason's theme, but I may take the initiative to frow in a few of my favorite fongs. Ah hmm. So whoth giving her away, and who would take her?"

I peered up at the podium. My God, the minister was drunk. I was so far past mad I was edging over to hysterical and beginning to get the giggles. This started Bill and Christy off. Bill showed no further signs of intoxication. The rest of the group followed, and soon everyone laughed. Sam gazed up and chuckled, and I realized this was all a joke on me. They suddenly appeared to be sober. Colin stared smugly at me and winked.

Bill said, "I'm getting rid of her." Bill kissed me and walked me to the edge of the podium.

Colin extended his hand and helped me walk up the steps to stand beside him. He put his arm around my waist as I stood by his side. "If no one else objects, I'll have her."

My son, Brandon, stood, turned to the crowd, and announced in front of even the grandkids. "Think twice, Collie. She's a ball-buster." I rolled my eyes, thinking of the grandchildren still playing dodgeball.

Colin squeezed my waist. "I think she's met her equal. The cowgirl reeducation and enlightenment classes are in session. I think I've matched the hatch."

I shook my head, recognizing I'd been fooled for weeks. After a prayer and a reading from the Bible, Sam asked us to say our vows. I went first.

"Okay, beautiful boy, I want you to know that I love you with all my heart—true as true. I feel like the luckiest woman on earth at this moment. You make me laugh, and you make me feel safe. I pledge to support, love, and care for you forever. If you planned for anything else today, darling, the operative word is gelding—you know—the verb."

It was Colin's turn. He held up a finger. "Well, I don't want to waste any time at my age." He reached into his pocket, brought out several sheets of folded paper, and opened them. "Oh, hell." He threw them down. "Maggie, Margaret, Magster, Maggot, and, let's not forget, Darlin'. Despite the facts, I love you. So, what are the facts? Maggie likes to trespass on other people's property. She can't hang a gate to save her soul. You can make a sailor blush with your use of the entire vocabulary of known swear words. She casts a fly like a girl, yet she dresses like a boy."

Colin stopped, looked at me, and laughed. "Well, maybe not today. You seem to get yourself into all kinds of dramas. You make my poor grandson work for a car. Enough of the questionable points. What you can't do in a tight squeeze is nobody's business." Colin turned to take my hands. "You make me laugh. Darlin', you make me feel loved, and you have brought joy to me and my family's lives. I will honor and cherish you, and I'll never ask you to obey, as I know I'd waste my breath."

I had tears. Colin had tears, and even Sam wiped his eyes. "Now for the rings."

Colin reached into his pockets and searched on the ground. He pulled his pocket out of his pants, displaying a large hole. Colin turned to his two sons, who shook their heads while searching their pockets. I glanced at Luke, who appeared to be genuinely upset. Luke went to the back of the podium and searched under the structure. He stood and shook his head as he returned to his grandfather's side. Luke whispered to his grandfather, who turned to Sam. "How soon do you have to leave? Do we have to have rings to make it legal?"

I gazed out at the uncomfortable, murmuring crowd. My tears of joy were turning into different tears. Was Colin beginning to show signs of memory loss?

Sam shook his head. "Colin, you know I have another wedding. Can you borrow someone's ring? No ring, no wedding—you know my rules."

Colin turned away from me and gave an ear-piercing whistle. I heard a horse approaching the venue from a distance and saw a riderless Digger gallop up to the podium base. He was groomed with a garland of roses over his saddle. Around his neck was a satin sash. Dangling from it was a small gold purse. Luke walked down, untied the bag, handed it to Colin, and returned to the podium. Gabe walked up to lead Digger away. Colin removed the rings from the purse, placed one ring on my finger, and said, "For better or for even better." His hand shook as he put the ring on my finger.

I took the second ring from Colin, placed it on his finger, and gazed up to his eyes, which brimmed. I smiled. "Game on, beautiful boy, saddle up, and get ready to ride."

Sam pronounced, "Done deal. Kiss your heathen bride and get me some alcohol." The ensemble played the traditional wedding music and abruptly switched to "Walk Like a Man." Colin and I stepped from the podium as the wedding guests sang. The entire audience was high fiving one another. I then knew they were all in on it. I'd been pranked.

Chapter 6

Colin's boys were the first to kiss me, but my actual intention was to get to Luke. "So much trouble, mister. So much trouble. I'm pretty sure back tickling as you know it is over for at least two months."

He smugly replied, "Totally worth it."

Jodie and her husband were at the front of the queue. "And I thought you were my friend. No secrets? I think the Uber will be here in a few minutes to take you to the airport."

"If I had to walk to the airport, I would still have gone along with it." Jodie hugged me and whispered. "Payback is a bitch."

Lauren and Jim Kennedy and Lauren's father and mother were all giggling. I walked over to them. "I suppose you're wondering if life is like this all the time?"

Dr. Harper hugged me and whispered, "One can only hope. I wish Becky could see you."

The tears began again. "Me, too."

Mrs. Harper was in awe of Colin. Of course, she watched *Comstock* years ago and never realized how young Colin was in that show when he played the patriarch. Mrs. Harper had already secured a dance later in the evening. "I wish my sister could have been here."

I recognized Sandy, my clever friend from the South. Before Charlie McLeod's death, he'd arranged for her to receive a large disbursement from the now-defunct CLM Enterprises to fund her school for disadvantaged students who wanted to attend college. I waved, and she returned the gesture with a laugh and a thumbs-up.

Fewer than fifty people were present, but it took an hour to thank everyone. I finally heard the complete story from my friends, Sylvia, and Trent West, who owned a working ranch down the road. Colin arranged this charade weeks ago. Everyone knew and was sworn to secrecy. Colin's and my kids helped plan the entire event.

Patty Tilmouth, our local vet, and her brother, Dr. Eric Travers, only found out that day. I wagged my finger at Eric. "Gee, you're going to have to find a new place to fish the rest of the season." He held his hands up in the arrested mode and pleaded, "I was shocked that your husband would do such a thing. You know I would never have approved." Then he and Patty high-fived one another.

Colin had hired a photographer, who videoed the entire ceremony and now was taking pictures of the initial reception. There were several of Digger, Colin, and me. Clouds and the threat of rain were increasing.

The wedding party would move back down to the main ranch, while Colin and I would have our photos taken with the official wedding participants and our grandchildren.

Colin and I were finally on our own for a minute. I turned to him and smiled. "Forever and a day, beautiful boy."

Colin laughed. "Anytime you think you're bored, remember this day. I want you to be safe, and I want you to be happy. How am I doing so far?"

"So far, you get a pass. How the hell did you pull that off?"

"It wasn't easy. The kids wanted far more. They're evil, and my boys were just as bad as yours. Luke was on your side the whole way. He was afraid you might call it off. It would have gone on far longer, except Luke said you had limits and would turn around and leave."

"Never. I admit I was so pissed at my family for drinking so much, especially Christy. So how did they do that? I swear I saw them drinking."

"They poured it down the sink when you turned away. Well, some of it. I think Miles was fairly lit when he arrived."

"I guess we have to be the hosts. Shame we can't just sneak off." I pulled Colin toward me, and we had our first proper kiss of the day. "So much trouble."

"It's payback for leading me on about fetish Tuesdays. I don't know if I'll ever get over the disappointment of learning you were kidding."

"Gelding, Collie."

A golf cart was waiting for us, in which we returned to the main compound to shouts and hollers. There was a suggestion that we had been gone so long that maybe we had sealed the deal. Colin quickly replied, "Don't think we didn't consider it."

Mrs. Gillard and her husband were present as guests this afternoon, but that didn't last long. Sylvia West whooshed me out of the kitchen. She and Mrs. G. assumed command mode and had us all helping her and the catering crew. Mr. Gillard, Colin's retired ranch foreman, tended the bar. He was much older than Mrs. Gillard, and I had never met him until today. He was Digger's original trainer.

"So, did you like Digger's participation in the ceremony?" I was curious whether he missed working on the ranch.

He handed me a glass of champagne and smiled. "Yes, of course, but that isn't his first wedding. Gabe and Betty Lou used him when they married."

"He's a wonderful horse, and I think I have you to thank, Mr. Gillard."

"Hardly, ma'am. Your husband did most of the stunt training. I just started him."

"Oh, really? I didn't know. Did you see the new colt up at the barn?"

"Not yet. I'll go up after we get the party all sorted. I was busy fooling a particular young lady. Someone had to hold Digger until they summoned him. May I kiss the bride?"

"Only if you call me Maggie."

Colin was already talking to Dr. Harper. I hadn't heard if he'd been successful fishing this morning. I strolled toward them but was instructed to take a phone call. "For me?"

"I think it's an international call, ma'am." The caterer had heard my cell phone ringing and thought it was hers.

"Hello?" There was a garbled, crunching sound. The altered voice suggested it was overseas. It must be my former Australian staff, calling to congratulate me. "Hey, you guys. Redial. We have a faulty connection." I hung up, and the phone rang immediately. Again, the voice sounded distorted. "I warned you. Now you or someone dies, bitch." I hung up immediately and turned my phone off. I took it to our bedroom and placed it on the nightstand. The voice was so muffled that I wasn't sure whether it was a man or a woman's voice. I quickly returned to the party and tried to act as if nothing had happened.

I sat with Mrs. Harper. She was now in her mid-seventies, yet still appeared athletic and much younger than her actual age. She hugged me and thanked me for the invitation. "This is such a wonderful time for us both. Jeff even caught some fish. It's been a while since he's fished." She paused and gazed at my wedding ring. "I'm sorry I wasn't there when Jeff and Becky married. I heard you were at their wedding, and I'm glad we can meet. I know you and Becky were close during vet school."

"Yeah, we were roommates in our freshman year. I have to admit when she went missing, I was involved with my Australian fiancé and, I sadly concede, I rarely thought about her. I see Lauren seems at ease with it all."

"Jeff and I were worried when she moved to Nevada, but she found Jim, and now we're only waiting for some grandchildren."

I looked at the children playing and counted my blessings. Colin's son, Jake, had older children sitting at a table with Luke. Great-grandchildren were a few years off. I excused myself to return to Colin. The phone call shook me, but I hoped it was traceable. I'd wait until tomorrow or the next day to tell Colin.

I noticed Dr. Harper was finally sitting alone. Colin chatted with Lauren and Jim Kennedy. I took a plate of cheese and crackers. He sipped on a beer, and I limited myself to tonic water before the initial champagne ahead of the main meal.

I sat down next to Dr. Harper, who greeted me graciously. "Ah, my second favorite student in the class of"—he paused—"eighty-one?"

I nodded. "My favorite teacher."

"Hardly." I could see it pleased him while deflecting the compliment. "So, you moved to Australia and practiced until last year? Why'd you come back?"

"In my second-to-last year of vet school, I took a trip to help Becky's father with the colts. I learned to castrate horses and, sadly, the instructor got me hooked on fly-fishing." I stared at Dr. Harper, who smiled and nodded as he remembered the trip and his attempts to teach Becky and me to fly-fish. "It seemed so innocent and dull until I caught my first fish. Unfortunately, it became an addiction only surpassed by the primordial urge to seek a mate and reproduce. When I understood this took me to a place where the trout were noncompliant, and I'd pair-bonded with the wrong male, I sought suitable companions. None met my criteria, so I gave up. I realized fishing was now more important than grandchildren, and here I am."

Dr. Harper laughed so hard that he spilled his beer. "Why not New Zealand?"

"Wonderful place. Colin and I own a fishing lodge there. We hope to resurrect it to fish there in the Southern Hemisphere during its summer and escape the Northern Hemisphere snow. We went there last Christmas, where we fell in love. Fishing in New Zealand is challenging, as you know, and we aren't getting any younger. Anyway, here I am, married to the man of my dreams. How about you?"

"Ah, yes, me. Not quite what I had planned, either, but I've made the best of my lottery ticket. I'm fortunate. I found love twice and, despite a recalculation in my career, I'm lucky. Sherry isn't Becky, but we had two more beautiful children, and I can die a happy man." Dr. Harper stared out toward the mountains. "Maybe one more fish." He smiled and placed his hand over mine and squeezed it.

"Sir, Colin and I hope to give you that fish tomorrow. I know you caught some today, so stand by. He knows you mean the world to me. Did he tell you about our dystocia a few weeks ago?"

"Yeah, how the hell did you get kicked?"

My face reddened. "Tattletale. It wasn't a real kick. Her hock came up and caught me in the chest. Hurt like heck."

Jodie walked over to announce she was stealing me for a moment. She had borrowed Colin's computer to Zoom with the staff, who were all in their homes, waiting for the call. I chatted with everyone who all wished me well. Jodie brought Lauren, Jim, Colin, and Luke in to greet them for a minute, and we received congratulations from everyone.

As we closed the Zoom, Jodie mentioned she wasn't allowed back in Australia if the clinic staff had not congratulated me on the wedding day. She gave us a box, which contained Vegemite, Harris coffee, and Tim Tams, and a single bottle of Penfolds Grange Hermitage.

The wine reminded me of my first meeting with Charlie McLeod, who asked me to guess the wine by sipping it. I didn't recognize it, but guessed it was a well-known wine. I was wrong, yet he didn't tell me until weeks later when he left me a bottle of the Penfolds wine.

Luke reached over to grab the Australian biscuits. "The Tim Tams are mine. You guys are too old to be eating this junk food."

Colin quickly put him in a headlock. "Eat those at your peril, Lukey Boy."

We reentered the reception, where I strode over to Sandy, who was chatting with my sister. "Are you recruiting Christy? She needs to stop sitting around and making normal white blood cells. She needs a new purpose in life."

Christy was sipping a nonalcoholic margarita that I'd suggested she try. Christy also had helped at a nonprofit for educating disadvantaged kids in San Francisco.

"You might say the same thing, Maggot. Society won't miss you when you die at the rate you're headed. Fishing does not contribute to society."

"True, but Luke will. I think that's about all I plan to do for the foreseeable future."

Both Sandy and Christy rolled their eyes. "Yeah, living with another teenager might be a worthy endeavor—that's if you survive. Have you got enough alcohol?" Sandy tipped the last of her drink into her mouth and tried not to spill it while chuckling.

I made the rounds with the staff and neighbors. Whit told me he was under orders not to discuss any adverse findings about his trip into the woods this morning, which concerned me, but his smile comforted me.

Trent and Sylvia were still laughing about the wedding ruse and the theme. "Maggie, there's no way you're going to be bored. Between Collie and raising another teenager, you're in for it, for sure." Sylvia eyed the food, which was being carried on enormous platters into the dining room.

"I may need to seek refuge in a certain day spa." She realized I was referring to the hot springs where we visited when I first arrived last year.

"Anytime, sister. I have some new geldings to ride. So, let's make it a regular event."

Finally, I approached Eric and Patty. Both put up their hands and shook their heads. "We swear." They both grinned.

"Yeah, well, I swear too, but that's not the point. If I didn't need a good doctor and a vet, you'd be kicked to the curb. I thought we were a team."

"In your dreams, Maggie. Colin has us in the palm of his hand. Just like you, in case you're living in a vacuum."

The bell rang, and they announced our wedding dinner.

Chapter 7

The guests were escorted to the reconfigured games room as they entered the house. You name it, and it was there, including trout, duck, and prime rib. Colin had organized the food. I simply wanted a plate of mashed potatoes.

Colin and I stood outside the room and shook hands or kissed our guests as they entered. "Move along. I'm starving." I could only whisper that to my kids, who had to juggle their own plates, along with those of our grandchildren.

Sam Hampstead, the not really inebriated minister, was now well on his way to what he pretended to be during the ceremony. He kissed

Colin and me on the lips. Colin could detect my irritation and squeezed my arm. "Darlin' give him a break. He's been under pressure all week."

"From?"

"Me, darlin'. I missed my true avocation. All week before the wedding, I coached him on how to act drunk. I should have been an acting coach."

"You sure fooled me. I was furious with you all."

"I love it when a plan works." He rubbed his curled fingers across his chest and pretended to spit.

"Don't overdo it, Mr. Chandler. Remember, Ryan Reynolds could always replace you."

"Which reminds me." Colin paused, and I thought, *Oh boy, he's invited, Ryan Reynolds.* "You're officially Dr. Margaret Chandler."

"Sure am. Sounds pretty good to me." We took each other's hands and walked into the dining room. The guests all stopped and clapped.

When the speeches began, I braced for more slagging. Colin and I sat as he put his arm around my waist. He whispered, "I don't know what they planned to say."

Colin's oldest son, Jake, was first. He stood and held his glass up, signaling the beginning. "Your attention, ladies and gentlemen. I wish to toast the union of this couple. Who would have thought our dear old father could haul in the season's best catch? But enough about the fish he caught yesterday." There was a pause for laughter. "Oh, and he seemed to score well in the wife-procurement department. He appears to have found someone who will not only put up with his antics, but someone who can also deliver the goods. A case in point is the foal running around up at the barn. We all know that I would not consider most men a good long-term catch at eighty, but Maggie seems prepared for the long haul. He held up a bill from a fly shop and noted a thousand flies. We know she ordered enough fishing flies for at least ten years last week."

I interjected. "That's only for this month, Jake. I have a standing order. Have you seen me cast?"

The jokes and teasing proceeded for several minutes. Finally, Luke asked to speak. "She's not all bad. She has good points, too. I've learned more cuss words from her than anyone in my family. She introduced me to the classics when I first met her. She broke several child-protection laws by letting me work for her. She tortured me by playing old people's music for hours every day until I gave up and talked for the first time in years to save myself from any more 'sixties' music. She taught me the finer things in life, like the multiplication tables and punishment and reward. I can't remember how often she took my phone away or refused to tickle my back for some minor transgression, such as not memorizing the periodic table. But she's made me a better person. She's made my grandfather so happy. I want to be just like her when I grow up, although I promise not to torture my kids with that music."

I stood up, went over, hugged Luke, and quickly whispered, "Thanks, Lukey Boy."

"Can I get my back-tickling privileges restored?"

"Nope, I'm your worst nightmare. 'Walk Like a Man' is not just a song. It's a way of life."

Colin rose and held out his glass. "To Margaret, Maggie, Magpie and you all know the rest of the names, and the joy in my life. Darlin', you saved me and brought excitement to our family that we hope has ended. I promise to teach you to cast a line like a pro and only use you for vet stuff when Patty and her vet crew are unavailable. I'll let you drive any of my vehicles from now on, and I hope we can last a year, but I won't say no to twenty. I wasn't supposed to say 'obey' in the vows.

Still, knowing her penchant and expertise in the horse- emasculating business, I promise to obey. As for her, she can do what she wants and when she wants. To the moon and back. So, here's to Dr. Chandler."

It was my turn. I wiped my tears and stood. "Thank you all for coming, including my office manager, and my former vet-school instructor and his family. My immediate family includes my siblings, children, and grandchildren. Thanks to my friends, new and old. My children didn't want me to move here. They were sure I'd die with the guns and violence pervasive in the news about the mad, gun-packing Americans. They were right.

"Although I survived, it's been a ride and a half. Thankfully, I fell under the watchful eye of my neighbor and his gun-toting ranch hands. I'm not just marrying Collie. I'm marrying an extended family. I'm marrying Mrs. Gillard, who makes domestic life easy. I'm marrying the men and women who work here, keeping our family from harm and the horses healthy and safe enough for an old lady.

"I'm marrying a community that takes care of one another and who finds joy in the simple things in life, such as a warm spring for skinny-dipping and neighbors who allow your children to have work experience and teach them the 'cowboy ways.' I'm marrying the town doctor and vet who both make house calls.

"Thank you all for the acceptance you have shown me, and I look forward to many more years of personal drama and excitement. Just kidding, I promise only boring stories. You'll want to walk on the other side of the street to avoid hearing about my aches and pains, horseback rides, and fishing stories. But, more to the point. I love this man, and I would take a bullet for him." I didn't mention I took a bullet, but it was in New Zealand and not the United States, and it was only a crease. I laughed to myself, remembering how many times the characters on

Comstock were shot, but mentioned it was 'only a crease.' "So, to my beautiful husband."

Colin stood, took me in his arms, and kissed me.

"Hear, hear! To Maggie and Colin." The formal festivities concluded.

Colin and I danced, chatted, and spent another hour with our guests. He finally announced that we oldies needed our sleep. It was only nine, but Colin needed to steal his bride. We said our goodbyes and received kisses and hugs from our family and guests. He took me up to the barn. We walked through the stable and noted that Digger was at his door, waiting for someone to recognize his role in the wedding. I opened the gate and walked into his stall. "You are the best horse in the universe, old man."

"Hey, I thought I broke you off that old-man talk. It goes for your horse, as well." Colin put me in a playful headlock. Digger was confused and tried to intervene. "Get back, you mongrel." Digger was not having any of this and forced his muzzle between Colin and me, giving me horse kisses.

"Attaboy, Diggie. You know you're my favorite. My beautiful horse has come to my rescue."

At that moment, Colin clicked his tongue twice, and Digger backed away. I realized Digger was playing a game and performing the trick at Colin's command. "If I can teach a horse to kiss on command, it won't be long before I have you trained."

"I have no hope." I saw my future.

"No, you don't, and the good part is you won't even realize it. It's part of the cowgirl reeducation program. Want to take a walk with me?" Colin escorted me from Digger's stall.

"Do I have a choice?" I gazed up at Colin and realized he was in tears.

"I want to pay my respects." Colin took my hand, and we walked up to the site where the ashes of Colin's former wife and deceased daughter lay. I wondered how often Colin and Luke thought about Sarah's murder. I couldn't imagine losing my daughter, but to see your mother murdered was inconceivable. I felt so terrible for Luke. Helen's recent death was still raw. Colin loved his former wife even after Helen left him for another man. We sat on a bench and said nothing. Colin held my hand, and I could see his eyes brim. Colin finally stood, took me in his arms, and kissed me again.

As we returned to the house, he mentioned that Whit and Gabe reported the strange camp back in the forest. "I know you went into the woods. What did you think?"

"It was bizarre. That's for sure. What did Gabe and Whit report?"

"There were around ten boys from maybe ten to fourteen years old. They were dirty. None of them said a word. I'll call Tom Sutton to see what he knows tomorrow. The sheriff's department would know what's going on."

"You'd think, but maybe it would be under the national park rangers?" I'd never seen a park ranger since I moved here, but there must be some somewhere.

"Darlin', it's our wedding night. I can think of other things we might discuss." Colin reached out to me, and we felt the first raindrops that would change our plans.

As we neared the compound, we could see the party was still going on. We snuck around the activity and headed for our bedroom. Colin took me in his arms and kissed me as I undressed. "Not so fast, darlin' girl. Grab a few things. We aren't staying here tonight."

"Huh? What about our guests?"

"Did you want me to invite them into our bedroom? It's just for tonight. We'll be back for breakfast. I have a feeling the fishing will have to wait."

Fifteen minutes later, we climbed into the Gator and headed up the hill into the woods. The road was rough and twisted, but it led to a dark, small cabin that appeared neglected. I'd never been there. I didn't know how far this ranch extended.

Using the truck lights for illumination, Colin opened the door using a code. He reached in and flicked on a light.

"It may kill me to do this." He swooped me up, carried me through the door, and quickly set me down. "This is our retreat from the world. There's no cell reception up here. You're free to do whatever you fancy." He raised his eyebrows several times.

The cabin was rustic, but had a fireplace, complete with a fire that needed a fresh log. There was a bucket with champagne on ice and two glasses. "I had Whit start the fire when we left the reception, but there's a standing order that no one will ever come up here without my permission. Well, you're the exception. This is where Helen stayed when she visited. The cabin is a no-go area for the kids. Luke knows it's off-limits."

"Is there anything else I need to know, beautiful boy?" I realized there was much more to the man I had married.

Colin raised his eyebrows and smiled. "In due time. In due time. Champagne?" Colin loosened his shirt collar and sat on the couch in front of the fire, which now roared. He patted the place next to him and summoned me. "It's not Tuesday, but I thought we could pretend."

Chapter 8

"Good morning, Mrs. Chandler. Or should I say, Doctor?"

"I like darlin' preceded by 'here's your coffee.' FYI." I stretched and turned to rest my head on his shoulder.

"Funny, that's my preference, as well. Thanks for last night. Did I meet your expectations?" He reached for my left arm, took my hand, and examined the new ring that accompanied my engagement ring. He rubbed it with his thumb.

I laughed. "And then some. Should we return to our guests?" We could hear thunder and lightning. Rain would undoubtedly delay our plans. I knew my overseas guests would leave this morning. In addition, my siblings would depart. That would leave the Harpers and Kennedys, who hoped to go helicopter fishing with us today and stay for a few days. Despite Dr. Harper's age, he was getting around better than his daughter, Lauren, had predicted. He and Colin had quickly struck up a friendship. I realized this would not be his only fishing adventure with my husband.

"I hate to leave, Collie, but we should get back." I reluctantly sat up and was immediately pulled back into my husband's arms.

When we returned, another full breakfast was served in the games room. My brother and sister hadn't come, so I drove to the house to retrieve them. It was bucketing down, and I knew they would be reluctant to walk over.

I drove out of our gate, down the road, and then up the driveway to my property. Thankfully, it was locked. I got out of the car, went to the still dented structure, and saw a plastic bag with a note. I unlocked it and returned to the car. I opened the bag and unfolded the enclosed note, which read, *I told you, bitch. Clearly, you don't take directions. Now you will pay.*

I put the letter back in the bag and went up to retrieve my siblings. When we were alone, I wanted to tell Colin. I know he would alert the authorities and ruin the day. I didn't want anyone to become alarmed. It still could only be a prankster.

I entered my cabin. "Hey, anyone hungry? Your chariot awaits."

"OMG, thanks." Bill was weaving. "I'm starving, and all we have are Bloody Marys to stave off near famine."

Not again? I suspected a repeat performance of yesterday's activities. "Bill, you'd better be sober."

Bill straightened up and laughed. "Yep, but don't test my limits."

My siblings and partners piled into Colin's truck, and we drove back to the ranch. Taking no chances, I stopped and locked the gate as we drove over to my new home.

The rain continued all morning. It would put a dent in our plans. My kids and grandchildren would go to Disneyland before they headed back to Australia. Colin had hired a bus to transport them to the airport. They would leave in an hour.

I had private chats with each of my children. I explained what I understood to be financials in case either Colin or I passed unexpectedly. Colin had already informed them, and my kids were satisfied that I'd be cared for until my death. They all laughed at the idea that Colin would precede me in death. "Mum, he'll outlive you by ten years. He promises to bring you over once a year, and we have full access to your cabin whenever we want. We plan to hold a reunion next year." Brandon was satisfied with Colin's efforts to care for me and my family in the future.

Colleen was her typical self. "Mum, watch yourself and try to make him happy. If you two split the sheets, for any reason, we'll go with Collie. You're out."

"Okay, duly noted." As I turned away, I smiled. I wanted to hug all the grandchildren. I realized it would be six or more months before I could see them again.

I remembered the note in my pocket. This threatening intrusion into my new marriage was in the back of my mind. *Was it a hoax? Was there a credible threat that would turn my wedding into a nightmare? Who would go to such lengths?*

After my children left, Colin and I drove my siblings back to my cabin. Lonnie and Bill packed while Miles and Colin went to the basement to check out a leak in the bathroom that had appeared since the previous evening.

"You and the old geezer. In a million years, Maggot." Christy and Lonnie sipped coffee while we watched the rain.

"Yeah, who'd a thunk." I smiled, remembering our first Google search of my elusive neighbor, the famous Colin Chandler. I knew Christy would remind me many more times in the future. *Yeah, who'd a thunk.*

"I could nearly forgive you for not moving back to California. Almost."

"Yes, it was a trade-off—smog, traffic, fires, and prices of land and houses. But I've made do with far less, and I'm happy. If you and Miles care to join us in this God-forsaken place, I know a good realtor who's not busy now."

My realtor was in jail, pending a trial for the murder of the former owners of my cabin. I'd purchased the place at a significant discount because it was the scene of a murder-suicide.

"Carol seemed so lovely. It's difficult to believe she did it."

"What's hard to believe is we were all duped. Colin was Charlie and Linda McLeod's biggest supporter. To think Charlie was running drugs from Mexico. Then, poor Linda was dying and yet sought to avenge Charlie's marriage betrayal. Asking her sister, Carol, to kill the couple was inconceivable."

"I'd kill Collie for you if he was playing around. After all, what are sisters for?"

"Good, I'll warn my husband that blood is thicker than..." I was interrupted.

"Darlin', Miles fixed it. They aren't leaving now. He and I will spend the day going through our houses."

Miles clapped him on the back. "You can't afford me, Collie."

"Darlin', what do you call it in Australia when buddies help buddies?"

"Mate's rates. I wouldn't count on any from my family. 'Take no prisoners' is our motto."

I stayed to help my sister and brother lug their bags into the car. The rain had increased, and my family gave me a quick kiss, hugged us, and ran for their SUV. Colin turned to me and smiled. "How long can we stay here alone before the rest of the crew gets hinky?"

I detected that mischievous smile and admonished him for even thinking about such things. "Collie, don't even think about it. Once a year is plenty. I'm not letting you die of exhaustion in the first week."

Retribution was swift and promising, but we heard Luke yell Sandy was leaving, and she wanted to talk to me. "Later, dude."

"With any luck, Dr. Chandler." That made me smile.

We picked up Luke, who had ridden over on a bike, and returned to the ranch. I recalled I needed to talk with Colin about yesterday's messages. It could wait until after dinner. I greeted Sandy, who was preparing to drive back to the major airport with Doug. She looked so radiant. "I feel bad I didn't spend more time with you. Will you come back?"

She looked at Colin, who put his arm around me. "Sandy and I had a little talk last week. She'll come back next month. There're some arrangements we need to make. On the Margaret and Colin Chandler Trust. You two can talk then."

"Oh, really?" I stared at Colin, who nodded his head.

Sandy grinned. "I'm set for several years unless they ask us to refund the trust money from CLM. Your contribution won't begin for at least five years."

CLM stood for Charlie and Linda McLeod. They were both dead, and the charitable organization they started was now defunct. It turned out that the funds came from Charlie's drug-smuggling enterprise, which was currently going through the courts. Colin and I would have to testify regarding our involvement. I was a witness because I had been taken hostage by some men who now faced court trials. We wondered if the feds would ask the recipients of the charitable trusts to refund the money but, so far, they had not.

"I'd like to say that's your wedding present, darlin', but I had something else in mind. Sandy, we'll see you next month, when the two of you can plan another adventure."

We hugged Sandy and ushered her into the car so Doug could get her to the airport.

The rain continued, and we had to figure out what to do with our remaining guests. We should not have worried.

Chapter 9

We walked into the house, where Luke and the Harper-Kennedys played gin rummy. Colin's family had departed while we were sending my side of the family off. They planned to return for a reunion the next month.

"Jeff, I hope you're prepared to lose the ranch. My grandson takes no prisoners." Colin peered over Luke's shoulder and patted his head. "That's my boy."

Dr. Harper smiled and announced, "Gin." He stood up from the table. "Read 'em and weep, oh young one. Maggie, how about a tour of your barn? I need to smell a horse."

Lauren stood along with him. "May I join you?"

Mrs. Harper, Jim, and Luke continued to play cards. Mrs. Gillard sat down at the table and announced lunch would be served in an hour. "Deal me in for one hand, and then Luke, you and I have work."

Before I could talk, Dr. Harper took my arm and announced he would speak to me only if I called him by his first name. He gave me "the look."

"Yes, sir."

We walked through the barn where a few horses were stabled. I asked for Lauren's opinion regarding the foal initially presented with knock knees. They were almost straight. We had delayed surgery as they continued to improve. The colt was reaching the age when a decision had to be made. The growth plates would respond to surgical procedures only if they were still active and elongating.

We had a month or two more but, by trimming the hoof and taking the pressure off the short side and increasing pressure on the long side, we'd made significant progress. The consensus was to wait one more month. By that time, if the front legs weren't straight, Patty Tilmouth would conduct a surgical procedure to release the tension on the short side and allow the bone to grow.

"Have you performed any periosteal elevation surgical procedures in foals?" I was curious about what Lauren had experienced in her career. She'd just been out a few years.

"Yes, my bosses in Nevada did most of them, but they finally allowed me to do one. It went well, and the foal improved quickly."

"I'm curious. Why do you stay in Nevada?"

Lauren laughed. "Did my dad put you up to that?"

Dr. Harper chuckled. "I did not, but I certainly will try to talk you out of that place if it would bring you closer to your mother and me."

"Maggie, I stay there for several reasons. I like the people at the clinic. Jim does, too. Besides that, we have friends. I don't even have to own a horse. They provide me with magnificent horses to ride. We also like the access to the mountains and the wilderness. Jim and I go up for a couple of weeks every year. Have you ever heard of Miner's Meadow? Even Dad went there twice. If you can go when it isn't overrun by Boy Scouts, it's heaven." Lauren looked away, and I thought she was in another world.

I had learned that was where her mother had been caught in a rock slide and was never seen again. I wondered if she spent time in the mountains, searching for her mother, as Becky's father did for so many years. Maybe she felt close to her mother by living near her never-found body. I didn't pursue that thought in front of her father.

"If it's an easy ride, Colin and I would love to see it sometime."

Dr. Harper laughed. "I made it up there two years ago. If I can do it, so can Colin."

"What makes you think it's Collie? I'm choosing easier horseback adventures, too." I looked skyward. The clouds appeared to thin out, and the sky brightened.

The rain stopped for a minute. Lauren excused herself. "I want to get back to the house to make sure Jim isn't betting on the ranch with Luke."

We were alone, and I showed Dr. Harper the last mare due to foal in a week.

"Maggie, do you have any of your yearbooks from vet school?"

"Of course. Why?"

"May I have a quick look at them? I never had them, and I thought the pictures of Bec might be a lovely gift for Lauren."

"It's not raining. How about I get the yearbooks and bring them over?"

"No, I want to surprise her. Could we go now?"

"Doc, I mean Jeff, I could photograph them and send them to you."

"Yeah, that would work. Something came up, and I want to see what Becky looked like near graduation. If you see any at all, will you do that for me?"

"What are you searching for?"

"I'm reluctant to say anything, but I think you can be trusted. In a million years, this is so crazy. I'd never tell my family what I saw."

"You can trust me, Jeff. I think you know that. I knew about you two from day one and told no one at the vet school that you two were dating. Pretty scandalous, if my memory serves me."

Jeff laughed. "Okay, you're right."

Jeff opened his phone and scrolled through his photos. It took awhile, but he finally stopped. "When I lived in Kentucky, I became interested in the Civil War. I would take Sherry, and we would visit museums and watch reenactments of battles."

He stared down at his phone. "No, it's baffling. You would put me in the loony bin if I told you what I was thinking."

"What has this got to do with Becky?"

"Nothing. Forget I mentioned it."

"Do you think she's alive?"

"No." His voice was firm and final.

"Jeff, if you want to talk, I have an open mind. I have no skin in this game. If you change your mind."

But he cut me off. "No, forget it. I believe lunch is probably ready. Do you think we'll be able to fish tomorrow?"

"It's hard to tell. The weather isn't easy to predict out here. At least the wedding went off without the rain."

"Maggie, I don't remember when I laughed and cried in the same fifteen minutes. You're lucky to have found each other. Colin told me how you met and about the references to trespassing and gate-hanging."

"In my defense, I rarely swear. That's all I'm saying. And, for the record, I'm the lucky one. Collie is the best thing to happen to me in many years. I always ask God to give us one year together, but I won't say no to ten. Twenty would be better."

Jeff squeezed my hand. "My goal is for some grandchildren. You might suggest that to Lauren and Jim on behalf of Sherry and me."

We headed down to the house and ate leftovers. The rain started again, and any hope of fishing was forgotten. Jeff and Colin went to Colin's office to peruse some historical books. I suspected cigars and whiskey may have been involved.

I took Lauren and Jim into town to visit Patty's veterinary clinic. It was Sunday, but we drove up and saw Patty's truck parked outside. Patty was on her way to see a colicky horse. She invited us to go with her. Lauren and Jim wanted to go, but I declined because the truck didn't have enough seats, and I wanted them to talk in case we could lure the Kennedys to move here.

"Can you bring them back when you're done? I'll run back and get some things from my cabin."

"Surely, you jest. I never plan to return them. They're mine—wa-ha-ha." Patty gave an evil grin, and with that, Patty and the Kennedys left her clinic.

Chapter 10

Yet another threatening message awaited me at the gate. *Crap, I never told Collie.* I took the note and tried not to touch it and destroy any fingerprints or DNA. I doubted the local sheriffs even had a fingerprint kit. No tire tracks led up to the house. I thought it must be some local loony who would stop soon.

I entered the house and checked to see if the security cameras worked. They appeared to be in order. I next checked the outdoor camcorder that Miles and Bill set up last summer. Many spikes in the recording suggested activity. I took a second to see what triggered the increase in activity.

I was shocked that two teenage boys emerged from the woods on three occasions. The man who had come to my house yesterday morning before the wedding followed them later. He appeared to be searching again. The boys seemed to walk toward the garage.

When I checked the camera, sure enough, the two boys went into the garage and upstairs to the room where Luke used to hang out before I moved in. Despite my desire to explore the garage, I decided that idea would not get a "pass" from my new husband. I would wait, and I used my phone to copy the videos for Gabe and Whit to check them out. I had a few minutes, so I opened my computer to find several messages that congratulated me on my wedding.

Unfortunately, there was one similar to the chicken-decapitation video I received a day earlier. That was it. I would return to the ranch to tell Colin straightaway. I was sick. This was far worse. It was the same video, but it was laced with a distorted voice that talked about death and revenge.

As I turned to leave, I remembered the vet-school yearbooks. They were in a box in the basement. I retrieved them, placed them in a box so no one would see them, and moved them to Colin's truck. I drove out, locked the gate to my cabin, and drove over to my new home.

After punching the code, I entered the ranch gate. I wondered what Jeff Harper wanted to see. I doubted it was simply to give Lauren the pictures. It was strange that Lauren showed little interest in her long-dead mother. I guessed Lauren was happy and thought her stepmother, Sherry, was all the mother she needed.

Phew. Yes, cigars and whiskey had been consumed. I waved my hand back and forth as the men emerged from Colin's office. I pointed to Colin to suggest that he sleep on the couch tonight. He laughed and shook his head. "Damn, I owe Jake twenty. He said I would not last forty-eight hours in the marital bed, and I was sure it would be longer."

Dr. Harper slapped Colin on the back. "Colin, you beat me. I was kicked out on the first night. Sherry was furious that I..." He paused. "You know, I don't even remember what my transgression was. Thankfully, I've slept only a few nights on the couch over the years."

"Collie, you have the whole day to sort yourself out and keep your twenty. Jeff, here are the albums." I handed him the yearbooks from vet school. I knew an extremely pregnant Becky and Lauren were included in the yearbook photos. Jeff took them and left for his bedroom while Colin went to his computer to check the weather. It appeared promising for a fishing trip the following day. "Collie, we need to talk." I hated to spoil the mood, but he needed to know about the threatening messages.

When I detailed the emails, notes, and phone calls and showed him the images from my security cameras, Colin called Gabe and Whit. He asked that they and any staff meet at the barn. I stayed with our guests while Colin and the ranch hands discussed the problem.

I knew Colin was reluctant to have anyone in the sheriff's office involved. Our faith in the local department was diminished after we realized that essential clues in the deaths of the former owners of my cabin were disregarded in the initial investigation. Tom Sutton was Carol Carter's cousin. No one ever believed he covered for her. Still, failing to investigate the evidence that might have led to an earlier arrest was apparent.

Lauren and Jim returned from their quick vet call and reported they liked the practice and might consider moving there someday. Patty's approach to a colicky horse was like Lauren's. Jim went through the small-animal clinic and noted it needed some newer equipment. He and

Patty would go through the equipment the next day if the fishing trip had to be canceled. Jim was keen to ride with Doug then to relive his Army days. He said he couldn't discuss what he did and where he did it, but it involved Blackhawks.

The rain had slowed to a drizzle. "Hey, Lauren. Do you want to have a ride on Digger?" He was my gift from Colin and the best horse on which I'd ever ridden. Recently, Colin had bequeathed me a saddle that belonged to his deceased daughter. I figured Lauren would like it. "I'll meet you up in the arena." Lauren went to her room to change.

I went up to the barn and indoor arena to prepare Digger for a quick ride. "Hello, beautiful boy." I greeted him as I slipped a halter behind his ears.

"Hey, I thought that was my name." Colin snuck up behind me as I brushed off some straw from Digger's back.

"Oops, sprung. I have three beautiful boys in my life. Get over it." We both knew the third was Luke.

"As long as I'm the only one you—" but he didn't finish the sentence as Lauren arrived.

"The one and only, Collie. Forever and a day." He took a quick glance and took me in his arms to kiss me.

"Grandpa!" Luke and Lauren approached the stall.

Lauren put Luke in a headlock and covered his mouth with her hand. "Luke, we'll review this in forty years. I don't think you'll feel the same then, and I'll be there to remind you."

We saddled Digger, who was his usual compliant self. Lauren had a wonderful ride. Luke stood beside Colin and me, so we couldn't discuss what transpired in Colin's discussions with the ranch hands.

Colin complimented Lauren on her riding and suggested putting him through his stock horse routine. She was reluctant, so Colin mounted him after lengthening the stirrups and did a quick performance of sliding stops and spins. "Now, get a crane to get me off him."

Colin quickly dismounted after he cued Digger to bow down, which allowed Colin to slip off by lifting his leg over Digger's neck. The stirrups were readjusted, and we watched Lauren remount to ride Digger again.

"So much trouble, mister." I didn't know that Digger could do that.

"So much to teach you and so little time, Dr. Chandler."

"I guess. Maybe we should head back to the house and leave these two cowboys. I think we need to plan a fishing trip for tomorrow."

The weather was clearing and, despite the rain, the river behind the ranch was still clear and had not risen. Jeff and I went down to the stream to do a bit of casting and reacquaint ourselves with fishing. I hadn't fished for more than a week to prepare for the wedding. Colin would remain and speak to Doug to plan the next day's trip.

We drove the Gator as close as possible to get Jeff to the river. He was steady and, using a walking stick, he could effortlessly negotiate the gravel bed and large stones at the river's edge.

He had fished down here before the wedding, so, using the same rig and fly, he began casting into a likely pool. I moved downstream from Jeff. I chose and tied a Parachute Adams onto my line. My initial cast missed my intended spot on the first cast, but I finally reached it on the third attempt. I looked upstream and saw Jeff bringing in a nice-sized fish. I set my rod down, scooped up his trout with my net, and removed the hook. "Picture?"

"Why not? You never know when it will be your last." I used my phone and returned to my line, which I left in the water. There were no fish on the line, and I recast to a spot I had successfully fished previously. Nope, but I heard Jeff *whoop*. Damn, this old geezer was showing me up on my stream. This one was small. I retrieved it, and we didn't take a photograph.

As I lifted my rod to recast, Jeff coughed. My heart sank. The old man was out fishing me, hands down. This was a big one—a massive one. It might be nineteen inches. Finally, after several minutes, I netted the behemoth fish. "Photo op. Get your *Field and Stream* smile ready." I took the photo, but Jeff wasn't ready to return the fish.

"Maggie, come here. I want a picture of us both." I handed him my phone, and I stood in front of him to hold the trout while he snapped a few of the two of us.

I returned the beast to the water when Jeff stopped to watch me as I fished. He suggested a stance that might aid my casting and smiled as I hooked a medium-sized fighting hen. I netted and returned the fish. I suggested we return to the house. Mrs. Gillard would have dinner ready, and I wanted to show Colin the picture of Jeff and his catch.

As we walked to the Gator, I asked Jeff whether he had examined the yearbooks.

"Yeah, thanks." He looked up at the cliff looming far behind the river.

"Are there any you want me to copy for you to give to Lauren?"

"Yes, several. I can do it. I saw a scanner in Colin's office." He paused. "Maggie, have you ever thought much about reincarnation?"

"Funny, Lauren asked about something similar when we were in Australia earlier this year. You know, I'm not much of a believer in the occult or anything that defies the law of physics. Why do you want to know?"

"May I show you something without your judgment?"

"No." I laughed. "Okay, I may secretly judge you, but I won't call the funny men in white coats to take you away." At least, I hoped I didn't need to call anyone.

Jeff opened his phone. "Two years ago, Sherry and I were in Gettysburg, where there were many historical photographs. I swear, one resembled Becky. This woman seemed to attend a casualty. I did some research, thinking this woman might be a relative. Lists of men were attached to the medical units, and in the list was a Dr. R. Harper."

Jeff showed me the pictures he took of the photograph and list. He continued, "I showed the picture to Sherry, and she thought it appeared to be a woman who looked like Bec. Sherry hadn't seen Becky for years and never as a grown woman."

"You think this is Becky's relative? Becky was a Lauder by birth, not a Harper. I don't remember any Harpers in her family until you two married. I recall she showed me an old mansion in her family, but the name started with an *M* or an *N*?"

"Merritt. We have the picture now." Jeff went back to his phone. "What made me think about it now was something else I found in the museum. I noticed your unusual ring. I'm intrigued by the images of the fish. The one I had made for Becky included the symbol of a tiny veterinary caduceus engraved in the ring when she graduated."

He showed me another photo on his phone. "Do you remember this ring?"

I stared at the image of a ring and nodded. "I wanted one, as well. Bec told me she thought she'd lost her ring one day. A few days later, she showed me the ring. I remember she was panicked that Lauren had swallowed it." I laughed, recalling the incident. "Did you know we planned to radiograph Lauren at the vet school if it didn't show up the next day, but then she found it and showed me what you had done? I was so jealous."

Jeff searched his phone again. "The first official use of the vet symbol was during World War I. This was on the battlefield near Gettysburg."

I was stunned. "I guess someone dropped it, and whoever found it didn't realize it was from modern days. It's the only logical explanation."

Jeff showed me a second image. On the inside of the ring, on its opposite side, were the initials JH and RAH. "Maggie, what are the chances that those initials and the caduceus would be discovered in a ring clear across the country from where Rebecca was killed?"

"Does anyone else know about this?" I had no conceivable explanation.

Jeff shook his head and closed his phone. "Well, I guess you know. I think it's best to keep this quiet. At my age, they'll be..." However, he didn't finish the sentence. I hugged him as we walked toward the Gator.

Chapter 11

We drove back to the house, where Colin and Luke greeted us. "I thought I lost my bride." He kissed me and wanted to know all about our trip to the river.

"He spanked me, Collie. He caught three, and I only got one."

Jeff beamed. "Hardly. Maggie, let me have the sweet spot."

I pulled out my phone to show Colin the images of Jeff with his fish. "Hey, send me the picture of you, Jeff, and the monster, darlin'. Too bad our artist friend isn't around."

Jeff shot us a questioning look. Colin told Jeff about Charlie McLeod and his artistic talents. The paintings were still down in the

New Zealand lodge. Colin had recently sent a crew up to start the repairs from the flooding and new renovations to begin our plans to reopen the lodge.

"We're set to jet tomorrow. We have a ten-hour window between rainstorms. Because Doug couldn't schedule another copter, he plans to take us guys on one trip and you girls on another, unless you'd want to divide it up differently. He has room for three passengers. Luke will work over at the Wests' cattle ranch tomorrow."

Sherry had previously expressed her concern about a helicopter ride. "That leaves Sherry here alone. I'll stay back, so you three can go. I'll take Sherry and Luke to the Wests' ranch. I wouldn't want to leave a guest alone."

Sherry stood up and shook her head. "No need, Maggie. Sylvia and I plan to go to the hot springs tomorrow. I need to stretch my legs, and we'll hike there. If it's as good as she describes it, I'll experience nature at its best."

Lauren looked up in surprise. "Mom, maybe I'll stay with you."

"As if. Lauren, I know where your heart lies. You go first and have a memorable fishing adventure with your father. You never know," but she didn't finish the sentence.

Jeff was eighty-five. He appeared to be healthy, although a little wobbly on his pins. I believed he had all his marbles until the previous conversation, but who was I to judge? I continued to search for a logical explanation.

I went to the kitchen to give Luke a hug. "Thanks, Grandma." He put his arm around my waist. "Can we renegotiate the car thing?"

"No way, Lukey Boy."

"Okay, Granny. I thought we might make other arrangements since we're family now."

"Call me 'Granny' again, and I will rearrange your backside with my foot, mister."

Mrs. Gillard put the finishing touches on dinner. "I'll hold him down for you, Maggie. Where did my sweet, compliant, quiet boy go?"

"Sorry, Mrs. G. I should have waited to introduce him to speech when he was past his teens. My bad." I put Luke in a headlock and kissed him.

"Gross. You're restricted from kissing me until I have a car."

"Fine by me. There's only one Chandler I want to kiss, anyway." I smiled with satisfaction.

"Double gross. You two are too old for kissing."

Mrs. Gillard, who had to be in her mid-seventies, and I glanced at each other and laughed.

"Luke Chandler, do you want to be sent to your room?" Mrs. Gillard stopped spooning the food onto plates and high-fived me. "United we stand, Maggie. Okay, you two, help me put this meal on the table. Dinner is served. Luke, take the rice to the table, and call your grandfather and our guests."

I carried the food to the dining-room table. When I glanced up at the massive antler chandelier, I noticed my wedding garter hanging from one of the antler prongs.

"Mrs. G., have I told you how much I love you?" The last thing I wanted to do was dust that light fixture. Despite her age, Mrs. Gillard was a spry and active woman.

"No, and I'm due for a raise. It's been a week since Colin gave me one."

We recounted the wedding prank during dinner. "You guys totally had me. I was so furious at you all." There were high fives once again. Colin sat next to Jeff and Sherry. They discussed their lives, their children, and Becky. Colin rarely discussed Luke's mother and her death, but I thought I even heard him mention her. I talked to Lauren and Jim about current trends in veterinary medicine. They told me about the cases they encountered after I left my old practice to head to Hamilton Island and on to New Zealand.

"You know, we treated two of your small colon impaction ponies and met the Navaras and Cindy."

"Oh, no. Did she have colic again?"

"No, Cindy had a grass seed in her eye, but they said she'd been sick and spent a few days at the clinic just when you retired." Lauren baited me.

"A few days?"

"She might have said a few weeks." Jim heard the story as well. "She said Cindy had spent several weeks at the clinic and ruined your retirement."

"Something like that, but it was one of the most rewarding and annoying cases I ever saw. Talk about iatrogenic complication."

Luke was listening. "What does that mean?"

Lauren answered. "It means a disease or complication caused by a doctor or veterinarian's treatment."

"I kind of like to say, 'bad vet moment.' It haunted me for weeks." I rolled my eyes.

"Jasmine mentioned Cindy contracted an infection from an injection, and it wouldn't improve."

"I hesitate to tell you for fear it puts you off doing what I call a lifesaving procedure."

Jim sat up and asked, "Okay, I'll bite. What procedure?"

I remembered Estelle Getty as Sophia in *The Golden Girls*. I extended my fingers and laughed. "Picture this—my last weeks of practice.

The new vets were coming in a month, and the last thing I wanted to burden them with was a pony with a chronically draining hole in her flank. The worst part was I caused it, and the pony was hospitalized at the Queen's pleasure."

Luke wanted to know what that meant, and Lauren responded, "I guess you were doing a freebie?"

"Oh, yeah—big time." I groaned when I remembered the stress. "Cindy came in with colic. It was typical pony colic. She probably suffered from a small colon impaction. I suspected it had been going on for longer than anyone had noticed. She was slightly dehydrated and mildly in pain. It wasn't so much that you could tell she was sick unless you watched closely. Cindy was stoic, and we all missed the severity of what was happening.

"We treated her with the usual oral and intravenous fluids and painkillers. I may have even sent her home, but she returned, and this time a young boy accompanied her. I think Jason was about seven, and the poor kid loved his pony. I understood this might be the last pony I ever treated for colic. There was no way I was going to let this pony die. Kill me now.

"The bad news was Cindy was older and, when she wasn't feeling pain, she could be a terrorist. This family was trying to decide about the treatment of a pony that was too small for the boy and difficult to handle. They mentioned they would not feel comfortable passing her on to another small child."

I paused. "Hand me the wine. This story needs alcohol." Jim refreshed my glass, and I noticed everyone was listening now. Luke held out his glass, and Jim poured a sip after Colin nodded. Luke tasted it, quickly washed it down with juice, and shook his head. Colin smiled.

"I treated her for two days, and she didn't respond. I realized surgery was off the table." Jim and Lauren laughed at the pun.

"Jason came twice a day to walk Cindy for us, and we even had him listen to her abdomen for gut sounds. This pony was killing me. You must respect the owner's decisions. We gave Cindy twenty-four hours, but she didn't improve. Jason was beside himself.

"I took Jason aside. The money his parents allotted might not be enough. I had to make a deal. I could see Jason was all in on the vet stuff. He was a clever boy, and I could see a potential veterinarian in the making. I asked him if he aspired to be an animal doctor when he grew up. Yes, he did, and we made a bargain. I would do what it took to save Cindy, and he would study hard and earn good grades, and he could become a vet. I told him it was okay to change his mind, but studying and good grades were not negotiable. We shook. Done deal. Pressure. I would report to Jason from then on.

"The owners left Cindy at the clinic, and I was given a small amount of money to perform one more procedure. My nurse held her while I completed the umpteenth rectal. Miracle of all miracles—the impaction could be felt rectally.

"Boom! Can you spell anesthesia? In fifteen minutes, we had her knocked out, and I lay down on the ground, with my arm inside her, attempting to massage the hard mass. It took an eternity, but I eventually eliminated the blockage. The problem was that while that one was small enough to pass through the small colon, there might be another. We would know in a few hours.

"Cindy didn't improve, and she was bloated even more than before the anesthesia. I was by myself in the middle of the night and knew there must be more than one obstruction. Her pain was probably worse than before we anesthetized her. I decided to trocarize her."

Luke asked what that meant.

"Lukey, it's a technique to relieve gas pressure when the pony can't fart. You stick a large needle into the intestine through the flank to release the gas."

"Do they do that to people?" I could tell Luke was worried.

"Knowing you, it will never be the case in this house."

Luke's face reddened, but he was relieved.

Jim tipped the bottle of wine in Luke's direction, but Luke shook his head. "Safe for another year. No, Luke, they don't do it with humans, to my knowledge." Jim poured the rest of the wine into my glass.

Cindy's story continued. "I was alone, and despite heavy sedation, I could see Cindy was in agony. I prepped both flanks and, using a large-bore intravenous catheter, quickly plunged the catheter and stylet into the left and right flanks. The gas came out, and the pressure on the intestines decreased but, toward the end, as I withdrew the long needles, some fluid came out, as well. More wine, please."

I saw Colin shake his head. "Jim, are you able to carry her to bed? There's no way Maggie can walk away from this table."

"Yeah, maybe we can finish this story another day." I stared into my wineglass and grimaced.

Jim poured me the last of the second bottle. "No way. I'll get her to bed, Colin. I want to hear how the story ends."

"Okay, but it didn't end well in the beginning. Of course, Cindy finally passed feces by the morning. The family all came to visit, and Cindy could nibble on some grass. Jason was beside himself. Cindy was on antibiotics in case some minor infection resulted from the trocar.

"In thirty-plus years, I saw only one other infection from this procedure. Lauren, I did at least twenty of them over the years in my practice, so don't let this deter you from doing them. Anyway, Cindy stayed with me for weeks, an abscess finally formed, and we opened it in several areas. Keep in mind she was eating and pooping, and never looked back. Oh, she looked back when I flushed her flank twice daily—for weeks and weeks.

"Eventually, I had to knock her out and remove necrotic tissue, and then the abscess finally healed. Days before the new clinic owners arrived, I sent Cindy home to a relieved vet-in-training. Within a few weeks, Jason was back riding and even went to pony club to compete with her." I was teary now and blamed the alcohol. "Sorry, I'm a light-weight in the alcohol department." But I was not the only one with tears. Lauren, Sherry, and even Colin wiped their eyes.

Mrs. Gillard had left, and dessert was awaiting us in the fridge. I got up and swayed. Jim caught me, and we went into the kitchen. Colin followed us. He and I held each other as Jim took the plates to the dining room.

"My beautiful, clever wife," was all he said.

"I think you forgot drunk."

"Yeah, that, too." He handed me two plates and smacked me on the backside. "No more alcohol for you tonight."

Chapter 12

The following morning, I was surprisingly sober. I had none of the usual telltale signs. No nausea or headache. Phew.

"Maggie, you snored like a walrus. I'm limiting your alcohol tonight." Colin had dressed in his fishing shirt and pants.

"Gelding, Collie." I observed him examine his upturned finger. "You don't have to. I am swearing off any mind-altering substances for the rest of the month."

"Tomorrow is the first day of June." He pointed his finger at me. "One more day, and we're alone again."

"Counting down the hours, beautiful boy. I don't remember what you said, but what do you make of the threatening notes and the campers?"

"No idea, but it must be someone who knows us and has your email and phone number. I doubt it would be any people from Charlie's drug running cartel. They're mostly in prison. I don't want you going anywhere alone." He stared at me. "Let me rephrase that. Please don't go anywhere alone, my beautiful wife. I'm only asking." Colin came over to the bed and pulled me up into his arms.

"You realize the cartel reaches into the government on both sides of the border. What if one of the cartel members threatened to talk? Whom do you trust?"

"I don't know. Too bad Charlie's already dead. I'd love to kill him myself." Colin peered out the window. "I wish it was just us, but I know it'll be a great day. I see some casting tuition in your future." We smiled.

"The rest of our lives, beautiful boy. I love learning."

"So much to teach you and so little time." Colin held my face and turned to the door. We entered the dining room, where everyone was already eating. Colin apologized and went to the kitchen to get us cups of coffee. I heard his phone ring. I placed food on both plates and waited for him to return.

"Everyone ready for the day?"

Sherry had finished her breakfast and sipped her coffee. "Sylvia will be here in an hour, and she'll take Luke and me. So, we're set. Just make sure you return my husband in one piece."

I noticed Jeff, Lauren, and Jim all wore traditional fishing clothes in varying shades of green and gray. Lauren was not eating much this morning, and I guessed she was nervous about the helicopter ride.

Colin entered and gave me my coffee. "All set. Doug will be here in thirty minutes. It's probably best that you all put on your waders, so we'll have room for the lunch and our rods."

Jim glanced over at Lauren. "Why don't you go with your dad, and I'll ride with Maggie?"

I observed Lauren consider the change and smile. "Are you sure?"

Jim took her hand. "You'll be fine. We'll be there within the hour, and by then, you and your dad will have cleaned out the river and be ready to come back."

The flight from the ranch would take thirty minutes each way, giving them an extra one and a half of fishing. "Or Maggie could go on the first trip, and we could follow them."

The actual distance wasn't that far, but the area that Colin had selected was inaccessible by horseback and a challenging trip on foot over a tall mountain range. Very few people knew about it, and Colin was the only person to fish there as far as Doug knew. "Nope. Guests first. Lauren, you go with your dad. Jim and I can catch the second trip."

Thirty minutes later, Jim and I waved goodbye to the rising copter. Sylvia arrived in her truck to collect Luke and Sherry. Luke was out of school, and he would stay with the Wests for several days. They would drive their cattle up to the mountains beginning the next day. I checked his pack to be certain he had at least one change of clothes and a toothbrush. Of course, he didn't. He had a copy of my book, which surprised me.

I went to Luke's room, where he was adding a few things to his pack, and kissed him. "Love you to the moon and back, Lukey Boy." He tried to duck my kiss. *Welcome to the world of a teenager.*

Jim and I waited for Doug's return and talked about practice and the life of a vet. He told me about his time before he met Lauren. He went to sequential veterinary practices, subbing for vets who needed to step away from their clinic for personal reasons. Jim enjoyed the challenge of walking into a situation in which he could help the practice owners, who were struggling from pressure within and outside their professional commitment.

Jim started in the Nevada practice when the owner was injured in an automobile accident. That was how he met Lauren. The practice owner eventually died, and the clinic was sold to a corporation. Jim and Lauren moved to a nearby mixed animal practice. Jim was a small animal surgeon, and Lauren was a horse vet like I'd been. Jim stayed this time. "I couldn't expect Lauren to lead a nomadic life. We want to have children and settle down."

"But rural Nevada?"

"I guess you'll just have to come and see the Eastern Sierras. We love the access to the wilderness. We 'go bush' for two weeks every year. Isn't that what you say in Australia?"

I laughed. "And you've been married for three years now?"

"Three years in June. Say, have you felt this lump on your dog?"

My rescue dog, Baxter, had become Luke's constant companion. I hardly ever petted him. There was a firm mass near his jowl. "That's new. I'll run him into Patty's this week to see what she thinks."

"How old is he?"

"We don't know for sure, but I thought he might be six or seven. What do you think?"

"You may be light on your assessment. I'd have thought closer to ten."

"It doesn't matter. Baxter's going to live forever like Jeff and Colin. Hey, we should get ready. Doug will be back in another fifteen minutes, and we need to get the lunch out on the landing pad." I went to the kitchen, where Mrs. Gillard had packed two coolers. One contained the food, and one held the beer. There were nonalcoholic drinks, as well. I still felt good with no lingering hangover. The copter ride would test my limits.

Doug returned and landed shortly at the heliport, where we loaded the food and drinks. "Let's get going. The river is perfect, and if we don't get there, there won't be any fish left for us. Their ride was smooth. Even Lauren enjoyed it."

"Phew. That's good news. Lauren can be the vomit queen." Jim was relieved.

"No, I'm the queen. She could only be a princess." I climbed into the copter and took a backseat. We all buckled up and put on headphones.

Doug and Jim were experienced, and they nodded to each other and gave the thumbs- up. Alarm bells went off. Was this going to be a wild ride? I tapped Doug on the shoulder. "Precious cargo, mate," I shouted into the microphone.

Doug gave me a mischievous smile. "I know. Collie said to be careful with the beer."

"Sheesh, I was thinking of his wife." I did laugh. "Hey, can we take a quick gander at the forest behind my place? I want to see if the kids are still at Saddleback Lake."

Doug banked the copter as I grabbed the edges of my seat. My stomach dropped two feet into my pelvis as I felt the lurch when we abruptly ascended. *Why did I ask for that?*

We took a quick look when we flew over my property. I could see both Whit and Gabe riding horses near my garage. They gazed up and waved. We climbed higher, and as we gained altitude, Doug flew north and toward the lake. No one was visible. The lake shimmered with a light breeze, causing isolated ripples on one side. A single cloud and our helicopter were reflected in the lake. Doug and Jim were experienced in heli-searches, and both shook their heads. We turned toward the river. Twenty minutes later, we arrived at the same river where I had been with Colin and Luke once before on his eightieth birthday.

I could see everyone down at the river fishing. Colin netted a fish for Jeff as we climbed out of the copter. Lauren wasn't in sight. I guessed she was fishing around the bend. Jim and Doug carried the food and drinks over to a sandbar away from the river. I spread out some blankets and recalled my talk with Colin.

Colin attempted to talk me into forgiving Charlie when I found a young woman in Charlie's house. I laughed, remembering Colin told me if he wasn't married, the appeal would be for me to consider him and forget Charlie.

I knew Colin wanted this fishing adventure to be for just us two, but he knew how important it was for me to have Jeff and his family here to share the fishing adventure. His generosity in sharing the day was one of the many reasons I loved this man. *One year, God, but I won't say no to ten.*

The day promised success. We all realized we had a limited time before we should return to the ranch to avoid the next weather front. The water level and clarity were perfect for fishing wild and ferocious trout. The average trout size was pleasing, and there was the occasional monster. My goal was for Jeff to catch a big one. Since he'd fished in New Zealand many times, where the trout were much larger than most native American fish, this was not a size contest. However, for our area, they were far above average and fought like tigers in a snare. Hence, Jeff appeared to be enjoying himself. I could tell he and Colin had bonded.

I thought about Becky and wondered how different things would be if she were still alive. Sherry was bright and fun and had the admiration of Lauren. I detected no evidence that Lauren missed her birth mother. When I mentioned Becky, I saw Lauren smile and noticed no hint of loss or regret at her passing. Jeff was obviously in love with Sherry. He'd held her hand whenever they were together.

Doug and Jim went to find Lauren. They returned two hours later as I spread out the food and drinks. Everyone had caught good-sized fish and loved the scenery. Jim and Lauren saw a grizzly far upstream and were glad Doug had a pistol to scare away any attackers. I laughed, thinking of my past year and dramas. A bear would not compare with what I had been through with Charlie.

After lunch, Jeff, Colin, and I hung back while Doug and the Kennedys returned to the river to head downstream. I knew they were concerned about Jeff and didn't want him to negotiate the terrain to get to the fish. Jeff eventually went back to the river's edge, and Colin and I sat together on a blanket. I fell asleep, leaning into Colin. I heard him snore and realized he was sleeping as well. When he woke, I admonished him as he had done last year.

"Farting, drooling, and snoring, beautiful boy."

"I won't deny the snoring, darlin', but the rest of those actions are your department."

We kissed and sat together for several minutes. I leaned into Colin with his arm around me.

"In a million years, did you think this would be how we would end up?" I fanned a fly away from us.

"Yes, I prayed and daydreamed daily for this moment." He reached over to touch my face. "I didn't expect it would be this dramatic, but I can't deny I'm not sorry about how it ended. Of course, it would make a splendid book and movie. I might have to come out of retirement."

"I may have to learn how to write a screenplay." I leaned forward and stood. "As much as I love you, Collie, some of the fish have my name on them." I pulled him up, and we walked to the river.

At the end of the afternoon, I understood we needed to go back to the ranch. It was decided that the men would all return first, and Lauren and I would wait for the second trip. Doug left his gun, and we walked back to the river to fish for the next hour before Doug returned.

Chapter 13

As the helicopter lifted off, Lauren gazed up as it flew out of sight. "There's no way Jim's going to out fish me." Jim had struck gold all day. He caught the biggest and the most fish. I watched him fish and observed a possessed man. The last fish he caught measured twenty-one inches—unheard of in this environment.

Lauren went upstream while I fished down from her. The light from the late afternoon faded. I wished we had sent the first group home sooner. We were testing the limits of Doug's ability to fly in the mountains.

Lauren caught three more nice-sized fish, and I hooked only one. There had been no more tuition from Colin that day. Still, I observed

Lauren and Jim fishing together. I was reasonably sure there was more going on than fishing lessons.

We sat down and waited for the whirring sound of the helicopter that would signal its return. We talked about Lauren's dead mother, and I wanted to know if she had any memories. She smiled and said she didn't. She changed the subject, which showed me she preferred not to dwell on a memory that would go nowhere.

After an hour, we each were alarmed. Doug was at least thirty minutes late. Lauren gazed in the ranch's direction. "What do you think is taking them so long?"

"Maybe Doug refueled? I know he keeps fuel at the ranch in case of a fire. It shouldn't take more than a few minutes." I stood and put on my jacket. It was becoming cold, and the clouds built behind us.

A minute later, we saw the illumination of the clouds showing lightning. It was at a distance, and we could not hear the thunder. I was officially ten out of ten on the scale of panic. "I hate to say this, but I think we need to find some shelter if Doug doesn't return tonight."

Lauren looked up and down the stream and remembered the grizzly she and Jim had observed earlier. "I guess you know how to fire your gun, and it has bullets?"

I nodded, knowing I had not shot a gun in many years. I examined it and realized it was modern with a magazine. I hoped it had bullets, but I wasn't about to test that theory. Lauren stared at me, holding the gun, and laughed. She took it and unloaded and reloaded the magazine, and suggested she be in charge. "I'm taking over, Mrs. Buchanan."

I looked at her quizzically. "Huh?"

She tipped back her cap and said, "Mrs. Sam Buchanan—*Comstock?* Your husband's television series?"

"Duh. I don't think about it much. I know your mom and Becky liked it."

"Didn't you watch it as a child?" Lauren was surprised at my response.

"Sure, everyone did in those days, but my family didn't have a television for many years. My parents bought a fancy hi-fi. They were into music. I know it was the rage, but we only occasionally saw *Comstock*. I never watched it when it was in color until a year ago. Did you know Colin was younger than two of his television sons, but he dyed his hair?"

"You should watch the reruns. They're on all the cable networks."

"Ca-ching. Don't I know." But the moment was lost when we heard thunder.

We looked behind us and could see the clouds approaching. "Shit." Lauren and I had only cotton sweaters and thin rain jackets. "We need to find shelter. Does your phone work up here?"

"No. That's one reason we like it here." I was sick with worry. I knew Colin would be here if he could. The unthinkable surfaced. *What if the helicopter crashed?*

"You don't think they've had an accident, do you?" Lauren gazed at the horizon.

"Lauren Kennedy, don't even think that." But that was what we now did. If the copter crashed, and everyone was injured, or…

"Maggie, who knows where we are besides Doug and Colin?"

"I really don't know, but that couldn't have happened. They're all fine, and Doug may have to wait for a day, but by tomorrow, I'll be back at the ranch, and you'll be on your way to Nevada."

Even if they had perished, Luke would have some idea where we were. I didn't say it, but I realized Doug would have filed a flight plan.

We would be rescued even if the unthinkable happened. "Doug will be here in the morning. I'm sure. I would know if they were…" but I didn't finish the sentence.

Lauren pointed downstream. "Well, unless there's a miracle in the next few minutes, we need to find shelter." We walked over to a rise and decided a grove of trees was our best option. It would be a wet and chilly night.

We gathered wood, and both of us laughed as we realized we had nothing with which to start a fire. Lauren searched until she identified two suitable rocks. She hit them together to create a spark. She had a fire going in less than a minute.

"Girl Scouts?" I would have spent the night cold and wet. My survival skills were dismal. I remembered the night in the New Zealand lodge when I couldn't even get the generator to work.

"Something like that. Let's create a barrier, so we don't set the place on fire." As she said that, we saw a crack of lightning and heard thunder, which informed us a storm was approaching faster than we expected.

I was beyond frightened. "Should we move?" *In the unlikely chance that I survive, I'll get a survival book.*

"No, stay low and squat. Can you do that? I can steady you." We both bent down and had only our feet on the ground. We hovered for several minutes when lightning struck several places in the mountains above us. The lightning finally seemed to pass, but the rain continued to fall.

"So, which is worse, the rain or the lightning?" I took some wood we had piled up at the base of a tree to ensure we had some dry wood for the fire through the night.

"Now that the lightning's moved on? I would say the rain. We won't die, but it's a toss-up. An hour of sheer terror or an entire night of cold and misery. Take your pick. We may be miserable, but we'll survive." Lauren searched the clouds as we watched the ever-receding lightning. "I know they're back at the ranch feeling guilty. I hope they have a backup plan for tomorrow."

"At least we have our waders on, and we'll be wet only on the top." We didn't have any further discussion about a copter crash. If the helicopter went down, we might both be widows. Lauren would also lose her father. *Oh, please, Lord, let them be alright. I promise to...* But I didn't promise anything. There was no point. If Colin was dead, I would live out my life as I had planned before we met. I would care for Luke and attempt to find joy in my life.

Neither of us had jackets that deflected the torrential rain. We maintained the fire, but we were soaked and cold. The water seeped down into the waders, but our body warmth kept our legs and midriff nearly warm. We huddled together as we attempted to support each other to stay warm. It was a futile effort, but the clouds prevented the temperatures from plunging to a range that might be dangerous.

As miserable as it was, we knew it would be over soon. We'd be rescued in the morning, and as we saw the early signs of dawn, we hoped our ordeal would soon end.

We were wrong.

Chapter 14

The rain had dwindled to a drizzle, which was heartening. Still, we understood Doug would need to fly below the cloud cover to reach us, and sadly, there was no sign that this was going to be early this morning. We were wet, cold, and hungry. We could remedy some of this while we waited for Doug to return.

The large canopy of conifers in the area behind us protected adequate dry wood from the rain. "Okay, mountain girl, you catch us some trout, and I'll get some more firewood. We may have to wait an hour or two." My bravado was pure bluff, and I didn't fool Lauren.

"All I want to say is that I've been in worse situations and made it out, so we don't have to pretend. I only need to know that the guys are..."

Lauren looked skyward, and we both heard the unmistakable sound of thunder once again. "Damn."

Lauren hastily went down to the creek with her fly rod, as I scavenged for more firewood. I occasionally glanced at her efforts to hook a trout. I saw her search in her vest and watched her change flies from a dry fly to a drop-nymph rig.

I shouted, "Match the hatch, sister."

She acknowledged me with a raised arm. "No hatch to match." A minute later, she cast into the pool where so many fish were caught yesterday. I saw her raise the rod, attempting to set a hook, but that one got away. I scoured the area for additional dry wood and tried to stoke the fire. It was not a blazing fire, but it would maintain our warmth, and we could cook a trout. We had nothing to hold water, and we understood it would be a mistake to drink the water from the river. Giardia was prevalent in all the streams in the state, and that would not be fun. I wasn't thirsty.

I watched Lauren cast several times and change flies at least three more times, with no success. I looked through my vest and discovered a streamer I'd never used. It was big and gaudy. The reason that fly was in my pack was a mystery. The good news was I found a beautiful fishing knife that a former veterinarian had given to me. I walked over and showed her the bright-pink, iridescent fly.

Lauren turned to me and saw what I offered. She smiled and held out her hand. "Ah, a Bec Beauty. Did my dad give that to you? He loves those. He said my mom designed them."

"He must have sneaked it into my vest. I've never seen this before in my life. Want to try it?"

"I couldn't possibly do any worse."

"No pressure, Lauren. I may starve to death, and your life could be over if you kill Sam Buchanan's wife. I give you twenty minutes to be a hero, or else I will step in, and never fear that this story will come up in a book sometime."

"Pressure. Stand back, old lady, and let a pro at this. At least, I know the name of this big mama." She tied the fly onto her line and walked to the river.

I moved back to the trees, where our fire was trying to die, and gave the fire mouth to mouth. I was sure it would only be a few hours before we'd be rescued. Scenarios ranging from minor helicopter damage to crashes ran through my head. I was sick with worry, but for Lauren's sake, I didn't discuss the one scenario that we both contemplated. I walked downstream, found more firewood, and returned. Lauren smiled as she walked back with a nice trout.

I used my newfound fishing knife to clean the trout. Sadly, it was a female with eggs. Lauren went away and returned with some nettle and a plant she knew was safe, but she was not familiar with its name.

"How certain are you that this is edible?" I knew nothing about eating plants grown in the forest.

"Ninety-nine." Lauren appeared to know what she was doing.

"Percent sure?" I was dubious. Yet Lauren nodded, placed the plants inside the fish, skewered the trout, and held it over the fire with a long, green pine branch.

"Did I tell you I got giardia from eating trout that wasn't fully cooked?" I groaned internally, remembering that incident.

"Really? How sick were you?" Lauren continued to turn the fish by rotating the branch, supporting the trout. It smelled delicious, and I was starving.

"I could still fish, but I spent most of my downtime dealing with a gut ache and diarrhea. I don't want it again, that's for sure."

The trout was well cooked when we ate it. We each had a fillet, and in the end, I was not full, but I was no longer starving.

I walked over to the river and threw the leftovers into the water. I didn't want any smells that might attract a bear or a mountain lion. As we finished, we heard thunder again. It was accompanied by an icy wind this time.

We both made nature calls and watched another thunderstorm approach. The rain wasn't as heavy, but we were soaked down to our waists.

I could detect the strain on Lauren's face. She gazed in the ranch's direction and sighed. "It's the not knowing. If I knew Jim and my dad were alright, I'd think this was another *Comstock* adventure. We might endure a bit of discomfort or drama, but in the end, we'd know we will be okay. Maggie, what are the odds?"

I shrugged. "How many hours has it been? Maybe they had to put the copter down somewhere, and with the storms, they're waiting somewhere just like we are. Perhaps they're back at the ranch, and they're watching the weather and are ready to return as soon as they know it's safe. There are at least five other explanations that still mean everyone is alive, and they're simply being cautious. I would trust Doug with my life. I've never seen clouds stay more than a day, but we may spend another night here in the forest. We know no one is coming soon. Let's see if we can locate more shelter in case we're here again tonight."

"Or a fast-food outlet." Lauren giggled, and I joined in.

"Or a Howard Johnson's."

"Too bad we aren't at Miner's Meadow. There's a cabin there that would be perfect."

"Did you tell me about it? Didn't a large tree fall when you and your father were there?" Lauren stared away and sighed. I thought she must be remembering her parents and happier times.

"Lead the way, Maggie. I think we should stick to the stream, though."

"Upstream. You have the gun?" I hoped Lauren really knew about firearms. They were banned in Australia many years ago. Besides a quick tutorial from Colin, I verged on dangerous with one in my hand.

"Yep. My daddy didn't raise no fool." Lauren smiled as she examined the revolver.

We slowly crossed several streams that now entered the river. They weren't there the previous day, and we both decided it would be safe to drink the water. It was clean and sweet. Since they could be gone by the afternoon, we probably drank more than usual. Trying to urinate with waders was not a simple task.

After an hour of walking, we found no suitable shelter. We turned and followed the same path back to our base at the sandy bar of the river's edge. Lauren stopped short and pointed to the gravel bed. The imprint of a large animal was unmistakable.

"Cougar. We stick together from now on." Lauren checked the revolver once again.

"No prob. I've always enjoyed your company." I was worried sick that everyone on the copter had been killed. I was never worried for our sake. The forest was not Disneyland, and this reminded me of that.

Lauren assumed the lead now. I swear she has some hidden history of living off the land. When I asked Lauren, she laughed and said she read survival books in high school. It didn't ring true, but for sure, she knew how to survive.

We gathered a mountain of firewood and prepared to spend another night. I took Lauren's rod and a Bec Beauty fly to the river, which was swollen and was turbid. I hooked a nice one on my second cast, and dinner was served. Again, we took all the entrails and leftovers to the river to remove any enticing smells.

As darkness descended, the rain intensified once again. This time, we each took the watch while the other dozed. I thought about the warm springs that I had visited with Sylvia West. How I wanted my bath and my warm husband. After what seemed like several hours, I could not go on. Lauren was cold when I woke her. I rubbed her shoulders and attempted to warm her. I thought she might have a fever. Did she pick up giardia? Would it be something different, like salmon poisoning?

"Hey, are you okay? Do you think you're getting sick?" She appeared disoriented, and she finally responded that she thought it was from inactivity during her sleep. Lauren thought if she got up and moved around, she would be alright. We sat back-to-back, and I dozed off sitting up. The rain stopped, but we were soaked in and out of our waders.

I was sure I had slept for hours, but it was still dark when I awoke. Lauren had shook my shoulder. "Maggie, wake up. We have a visitor."

I shot forward, looking for the cougar, but it was a grizzly. The fire was only barely going. "Damn." I reached for some dry twigs we had kept under our fishing vests—too little and too late. The bear appeared to be a single male. He warily approached us and raised up on his hind legs as he saw us move.

"Get ready, Maggie." Lauren aimed the pistol into the air and fired it. It did not seem to distract the bear. We stood and prepared to run. This time, Lauren pointed the gun directly at the bear. A single shot was fired, and the bear roared and charged us. We ran, but as the bear took a few steps, he fell over. We stumbled over some branches we'd gathered the previous afternoon. After the bear paddled for a minute, he lay still. Lauren looked up and dropped to her knees. "Oh, Lord, please forgive me."

I hugged her and thanked her. "I forgive you, even if God doesn't."

"You can thank Sam and Jim for my riflery lessons."

"Who's Sam?"

"Your *Comstock* husband. Just kidding. He was an old friend who's long dead."

She was lying. I didn't know what she was covering, but there was no mistaking the telltale signs. "I'll worship at the altar of those two men, whoever they are. You must have hit the heart."

We quickly rebuilt the fire to get ready for another day. Lauren kept walking over to the carcass. "I'm afraid he's going to wake up."

"Me, too. I'll be happy when it is light enough to see Mr. Bear's dilated pupils. How game are you?" I had a brilliant idea.

"Let's huddle up with him to share some of his warmth. We can skin him in the morning and use his hide to protect us today." I saw stars and hoped we would not need to be here much longer. Doug would be here by daylight, which he was.

Chapter 15

We could scarcely detect the flashing lights of the helicopter in the distance. I attempted to set some pine-tree branches on fire. When they finally lit, I waved the flaming branches. Lauren and I hugged. The copter landed after another several minutes. Doug and Jim jumped out and ran to us.

Okay, I'll admit it. I cried. Lauren did as well. I hugged Doug and stared at him without speaking. He walked over to the bear and whistled. "Which one of you slaughtered this poor, innocent creature?"

I pointed to Lauren, who pointed at me. "If it's bear season, Lauren shot him. If not, I did. We were kind of desperate."

Jim lifted the now-stiff leg and noticed the entry wound near the elbow and into the thorax. "Nice shot. Whoever did this."

Lauren curled her fingers, rubbed them up and down on her chest, blew on them, and coughed. "Thanks. Fair warning. We women should not be messed with."

We were freezing cold. The guys brought jackets but didn't think about the wetness. We endured another thirty minutes of freezing cold before we landed. When we arrived, only Colin was there to greet us. Alarm bells went off, but Jim and Doug had said everyone was alive. They announced they would explain everything when we reached the ranch house.

I descended from the helicopter as soon as the blades stopped. I ran into Colin's arms.

"Hell, you're freezing, darlin' girl. Let's get you into the house and let me draw a bath for you. Or would you two prefer to use the sauna?"

As we walked toward the house, I heard Lauren gasp. Jim had whispered to her what had happened. I turned to them. "What?"

Jim rubbed Lauren's arms. "He's fine, and he will be discharged from the hospital today or tomorrow."

"Jeff? What happened?" I was shocked, but they were all alive, and in a few minutes, we would be warm.

As I removed my wet clothes, Colin explained Jeff had a touch of angina, which is typical for him, but the pain intensified. "I insisted Doug fly Jeff to the regional airport. An airplane met him, which transported him to the critical-care hospital in the capital. He was examined, and the cardiac surgeons performed angioplasty. He has three stents. After Doug escorted Jeff to the plane, he couldn't leave the regional airport because of the storms. We've been sick with worry. Darlin', I'm so sorry you had to suffer through that ordeal."

"It was so hard to wait and not know why Doug hadn't returned. You can guess what we imagined." I cried again. Colin took me in his arms and reiterated how sorry he was. He walked me to the bathroom, kissed the back of my neck, and left me to soak. He returned to Jim. Lauren took a shower. One of the ranch hands would drive them to the hospital. Jeff could not fly for a week. He and Sherry planned to stay in the city while he recovered. Lauren and Jim would join Lauren's parents for a day. They'd fly back to Nevada the following day to return to work.

Colin suggested we visit Jeff and Sherry during his recuperation. "I think he'd like to see you one more time, but let's give them a day."

Mrs. Gillard was back in the kitchen, where she served us some soup. I was finally warming up. Lauren appeared, and we shared soup and coffee. Lauren described how we survived our ordeal and our futile attempts to stay warm and dry. In the back of my mind, I was certain Lauren had endured something like this previously. She denied it, but Jim didn't seem surprised.

Whit drove up to load their bags into the truck. We hugged them and wished them well. Lauren said she'd call me that night to report on her father.

"Thank you for the most unusual wedding we've ever attended. Thanks for the adventure I won't soon forget and please come out to join us for a tour of Miner's Meadow either this summer or the next. We'll be away for much of July, but August is always nice."

As they left, I turned to Colin. "How many days before Luke returns?"

"Two or three? I think, but I don't know for sure. I'm sending Mrs. G. home for two days, if that's all right with you."

"Sounds like a plan. Could you give me thirty minutes for a quick nap?" I slept until the following morning.

I'd dreamed of lying in my husband's arms during our short and miserable ordeal. "You don't know how stressful that was for me. Not knowing why Doug hadn't returned was torture."

"Jeff called last night when you were asleep. He wanted to know if we could have a repeat next summer. I said we could discuss it tomorrow when we visit him and Sherry."

"I'll bet Sherry is dead set against it."

"No, she and Sylvia hit it off, and she loved the warm springs. She was grateful we flew Jeff to the hospital, and he now has the stents. She thought his local cardiologist had blown him off because of his age."

"Really? When was the last time you had a checkup, mister?"

"I'm probably due, but I was kind of wondering if we might try a cardiac stress test right now?"

Chapter 16

After breakfast, we walked up to the barn. The final mare had waxed, and the impending birth was imminent. "I wish Lauren was still here. I don't relish another dystocia."

"I'll have Gabe call Patty Tilmouth to put her on standby." Colin turned to see if Gabe was nearby.

"Which reminds me. Jim felt a mass on Baxter's jaw. I need to take him into the vet clinic to have them check it out." I reached down to feel the enlarged, non-painful mass. I didn't want to say it, but bone cancer was my initial thought. What I knew about bone cancers on a dog's mandible would fit in a thimble.

The mare's vulva and tail muscles were relaxed. Her abdomen had lifted, indicating the foal was now sitting up in the birth canal. I lifted her tail and noticed a pinkish mucoid discharge. "Show. Twenty-four hours or less." I tested the alarm. I explained that "show" is a term for the mucoid plug in the cervix, which is an ultimate barrier between the vaginal birth canal and the safe environment of the uterus. The plug is passed before birth and is another sign the birth is imminent.

Dixie had a foaling alarm, which comprised magnets sutured on each side of her vulva. When the foal emerges from the birth canal and divides the magnets, a signal is sent to an attendant's phone. I needed to be added to the other recipients.

When I separated the magnets, a buzzer went off inside the office. Gabe's wife, Betty Lou, came running from the office, holding her baby. Seeing us in the barn, she realized it was simply a test.

"Hey, Betty Lou, can you put the alarm code on my phone? I want to be on standby. She has a bit of show, and I don't want to miss the birth." I handed her my phone.

"I can add a link to the video, too. Would you call Patty's clinic to make sure they are on standby?"

Betty Lou nodded as she held her sleeping daughter. "Sure thing, boss-lady."

That was new. I was always called 'boss' at my clinic, but never here.

Colin brushed the mare and felt between her udders. "Best to wash her up a bit. She's pretty dirty down there." He pulled out a sizable chunk of dried smegma. "Hors d'oeuvres, anyone?"

Betty Lou took the piece and said she would give it to the baby later. I saw her throw it in a waste bin. She returned to the office with my phone, and in a few minutes, she emerged and handed my phone back. "Set to jet, boss."

"Hardly. Collie's still the boss. I am only the 2IC." I smiled at the thought.

"2IC? Second in charge." Colin grinned. "I like that term."

I glanced over at Betty Lou and smiled. "Well, I may be further down the chain of command than second."

Betty Lou understood I was deferring to her, but she quickly replied. "Yep, Digger is definitely just behind the boss."

I identified the app for the overhead camera and realized it afforded me an excellent view of the entire stall. "Perfect way to watch a foaling from the comfort of my bed."

We went next door to Digger's stall. He whinnied and greeted us at the door. "Hey, ol' boy. You will get today off and probably tomorrow, but I'm putting you on notice. We both need to ride again." Digger walked to the back of his stall after we stepped away from his gate. Colin set the brush on the bench in front of Digger's stall. "He knows all the cues, doesn't he?"

"You trained him well." I took Colin's hand as we left the barn to return to the house.

"Yep. But my primary task is the wife-reeducation program." Colin squeezed my hand.

"You wish."

When we retired for the night, I set my phone on the bedside table. I didn't want to miss the final foaling. I didn't have to wait long. Right after midnight, the alarm went off. I watched the mare as she foaled. I could see three ranch hands in attendance. I didn't get up. Colin slept through it all. The birth was quick and textbook. The mare lay on her side, and in a few grunts and pushes, a tiny foal was out.

I'd instructed the ranch hands to let the foal lie and not disturb the mare, so the foal could receive as many nutrients as possible from the umbilical cord and placenta. The foal was almost lifeless and continued to lie for an extra twenty minutes, which alarmed me. The mare stood, which broke the umbilical cord, and sprayed some blood around the stall.

After several more minutes, when the foal had not risen, I became alarmed. I phoned down to the barn and asked the crew to help the foal stand. I watched as they got the foal up. The foal stood but didn't follow the mare or seek the udder.

I called the crew back, and by now, they were joined by Betty Lou, who was experienced in caring for foals. I wanted her to phone me if the filly had not latched on to the mare in another hour. I returned to sleep. I suspected I would receive yet another call.

I had my phone on vibrate and held it against my chest to allow Colin to sleep. The call arrived the second I fell asleep. "Maggie, it's been two hours, and we can't get this foal to drink for love or money." Betty Lou described her attempts to encourage the foal to suckle. "I think it's a dummy."

"Yeah, I'm watching now, and I'd agree. Have you seen the rope-a-dope treatment?" I had an ace up my sleeve.

"I think I heard about it. Shall we give the foal another hour? I know you're sleep-deprived."

"Sleep is quite overrated. I'm used to it. Could you text me some vitals? I need her temperature, respiratory rate, and a description of how the foal breathes. Look for labored breathing. Also, look at the inside of the ear, and check for petechiae or red pinpoint spots inside the pinna. Make certain the foal doesn't have a cleft palate. Oh, I almost forgot. Check the umbilicus and be sure it isn't thickened. I saw you dipped it in the chlorhex disinfectant. Dip it again. Report back, and if everything's good, I'll come down. If not, we'll need to call Dr. Tilmouth."

I was sure she could not have completed her exam so quickly, but Betty Lou informed me it had been thirty minutes.

"Maggie? Are you awake? No fever, no petechiae in the ears, the filly's breathing slowly, and she stands solely with help, walks around the stall, and has no interest in her mother. I think it's a classic dummy. Should I call Patty Tilmouth?"

"No. I'll be down in a minute." This procedure would take only a few minutes. I could set them up and return to bed. I laughed to myself, remembering the first dummy foal I treated nearly eight years earlier. When my vet friend in South Australia told me about this, I was sure she was off the planet. I became a genuine believer after trying this technique with one of my cases. I prayed this would help the little filly.

I quietly dressed, and as I was leaving the room, Colin woke and asked me what was going on. "I think we have a dummy. I'll go to the barn to set it up for treatment, and I'll be back in less than twenty minutes. Prepare to be dazzled, beautiful boy."

"You know what dazzles me. It isn't a sick foal. I swear this is the last mare I will breed."

I bent down to kiss him. "Be back in a sec. Do you want me to leave my phone so you can watch?"

"Yes, please. What time is it? Want some coffee?"

I glanced at my watch. "Three twenty. No. I'll be straight back. I'll need the human wheat bag, so keep yourself warm."

As I entered the barn, I realized that nearly all the ranch hands were present. "Showtime!" And this time, I hoped it would be true.

"Lady and gentlemen," I started, noting Betty Lou was the only woman present. Gabe must be back at the house with the baby. "I need a soft rope and maybe a towel to set under the foal's head, so she doesn't injure her cornea. How's the mare? Is she protective of the foal?"

Betty Lou quickly responded. "Well, that may be another issue. She's not in love with her daughter."

"Oh, great, two hormonally challenged horses. Kill me now. Do we have any prostaglandin in the barn?"

"No, for sure. We used it up on the cattle. I could run into town when the vet clinic opens." Whit, who oversaw all the cattle breeding, used the prostaglandin to synchronize the cows to shorten the calving season. Before I retired, it had become popular to use it on mares that rejected their foals.

"Let's see how this goes. We may need Dr. Tilmouth or one of her offsiders to come out, anyway."

"The boss won't like it if we have unnecessary vet bills."

I rolled my eyes. "Your boss is laughing all the way to the bank every day with me as his wife. My biggest need is flies for fishing, and I know where to buy them in bulk to save. He can afford a vet bill or two, and I need to support my fellow vet sisters."

While I reexamined the foal to ensure she wasn't just ill, I explained that for years, oxygen deprivation was thought to cause the dummy foal or neonatal-maladjustment syndrome.

"This clever vet in California figured out it was not oxygen deprivation in many, if not most, foals. It's a persistence of circulating neuro-steroids. Some progesterones cause all mammals to be rather sleepy or dopey before birth. That's why foals aren't galloping in the uterus and tearing through the womb. They are in a steroid-induced sleep.

"When a foal, or any mammal, passes through the birth canal, it receives a stimulus to stop the steroids and wake up. Some mammals, including humans, benefit from the pressures exerted during the passage through the birth canal. A quick delivery might mean the stimulus to stop the steroids is missed. I watched the monitor, and that delivery was pretty quick, wouldn't you say?"

Betty Lou handed me a rope and nodded. "Damn quick."

"We'll do a rebirthing of the foal to see if we can wake her up. It's called the Madigan Squeeze, after Dr. John Madigan, who figured it out, but I call it rope-a-dope."

I placed a rope around the tiny chestnut's neck and tied a bowline knot, so the cord would not tighten and choke her. I ran it along her back and behind her withers, where I tied two half hitches around her chest. As I pulled the rope, the half hitches squeezed her thorax. She dropped to the ground and Whit caught her and helped her to fall. We placed her head on the soft towel. I showed Betty Lou the way to maintain the tension on the rope to ensure the filly remains recumbent for twenty minutes.

"At the end of the twenty minutes, let her go. Sometimes the mare rejects her foal because she thinks something is wrong with the foal. If she still rejects the foal, and the filly acts as a foal should and wants to nurse, twitch the mare and allow her to nurse if it's safe. If not, call me back. I'm going back to bed. Remember, twenty minutes. Do we have a recording going on the camera?"

Whit nodded. "Sure do. It's for security."

I returned to bed. Colin was looking at my phone when I returned. "Everything okay?"

"I hope. I'll sleep for a while. Your ranch is a dream come true. I had to do it all by myself in Australia. Now I can go back to bed." I kissed Colin and went to sleep.

He spooned me and held the phone, so he could watch the squeeze. "Want me to wake you up when it's over?"

I know I heard him ask, but in the morning, he said I didn't respond. Colin reported that thirty minutes later, the foal got up and went straight to the mare, which tried to kick her foal. "I saw the guys put a twitch on the mare, allowing the filly to nurse." Colin was dressed and headed to the barn.

"We'd better call Patty. We'll need some prostaglandin. Could I have a few more minutes?" I was not yet caught up in my adventure two days earlier. We planned to go to the big smoke to visit Jeff and Sherry.

"Do you want me to cancel? I know Jeff would understand."

"No, but let's go later." I was eager to talk to Jeff one more time, and I knew Sherry was enthralled with Colin.

When I emerged from the house an hour later, Patty Tilmouth was leaving. "Too early to do a colostrum test. I left a vial and a test kit for you in the barn. The mare responded beautifully to the prostaglandin, letting the foal nurse. I've instructed the staff to keep the foal separate for a few more hours. They have a barrier to protect the filly but permit the foal access to be near the mare.

"Good job on the squeeze. What a game changer that's been in my life."

"For sure. Collie and I are headed to the hospital to see Dr. Harper. He suffered a mild heart attack when we went on the fishing adventure. If anything's needed, please do whatever it takes."

"Oh, I forgot. If Luke is keen this summer, we need kennel help. Our regular kennel man will have surgery and be out most of the summer."

"Great. I'll let him know. I think he'll be back tomorrow or the following day from the cattle drive. Is it okay if he calls you then?"

Patty nodded and left. I hoped the job offer would lessen Luke's disappointment about missing another extraordinary foaling drama. It almost did.

Luke returned a day early, stating that the rain made the going too hard on the cattle, and they would resume moving them in a day or two. He watched the video of the squeezing procedure and the foal's abrupt return to a more normal pattern of seeking milk.

"I'll never learn how to do this if I'm always gone," he wailed.

"If you become a horse vet, I'm sure you will do plenty of these procedures. It became known only during the last few years of my work. You'll see more than you'll like in your time."

"Why did the mare reject her foal and accept it later?"

"We altered her hormones by giving her something to increase her oxytocin. You know, the exact mechanism of the response isn't entirely understood, but prostaglandin increases oxytocin. Oxy's known as the 'love drug.'"

Colin came up behind me and put his arms around me. "Listen to her, son. I'm convinced that's how she roped me in."

"Pun intended? Anyway, Lukey Boy, you need to go to Patty's clinic on Monday to report for duty."

Colin and I went down to the barn while Luke washed off several days' worth of dirt from his cattle-driving experience. Gabe held the filly while I took the blood for the colostrum test. It was a strong positive. "She's small, but she's strong. We have our hands full with this little pocket rocket. I'd suggest we get her halter broke soon."

Colin agreed. "I think I'll assign Luke to this one. I'll bring him down tomorrow, and I'll give him some wrangling education. We need to get going to see Jeff and Sherry today. They sent me a message about the place they're staying since he was kicked out of the hospital."

We returned to the house to change. Since Mrs. G. was off duty, Betty Lou would assume the kid-wrangling duties. Luke loved hanging out with Gabe and Betty Lou, but he wasn't excited to spend the night with them. "It's only until we're back at the house tonight. You'll be fine, ol' boy. Tomorrow, you and I will work with the new filly. Come up with some names for the foal."

"I get to name her?"

Colin put his hand on Luke's shoulder and hugged him. "I'm counting on you to carry on the family tradition of wrangling."

"Grandpa, who else likes horses in our family? Aren't you the only one?"

"Your mother was a hell of a hand until," but Colin didn't finish the thought

Chapter 17

We left for the big smoke and arrived in the middle of the afternoon. We located the Harpers at a motel near the airport.

Jeff repeatedly apologized for stranding Lauren and me in the woods. "I feel bad about the fright I put you through."

"The Bec Beauty you left in my vest made it all worth it, Jeff. I will order some tomorrow. And thanks for the knife." I was facing the window, which furnished a view of the swimming pool.

"You can't get them online, Maggie. I tie them myself. I'll make some for you at home."

Sherry rolled her eyes. "At least it keeps him busy. He is restricted from walking around the block, and he may not cross the street. I will put a tracking device on him when we're home."

I stared at Colin. "Interesting concept, Sherry. Let me know how that goes. I may need one, as well."

"In your dreams, darlin' girl." I could see Colin thought the concept amusing, but he had his limits.

Jeff and Sherry thanked Colin for arranging such an excellent place for Jeff to recuperate. Jeff appeared stronger than I'd noticed on our fishing trip. He wished to be invited again next year.

Colin put his hand on Jeff's shoulder. "Jeff, you're one of the few men older than I am, so I have to defer to your wishes. Let's make it August, so there's less chance of rain. But better yet, why don't you join us next January in New Zealand?" We all knew that was a long shot, but it gave Jeff something to consider.

Jeff stared at me, and I understood he wanted to have a private conversation. "Colin, do you and Sherry mind if I chat with Maggie?"

Sherry was quick to respond. "Only if I can steal Collie for a minute." They left the room.

"Maggie, you know what I told you about the ring?" He seemed embarrassed as I nodded. "Will you forget what I told you?"

"Probably not. It's kind of hard to dismiss it. You know, I mean, it must be the same ring. Obviously, it traveled from the mountains in Nevada to the South. When Becky went missing, and with all the publicity, why would someone find the ring in Nevada, not report it, and simply lose it on a historical battlefield? Was it discovered in Gettysburg, or was it only displayed at the museum?" I sat next to him and saw he was upset.

"The museum attendant said the collection came from several battlefields. They may have a specific location, but that would be in the archives. I didn't mention the caduceus insignia was modern. The man was just an attendant guard, and he didn't realize the significance of the image."

Jeff nodded and opened the images on his phone. He scrolled through his pictures for what seemed like forever. He finally found the picture as Sherry and Colin entered the room. He sent the photo to my phone and checked to see if any others were in his camera. There was one of President Lincoln making the address, but I saw only men in the audience. I handed the phone back to Jeff.

Colin had a trolly to bring up the bags from their car. Colin excused himself for a few minutes. I had a feeling I knew what he was up to. I'd find out during our drive home.

Since it was close to dinnertime, we headed to the restaurant. We all felt guilty and ate heart-healthy food. We discussed our plans for the next fishing trip and the progress toward opening the New Zealand lodge. Access to the river at the fishing lodge, which had wild trout, would be easy for Jeff.

When Colin showed him some photographs, Jeff and Sherry immediately recognized the place. Sherry was the first to respond. "You own this place? I can't believe it. We went there every year that we were able until it shut down. It's our favorite destination outside the States."

Colin put his hand around me and squeezed my shoulder. "Well, Maggie owns it. It's a long story." Colin briefly explained about the not-so-dearly departed Charlie McLeod and CLM Enterprises.

"Colin and I own it together. It's a joint project. I love winter and snow, but after a month, I'm ready to head to warmer climes. It's a great way to visit my family and fish at the same time. We hope you can join us next year."

There was no mistake about my admiration for Jeff. He was the man who introduced me to fishing. The surprise was how well Sherry and I got on as well. I could tell she was mesmerized by Colin. Still, she genuinely seemed to enjoy her time with us, and I could imagine her as a co-conspirator in the unmentioned battle of the sexes. She was so much like Becky.

We left them, and of course, Colin paid for the dinner. As we walked to the car, Colin handed me the keys. "I'm stepping down tonight. I'm exhausted. I need to preserve my energy. Maggot, you're one exciting woman, but I need a nap." With that, he lowered the seat and was asleep in minutes.

Colin woke when we stopped for the automatic gate opener. A plastic bag was taped to the post. My heart sank when I opened the door to retrieve it. I only touched the corner of the bag as I tore it away from the bar and returned to the car. We stared at it and the paper contents.

"Should we open it?" I turned to Colin, who was now fully awake.

"Why don't we wait to give it to the sheriff's department tomorrow morning?" Colin set the bag on the console and immediately called Gabe and Betty Lou.

When Colin called the office, Betty Lou answered. He informed her about the message and suggested they check the security cameras, assign someone to stay at the barn, and keep a twenty-four-hour watch on the monitors for the next few days.

Betty Lou reported the new foal was bonded and nursed aggressively. "We have our hands full with that one. She's a firecracker."

We were on speaker phone. "Uh, that will be Luke's problem. He and Collie will be at the barn tomorrow to begin the foal-wrangling lessons." I smiled as I gazed at my multi-talented husband.

Betty Lou responded. "You may want to delay the lessons, boss-lady. The mare's done a one-eighty, and she attempts to kill anyone who goes near the foal. Luke was up twice to see the foal today, and she nearly cleaned his clock. Luke was ready to start, but I talked him out of anything until the guys could give him a hand."

Colin readjusted his car seat. "BL, I don't want anyone in the stall for another two days. She'll get over it. We can wait. It will take me a day or two to recover from this wedding week, anyway." After Colin hung up the phone, we entered the house.

"BL? Is that short for Betty Lou?" I didn't remember anyone calling her by that name previously.

"She asked me to call her that years ago. I guess you didn't hear me say that before. BL also stands for boss lady, but now that's your moniker."

I noticed the remnants of a gin game on the kitchen table. I opened the door to Luke's room, walked over, and kissed him. He batted me away, and I quickly retreated. As I closed the door, Luke said, "Sweet dreams, Maggie."

"Sweet dreams, Lukey Boy. Prepare for goodnight kisses for as long as I live."

Chapter 18

"I love waking up next to you." Colin rolled toward me and pulled me into him. There was no mistake about his intentions.

"Mr. Chandler, I married you for better or worse, but at your age, really?"

"This is the better. But remember, darlin', I promised only better or even better."

When we entered the kitchen, Luke rolled his eyes and covered his face. "Will you two always be late for breakfast?"

I quickly replied, "No."

Colin turned to me and said, "No promises, but I hope so."

Mrs. Gillard rolled her eyes and asked how we wanted our eggs. Colin and I, who thought about Jeff, both declined eggs and bacon. I knew that dietary consumption of bacon and eggs was not nearly as significant as other factors, and we were both lean. My cholesterol levels were checked a few months earlier, but I didn't know about Colin's test results.

Colin instructed Luke to run to the barn to check on the mare and foal. "Don't go into the stall, Luke. A foal-proud mare is unpredictable, but make sure the foal is nursing and bright. I think Patty Tilmouth wants you today. Get back and get ready, so I can run you into town."

After Luke left the room, Colin called the sheriff's office. He was notified that Tom Sutton was no longer the sheriff, and a new sheriff had taken his place. I watched Colin's reaction to the replacement—thumbs-up. Terry Simpson was the new sheriff. Colin and I assumed it was a man, but when Colin asked to speak to him, he was quickly informed that Terry was a woman. His hand rotated, pointing his thumb down.

Colin received my response. He caught my foot with his free hand before it hit the mark. I almost went down to the ground, but he grabbed me and put me in a headlock in front of Mrs. Gillard. Colin waited for the sheriff to come to the phone.

"This is Sheriff Simpson. How may I help you, Mr. Chandler?"

Colin explained that we'd received some threatening phone calls over the wedding weekend. We believed it was time to involve the authorities.

"I see. I'm new to the area. Do you mind if I come out? It's probably best that I assess your security."

Colin cocked his head, considered her proposal, and seemed agreeable. "Okay, that would be great. I need to run my grandson into town for a minute. We'll see you at ten if that suits you."

Colin turned to me and rotated his thumb upward again. "Darlin', get your computer and phone, so we can show them the messages. I think I'll talk with Luke on the way to town."

Mrs. Gillard appeared to be worried. "Is there something I should know?"

I rose to retrieve my computer and phone while Colin described the situation. When I returned, Colin smiled. "What do you know about handling a gun?"

I recalled my recent interaction when Lauren and I were left along the river. I was clueless when Lauren demonstrated her advanced knowledge about using a pistol. "Uh, I know as much as the average Australian does about guns."

"Perhaps we need a firearm session. Maggie, I know you took a lesson with the rifle, but I never thought it might not include using a handgun."

"If I need to learn these things here, my children will capture me to take me back. You won't even know I'm gone before it happens."

Colin took Luke to the veterinary clinic for an interview. I hoped they would keep him for the day. Colin planned to drive up to my property to be certain no new messages were on the gate.

"Idle hands are the devil's workshop, Maggie." Mrs. Gillard opened the swinging door between the kitchen and the dining room. "Hopefully, he'll come back when he's twenty-one."

"Mrs. G., my boys weren't even remotely socialized until they were in their mid-twenties. I think you're dreaming as if they would ever be human." I loved my kids, but they were a tough gig as teenagers.

"Maybe, but Luke keeps me in a job. That's for sure." Mrs. Gillard refilled the salt and pepper shakers as I checked my phone for new messages. Thankfully, there were none.

"You have no fear of me, Mrs. G. You're set for life as far as I'm concerned."

She placed her hand on her hip and looked up at the ceiling. "That's a relief. Before the wedding, the boss wanted to know if I would accept you into the house full time. I had my reservations, Maggie. After you cooked a meal for him, the question became a plea. He said you couldn't cook if your life depended on it. FYI, you would have been sent packing if I'd said no."

I doubted this. Considering the early morning activities, I was convinced Colin would accept my lack of culinary talents. Still, there was no sense in irritating the kitchen goddess.

"Mrs. G., as the only women in the house, we should stick together. You can always count on me to stand behind you."

"United we stand." We fist-bumped.

Colin returned a few minutes before the sheriff's scheduled arrival time. He checked his phone and noted both Betty Lou and Gabe said they would meet us at the barn.

"I'll bet she's five foot two, 160 pounds, short black hair, and a shirt so tight her buttons are in danger of popping off." I had never heard Colin pronounce such a sexist opinion.

I was shocked. *Who the hell did I marry?* "I see couch time in your future, Mr. Chandler."

He nodded. "As long as she's not related to the perps, I'll be happy." The former sheriff was a cousin of Carol, my realtor, who sold me the house and murdered the previous homeowners. The former sheriff never properly investigated the deaths until new clues surfaced years later.

Chapter 19

Sheriff Simpson's Land Rover pulled up in the parking area beside the house. Colin and I walked out onto the porch to greet her. I observed a tall brunette with shoulder-length, straight hair, who wore dark glasses that rested on a perfect nose and chiseled face. There was not a trace of extra weight over her curvy body. She might have come directly off a movie set.

Mother of God was all I could think.

Colin looked down. "Not exactly what I was expecting." I could see he was pleasantly surprised.

Pleasant was not how I felt—more like threatened. I softly hummed the "D-I-V-O-R-C-E" tune from Tammy Wynette.

"I think we'll be in expert hands now." Colin squeezed my shoulder.

All I could do was shake my head.

"Mr. and Mrs. Chandler, I'm Terry Simpson, and this is my deputy sheriff, Dwayne Thomas. Perhaps we should quickly discuss your concerns and check your security setup."

Colin went into command mode. His hosting skills exceeded anything I ever remembered receiving. I didn't even think about searching for a ring. Maybe she was married to an Adonis of a lumberjack or an Atticus Finch. I mean, who could blame Colin? *Heck, I would turn gay for this woman.*

When we were seated, Mrs. Gillard brought coffee and some cookies. Terry Simpson did not have a ring on—damn. She was a no-nonsense sheriff. She wasted no time in chitchat.

"Would you show me the messages you received?" She tapped her pen on the table as she sat forward and examined the paper notes, including the one from this morning. She then peered into my computer to watch the video of the chicken being decapitated.

After she examined the evidence, she stared at both of us. She wanted to know whether we had received any more messages and if we had any ideas about who might have sent the others. I described the garbled phone calls. Terry reviewed my phone-call log to record some notes. Her deputy assessed my emails. When they asked about my social media, I explained I had several accounts but used them only to sell books. My agent handled it.

"I think it's best to keep this situation to ourselves. I'm new to the area and station. I know there's been some lack of follow-through, and whether it was intentional or just poor policing skills is yet to be determined. Basically, these are good men and women, and while crime is not enormous in the county, there is an upswing, compared with a few years ago. So, you got married this last week?"

"Yes, we did." I took Colin's hand, and he put his over mine and nodded.

"It was touch-and-go for a few months, but my darling bride finally submitted and allowed me to marry her. Are you aware of the murder of the two occupants of my wife's property and Charlie McLeod's side business?"

"Yes, that's part of why I'm here. I was FBI in a former life, but I needed to step back from the fast lane."

Mrs. Gillard asked if anyone else needed anything. She planned to go shopping and wouldn't be back for a few hours. "Maggie, I can pick up Luke when he's done. Just call me. I'm going home for an hour as well."

I nodded and thanked her. "Will do, Mrs. G."

"Say, Sheriff Simpson, are you familiar with the boys' camp in the forest behind my property, near Saddleback Lake?"

"My friends call me Terry, and I'm not one to be too formal. And yes. We're aware of the activity. I have to say they were a strange lot. I rode out to see what was going on. The lake looks fishy. I'm always searching for places to fish."

Colin sat up and leaned forward. I closed my eyes and shook my head while Colin put his hand on my shoulder. "Well, Terry, you've come to the right place. Have you met our town doctor? Eric is a fishing tragic. Maybe you could join us for a fish one evening."

OMG, why didn't I think of that? "We'd love for you to join us. We're a bit busy right now, but next week we'd like for you to come." This was perfect. I could have another fishing partner who would not challenge Colin for my affection. I might get Eric someone new to consider. *Match the hatch.*

Colin quietly rubbed his leg against mine. "Shall we head up to the barn to view the security system and meet some of the staff?"

As we walked toward the barn, Terry surveyed the surroundings. "I guess you've considered the staff as the source of the threats?"

"Yes. These people have worked for me for several years. My grandson was the subject of a custody dispute following his mother's murder. I brought him here and hired former military personnel to run the ranch. Their jobs are twofold. We have a cattle and horse ranch, but their primary job is to keep my family safe. With my recent marriage, these men and women have had to double their workload. Keeping this woman out of harm's way is a job and a half." Colin put his arm around me and smiled down at me as we entered the barn.

Terry observed a young gelding being saddled. "Do you sell horses? I want a horse to ride. The reason I worked here is the accessibility of riding trails and the rivers."

Be still my beating heart. "Terry, we need to be better friends. I'm always looking for riding and fishing partners. Is there any chance you can come to dinner next Tuesday? We'd love to have you." I was already planning the wedding. Phew, Eric would be perfect for her. *Cue the wedding bells.* "Tuesdays are the best days, but this week isn't great. One of our wedding guests is in the city, and we promised to visit with him once more before he travels home."

"Did I know this?" Colin glanced at me as we entered the barn office.

"You should. We can discuss it later." I was sure Colin was present when Jeff and I suggested meeting one more time.

We introduced Terry to Betty Lou and Gabe Turner, whose baby was sleeping in a cot near the monitors. Terry surveyed both sets of monitors of the ranch and my cabin. "Impressive. This system is better than the one back at the office. I guess there isn't any recent activity?"

Betty Lou showed her the pre-wedding videos of the boys entering my garage and the men who arrived to search for the lost boy. Terry wanted a copy of the video. The faces of the men were detailed, and she thought she might run it past her crew and a photo ID database she could use.

Colin showed her some horses we owned but suggested she contact Trent and Sylvia West at the Bar Double X Ranch. "We have reduced our stock, but the Bar Double X constantly breaks in fresh horses, and they'll have something to suit you. They're our friends, and they occasionally employ our grandson."

My phone rang. It was an unknown number. "Hey, this might be another call." Terry said to answer it and put it on speaker. She turned on her voice recorder to prepare to record the voice.

"Hello?" I responded.

"Hello, Dr. Kincaid?"

"Yes?" Kincaid? Should I correct the person on the phone?

"This is Alice from the vet clinic. Can you talk for a moment?"

Terry turned off her phone, and I took the phone off the speaker.

"Yes, sure. Is Luke alright?"

"Oh, I don't know. Luke's on calls with Dr. Tilmouth. This is about your dog, Baxter. I'm afraid we have some bad news."

I felt my stomach drop to my pelvis. "Go on."

"It appears he may have a growth. Dr. Bledisloe doesn't think it's bone cancer. It may be another invasive cancer, and he would like to do a biopsy. Baxter's going to need an anesthetic. Did you feed him this morning?"

"No. No food or water, so go for it. Would you call me when you're done, and maybe we should discuss the findings before we tell Luke? He's been through so much, and I want to protect him."

Alice said she would call when she knew something and not discuss anything with Luke other than they were investigating the lump. I returned to the conversation. I noticed one of the ranch hands saddling Digger. "Hey, don't tell me you're selling my horse?"

"No, darlin', I'm only endearing the sheriff to our cause."

Terry adjusted the stirrups and mounted Digger. He entered the arena, where she briefly rode him. "Nice. Does he have a twin?"

I was quick to interject. "No, none for sale. How about you and I ride over to Saddleback when you have a day off?"

"A day off? I'm not sure what you mean. With the crime rate here in our county, I'm lucky to get some sleep. Did you know we caught a ten-year-old stealing a *Playboy* magazine issue the other day? The paperwork took us two days to process. Poor Dwayne has a new family member, and he isn't even sure if it's a girl or a boy. I'll try to fit you in, but you never know when duty calls."

Dwayne rolled his eyes. "His name is Fred, and he's eleven months old. She prevaricates."

"Okay, crime wave aside, sounds like fun. Do I call you Dr. Kincaid or Chandler? I've read a couple of your books, and I have some ideas about how a sidekick can assist your crime-fighting vet."

"I'm Maggie. I'm always open to plot ideas."

Colin was quick to add, "It's Chandler now."

"Well, let's hope this little adventure isn't book worthy." Colin walked over to the stall where the new foal nursed. When the mare ran to the door with her teeth barred, he quickly stepped back.

Terry dismounted and thanked us. She recommended we take no chances and be vigilant about any unusual activity. She and her deputy left.

As they drove down the driveway, I laughed. "Five foot two, and was it nine hundred forty or sixty pounds?"

"Oh, really? I hadn't noticed." He smiled as he stared at the ground and kicked a stone.

"I'll bet. We're the only ones here for lunch. Roast beef or peanut butter, beautiful boy?"

Chapter 20

Colin wanted to attend to some business after lunch. Terry's visit reminded me I had a job of writing books. I would call my agent about my change of circumstances and the need to separate my public emails from my personal ones.

Luke was still out on calls when Mrs. Gillard returned. I received a call from the vet clinic that both Baxter and Luke were ready to go. The biopsy went well, and the results should be known by the end of the week.

Colin said he would drive to the clinic to pick them up. He wanted to tell Luke about our concerns regarding the messages and assure Luke that he was safe.

When they returned, Luke hugged me and said he would protect me at all costs.

"Thanks, Lukey Boy." I loved having two protective men in my life.

"Uh, Maggie. I mean, Grandma, that will depend on the reinstatement of tickling privileges."

I had never meant for the punishment to last for more than a few days. "I figure you have me over a barrel. I suppose we could open negotiations."

Luke walked over to his grandfather and held out his hand. Colin reached into his back pocket, pulled out his wallet, and handed Luke a dollar. Luke shook his head, pointed to the palm of his hand, and tapped it. "I seem to recall we bet five dollars I would be back in her good books in less than a week. Pay up, old man."

Colin reluctantly took the one to replace it with a five-dollar bill.

I shook my head. "Sheesh, if you gamble my inheritance away, will there be anything left for me?"

Luke grinned and put his hand around his grandfather. "United we stand. Isn't that what you oldies say?"

"Good thing I've given up swearing, because I would suggest you two need an ass kicking." I stared at the boys, trying not to laugh.

Colin covered Luke's ears with his hands. "Years of therapy, and now this poor boy will have to start all over again."

"Grandpa, fifteen minutes of tickling is worth two hours of any therapy."

I shook my head. Oh, how precious these interactions were to our family. "I'm going to make a bed for Baxter. He can sleep in the laundry tonight. I think we aren't long for dinner. Luke, do you want to shower or help Mrs. G. set the table?" I knew the answer to that. Luke would be thirteen in a few days. His need to be clean and extracurricular shower activities would begin soon, but he wasn't there yet.

He headed to the kitchen. "Collie, maybe I forgot to remind you, but I told Jeff and Sherry I'd come by before they left. I thought I would go tomorrow. Do you want to go with me or stay here?"

"I'm surprised you have to ask. Either I go or send a ranch hand to accompany you. We can't afford to take any chances until we know the messages were a prank."

It was a comfort to have such a kindhearted but pain-in-the-ass husband—the good with the bad. I'd endured so many years attending emergencies in the middle of the night for people and properties I didn't know. As good as it was, I had to adjust to living with someone who would control my life while making me safe. "Your choice, cowboy."

"I'll go. I want to see Sherry one more time. I have some pictures I know she'll like."

Funny, but I meant to search for more photos of Becky and her ring. It was time to confide in my husband. I'd wait until this evening when we'd be alone. I checked Baxter and called the Harpers to announce that we would both be back the following day to take them to lunch. Jeff had clearance to leave early. He mentioned he was feeling so much better and even suggested they return to the ranch to fish again.

I could hear Sherry yelling to me that Jeff was restricted from any serious physical activity for a few weeks. "Not gonna happen, Jeff. The next thing you will do is wash the dishes at home. I'm going to learn to ride the lawn mower."

"Sorry, Jeff, but I'm with Sherry on that one. You're under house arrest. Don't make me come down to enforce the orders. You won't like my methods."

At dinner, Luke described his day. He worked in the small-animal clinic and accompanied Patty on calls. Luke mentioned he couldn't officially work until he was thirteen. He could volunteer, though, and he was welcome to come whenever he wanted to see what was going on. Luke was shooting up, and his voice was transforming. He would be movie-star handsome like his grandfather.

He still tutored a girl from high school and said he planned to buy a Mustang or Ferrari.

Colin nodded, and I guessed this topic had been discussed. I performed my mother- like eye roll.

When preparing for bed, Colin asked me about Jeff's and our private conversation at the hotel. I didn't want to betray Jeff's confidential concerns, but I also didn't want to keep secrets from my husband.

"Collie, I want to tell you everything, but I know Jeff is embarrassed about anyone thinking he's gone off the deep end. He has some information about Rebecca and her disappearance. It's probably a coincidence and nothing earthshaking. I think he's worried it would stir up things with Sherry. I thought I would ask him to include you in his discovery tomorrow when we visit him. I don't know if we can help him, but I'd like to ease his mind. Is that enough to satisfy you?"

"Well, since you brought it up—I mean the satisfaction concept." Colin smiled mischievously and took me in his arms.

"Nope, not gonna happen, beautiful boy. I need to sleep. How about a back tickle?"

"That's what I intended. You didn't think—no way. Remember our ages."

"Eighty going on twenty-four, and sixty-nine going on eighty-five. Get into bed, roll over, and accept your tickle. I'll set a timer."

"Darlin' girl, if I even can roll over, once I'm horizontal, it will be a miracle if I last a minute."

Chapter 21

After we dropped Luke at Patty Tilmouth's clinic, we headed back to see the Harpers one more time. I'd identified some more photos, which I copied to my camera from both my picture albums and undergraduate-university yearbooks. She was so cute and such a "go-getter." Her death was a terrible loss. I wished I'd written to Jeff back then. I was so excited about my pending nuptials I abandoned my American friends. It would lessen my guilt to help Jeff understand his discovery as simply a coincidence.

The concept of Becky abandoning her family was ridiculous. If she'd been injured and suffered from a case of amnesia, I am sure she'd have been located years ago. Anyway, I had to admit the evidence was unusual.

As we pulled into the parking lot, I noticed Sherry getting into a cab. She waved and yelled for us to head to their room. She shouted she had to go to the pharmacy and hospital to pick up a monitoring device and medication. Colin asked if he could take her, but she didn't hear him, and the driver closed the car door.

Colin knocked on the motel-room door to announce our arrival. Jeff ushered us in and kissed me. Since he stared at Colin, it was obvious Jeff wanted to talk to me alone. Colin excused himself to go to the lobby but, at the last minute, Jeff asked him to stay.

We discussed the weather, their flights, Lauren, and Jim. I guessed Jeff had decided not to pursue the Gettysburg findings. I didn't bring up the subject. I was glad I had the photographs on my phone and not the actual yearbooks and photos. I could tell Jeff was struggling. Some things are best left in the past.

Jeff opened his phone. "It was my intention to keep all this to myself, but it bothered me so much that I think the stress of knowing and hiding it all may have contributed to the cardiac incident. I'm sure my catecholamines were sky high. It's not fair to expect Maggie to keep a secret from you, Collie, and yet, I can't let it go."

He explained his chance discovery of the ring and pictures in the Gettysburg Museum, the history of the veterinary caduceus emblem, and the initials inside the ring.

Colin appeared to be uncomfortable. "Do you think she's still alive? Or do you believe someone found the ring and lost it at Gettysburg?"

He examined Jeff's phone with the image of the ring. "And you say that veterinary emblem has been around only since World War I, but here it is in a museum from the Civil War?"

"There must be another explanation, Collie, but damned if I can figure it out. Someone must have found the ring in the Sierras and lost it on a battlefield in the South. I know it's the one I gave her."

I experienced a profound sadness for this man. It was as if Becky were missing all over again. "What do you plan to do? Is there something we can do to help?"

"There's even more. I did some research about the cabin that Lauren wanted to buy. Thankfully, she didn't, but I made inquiries. I considered purchasing it for her as a last gift from Bec. I told no one, but I received a small insurance payout from a policy we took out for each other when we knew we were having a baby. I put it in a trust to help her. In the end, I opted not to use the money. Sherry and I still hoped Lauren would return to Kentucky. Anyway, the title of the cabin was researched. A Dr. Rebecca Harper owned it in the late 1850s until it was deeded over to a couple in the 1880s. Now, don't you think that's a little on the improbable side?"

Colin's hand gripped mine. "I'm sure there's an explanation. Have you discussed any of this with Lauren?"

"No, and I won't. She's found such happiness in her marriage. I don't want to upset her for what's realistically a rather unlikely explanation for the reason we never found her mother."

I hugged Jeff. "I guess you haven't told Sherry, either?"

"Oh, no. I'd never discuss it with Sherry. She still grieves about losing her sister. She regrets leaving her when their mother died. I don't want to add to her guilt. I didn't tell anyone what I found out about the cabin title, and I'd have said nothing about the ring. Except with the two pieces of information together, the unthinkable is something to ponder."

I could tell Colin was intrigued. "Jeff, I'm not following this. Are you suggesting she died and went to the past or had a past life? I played a role in a movie about time travel, but we all knew it was only fantasy. There's no such thing. Is there?"

"Guys, I'm sure there's a logical explanation for all this. I mean, Becky's dead, or she never died and is playing a cruel joke on us all. Sorry to say, I vote for dead."

Colin put his arm around my waist. He stared at Jeff, whose eyes were brimming with tears. "Jeff, what can we do? I owe you the moon. You taught my beautiful bride how to fly- fish and get foals out of tight spots. I could never thank you enough."

This made us all laugh and took Jeff a step back from the emotional precipice on which he teetered. Jeff wiped his eyes. "I'd stopped even thinking about Becky. I'm blessed to have found love twice, but when I saw you, Maggie, it all came back. We had such good times, didn't we? Well, I guess this is simply one mystery that will never be solved."

The door rattled as Sherry entered. We all stopped talking and glanced at her. Sherry knew we were discussing a serious topic. "Hey, did someone die?"

Chapter 22

Sherry gazed at us and then realized what she'd said. She knew we must be talking about her baby sister. "Here's the monitor the clinic ordered, and I think I have enough medication to take us to Christmas. Darling, we should get ready to go. I've ordered a cab, and don't think I'm not annoyed at someone who already paid our motel bill." She looked at Colin and me.

I turned to Colin and smiled. He shrugged. "You understand I either cover some costs for this misadventure, or sleep on the couch tonight? I never thought about these things when I agreed to marry my little Maggot. Like her kids say, she's a ball-buster."

"I'm just getting started, darling. I'll make a poor boy out of you, and I won't increase my personal net worth by a dollar. Remember, your dear friend warned you."

Charlie was my original suitor when I moved from Australia to my new home. I was not above using his money to help friends with their own philanthropic needs. However, when I learned the source of his money, I was disgusted and quickly decided he was not the man I thought he was—enter Colin Chandler.

Colin wanted me to drive back to the ranch so he could catch up on some emails from friends and distant relatives. I knew he had cousins, but I thought they had all passed. Every year, a few fans broke into the inner circle and kept in touch with him.

"Hey, want to head to Virginia City?" Colin smiled as he read the email. "I mean, we're invited to a wedding. That old geezer's getting married."

"Who?" I didn't know who he meant.

"Henry Davidson. You would never have heard about him, but he is one of the Manhattan Project scientists. Henry is a physicist who worked on the atomic bomb. His deceased wife was one of my most ardent *Comstock* fans. He even created a replica of the original fireplace for their house, which was so prominent in the television series."

"Would any of this concern the information Jeff shared with us about Becky?" I wondered if Colin was going to consider the crazy notion of Becky either still being alive or transporting herself to the past. I had to admit the coincidence of the deed to that cabin near Tahoe and the ring on a battlefield in Gettysburg was difficult to dismiss.

"No, but it takes me back to the television series and the beauty of the area. I'd love to show you Miner's Meadow, where we filmed some of our remote scenes. I know it's public land, but when we filmed, no one had even heard about it. I stayed in a cabin built in the 1800s, and the fishing in the lake was divine. I even took Helen there, and we stayed on after they completed the filming. Helen and I spent a few days alone up there. It's where Kyle was conceived." Colin grinned, remembering that time in his life.

"Yeah, I could get interested if the fishing's good. What did you call the place in your television series?" I had to swerve to miss a skunk that was crossing the road back to our ranch. I smiled to myself as I thought about how naturally the phrase 'our ranch' came to me.

Colin stared in my direction. "What was that about?"

"What? Asking about your series?"

"The smile." He cocked his head and reached over to take my free hand.

"I was thinking about how our lives had changed." *A small lie.*

"All the names from the series came from my partner and coproducer, Alex Conrad. Now talk about a genius. He dreamed up the entire series. Too bad he's passed. I would have loved for you to meet him."

"Yeah, so you aren't considering mixing any sleuthing by attending a wedding?"

"Darlin' girl. I'm always interested in what defies logic, but time travel and what Jeff showed us are a bit too long of a leap for this cowboy." Colin moved the seat back and closed his eyes. "Although seeing you naked in the lake up at Miner's Meadow sounds interesting. We could pretend to time travel. I could be twenty-four."

"And that would make me thirteen. How about you be thirty-four?"

Colin smiled as he folded his hands together and began a rhythmic breathing pattern that was becoming quite familiar to me.

Chapter 23

I took Luke to work at the clinic the next morning. I'd received a text message from the vet clinic to bring Baxter back. The histopathology report suggested a type of cancer that might respond to chemotherapy. Some bloodwork was required to make sure he would tolerate the treatment. The vet would run the bloods, order the chemotherapeutic agents, and start his first treatment if the drugs could be sourced locally.

I stopped by the post office to pick up Colin's mail and buy some stamps for the thank-you cards I'd ordered for the guests and other well-wishers. He mentioned there was a package, as well. I stood in line, which took forever. An elderly woman in front of me struggled to pay the postage for a package bound for Australia. The address did not work, and the postmistress was annoyed, as were the other customers in the line.

"My son lives in Australia, and this is the address he sent to me." I heard the distress in her voice.

"Well, ma'am, this says it isn't an address. FSD won't work on my computer, and no town called Booligal is in Adelaide. How about you step aside so I can assist the people behind you, and then I'll try to figure out what you need?"

She stepped away. She stared at her package and at a letter in her hand. Her hands shook. I stepped out of line. "Ma'am, I lived in Australia for many years. May I help you?"

"My son lives at a cattle station near this town. He wants me to send him some things from home. I copied the address just like it says, but the woman says it's not a proper address. I haven't seen my son in several years. This is the first time he's written to me in a year, and I want to help him. He wrote to me only when his father died, which was several years ago. He wants his father's wedding ring, so he can give it to his friend. I would do anything to make him happy. The ring is valuable, and I know he wouldn't ask me to send it if it wasn't important."

"Is that all? May I see his address and yours, too?" The woman was clearly flustered, and she said she couldn't remember her own address. I immediately understood the problem. She listed the state as Adelaide, which is a city in South Australia and not a state. The town was listed as Booligal, which is situated in New South Wales. It took me just a few seconds to identify the correct spelling and postcode for the residence.

I rewrote the address on the overseas form and finished the form to send the package. I signed it for her and had her stand in front of me in the line, which was increasing by the minute. When she was called to the counter, she presented the box. I stepped up behind her, explained what had happened, and clarified I had used my address for the return.

The postmistress examined the package and shook her head. "It's on you if anything in here is not what's written on the declaration."

I smiled with a feeling of warmth that came over me. Mrs. Frost and I walked out of the post office. I suspected mild dementia. "Where do you live? I'd like to help you return to your home."

"Missus..." She paused, and suddenly she knew who I was. "Oh, you're the hussy who married my boyfriend. Shame on you." With steely eyes, she did not flinch as she watched me. Then she smiled. "I'm only joking. It was wonderful to have you assist me. I'll be sure to tell the others."

"Others? Who are the others?" I was concerned she might be behind the threatening messages. *How ridiculous. She couldn't even mail a parcel to her son.*

"Most of the townsfolk think you shouldn't have married him. Don't worry, I'll defend you." She peered up the road and again, she appeared confused. "No, I'd rather walk than be seen with you. I have an excellent reputation, you know." She walked away down the street. She crossed to the other side and returned up the street in the direction she had just come. She walked purposely, and I would swear she showed no signs of dementia. As I walked back to my vehicle, a car sped past me, and I swore she sat in the passenger seat. *Did she just give me the finger?*

When I returned to the ranch, Mrs. G. was dusting in the library. I told her the story about the package and the lady. As I described the woman, Mrs. G. shook her head. "She doesn't sound like anyone I know in our county."

This made me think about using my return address on a box that only contained a ring. *Oh, please, Lord, let that be true.* Thankfully, I had witnesses.

Chapter 24

I picked up Luke, but Baxter remained at the clinic. He received his initial dose of chemo, and all had gone well, but Dr. Bledisloe suggested that since he had a critical-care patient, he'd like to administer some meds to Baxter around midnight.

Luke was excited that he'd be hired as soon as he turned thirteen. In the meantime, he could volunteer at the clinic when he was not working for the Wests. Luke would spend a few days with the Wests to finish driving the cattle into the mountains, starting on Monday.

Oh, how I wanted to go, but our new sheriff was coming to fish along with Eric Travers, and I needed to be present to string cupid's bow. Eric was still single and one of the best fly anglers in the area. If I couldn't get something going for Eric's sake, I would be disappointed in myself—not to mention the threat of a stunning, unattached sheriff hanging around my husband.

I had Luke's bag packed, I drove him over to the Bar Double X, and while no one was watching, I hugged and kissed him goodbye for the weekend. Luke walked away, turned, and returned for a second hug. "Maggie, please make sure Baxter's okay when he comes home. Will you let him sleep on the bed?"

"I'll try, but last time he wanted to go back to sleep on yours. He's not my dog anymore, you know."

Luke smiled, but I could detect brimming tears. He turned to hide them and headed to the corral. He raised his hand to signal he understood. "He's yours when the vet bill comes, Grandma."

"In your dreams, Lukey Boy—in your dreams."

I returned to the ranch, where I couldn't find Colin. I went out to the garden shed, where we maintained the fishing gear. Colin was tying a fly and smiled when I entered. "Luke and Baxter sorted, darlin' girl?"

I put my hand on his shoulder and peered over to see what fly he was tying. "Yeah. Is that a Bec Beauty? Did Jeff show you that fly?"

Colin reached under a paper sitting on the table and produced one of Jeff's flies. "He said it's lethal to fish."

"It sure saved us the other day. We couldn't catch any trout to save our souls, but that fly caught food for us when Lauren and I were left to die—I mean, stranded. By the way, apparently Becky thought it up and made the first one. The rest is Harper history."

"A 'left-to-die' situation—hardly, darlin' girl. Did I tell you the bear hide has been retrieved? I took it to a taxidermist. Care for an evening in front of the fire this winter?"

"Yeah, me naked on a bear rug is a surefire way to the divorce attorney—pun intended."

"You can't blame a man for trying." Colin removed the fly from the bench vise to study it. "I think it's a fair replica. What time can we expect our fishing guests? I'll get the Gator and put it down at the house, and then we'd better get dressed."

"I do hope this works out for all concerned. I would love to help Eric find love again."

Shortly after I dressed, I heard Eric's car pull up next to the house. Terry Simpson was in the passenger seat. *Oh good, they've already met.*

Colin greeted them, helped them unload their gear, and took them around to the shed. I waved from the front door. I said I would meet them at the Gator. I had snacks and beer. I brought soft drinks in case anyone was on the wagon for the evening. Eric often had to remain sober because he was on call. Recently, he had partnered with a new doctor in the adjoining town, and they shared the emergencies. I was not sure about Terry.

"Hey, Terry. Welcome to fish heaven. I'm so happy you could join us. Don't let these men put you off. Why don't you sit in front, so you can have a good view?"

The fishing rods were secured above the cab. I placed two coolers in the back of the Gator, and we were off to the river. Eric and I sat in the back, and I watched him grinning like a fool. I hit his thigh and quietly gave him the thumbs-up. He nodded and smiled in return. *Oh, happy day.*

"Don't worry, Maggie. I have my cuffs if they give us any problems."

"Oh, can I borrow them?" I tapped Colin's shoulder. "I may have use for them if my new husband doesn't start acting his age."

"Only on Tuesdays, darlin'."

Eric knew what Colin referred to, but Terry cocked her head.

"I'd tell you about it, Terry, but then you'd probably arrest my wife for false advertising."

"If you don't stop complaining, you'll never have the experience." *Why did I ever mention fetish Tuesdays?*

Eric pointed to the trees that guarded the river. "Up here, and didn't I tell you?"

"Yeah, you're right. They're feisty for a couple of oldies."

The fishing was productive, and we all caught fish. Terry was no slouch. She and Eric went hand in hand. I spent the evening netting fish for them both. We watched the sunset and a band of orange cumulus clouds in the distance.

"Last call. Lady and gentlemen, time to reel in your lines." By my reckoning, Terry caught the most and the largest.

We returned to the house, where Eric and I gutted and prepared the fish for dinner. Mrs. G. had the rest of the meal done before she departed. "So glad to be back with the fifteen-minute-meal-master. How's married life, Maggie?"

"I'm hoping for boring, but so far, that isn't happening. I haven't had time to even ride to Saddleback Lake. Poor Digger's going to waste, and I'm under some restrictions regarding my adventures. Apparently, I have a stalker. And you? How's the new sheriff working out? I can see you're acquainted?"

"Handcuffs aside, she's just what the doctor ordered." Eric grinned like a teenager.

"Are you two an item? Can you pass me the flour?"

"I've had dinner with her twice. The first time, I had to leave early for an emergency, and the second time, she had to leave."

"Fingers crossed, my friend. What do the kids think? Are they with their mom or you right now?" Eric shared two teenagers with his ex.

"They will be with their mom for only a few weeks this summer, so we'll cross that bridge when they return. Any word on locating your stalker?"

"Nope, I hope it was a hoax." I took things out to the swimming pool so we could enjoy the evening outside. I enjoyed eating under the canopy. I remembered having Luke's birthday party, meeting Colin's family, and Charlie's arrival by helicopter. *How far have I come?*

Colin and Terry emerged from around the front of the house. Terry glanced at me, carrying a tray. "What can I do to help?"

"Nothing. Just enjoy yourself. You're the guest. We usually let the newbies have only one evening of relaxation before you become a working member. What do you like to drink?"

"Sarsaparilla for me, ma'am, because I might be called to help clear the saloon later." She patted her pants where her handcuffs were pocketed.

I returned to the kitchen for the wine Colin had selected earlier. Eric followed me with the meal, including freshly fried trout. He and Terry sat across from us, and he casually dished out the food for both him and Terry. Terry appeared to appreciate Eric's attention. Colin kicked me under the table, and I could tell he was happy with the pairing.

"Oh, Eric, I forgot to ask. I met a woman at the post office, and I wonder if you knew her. She's an older woman, with a son who lives in Australia. I think her name is Frost."

Eric stopped to consider this. "I don't think so. Maybe she's from out of town?"

Terry stopped eating to ask, "Why do you want to know?"

"It's probably nothing. She had trouble addressing a package to her son, and I overheard her mention Australia, so I helped her. She seemed confused and couldn't remember her own address."

"Did you help her sort it out?" Terry wiped her mouth and drank from her bottle of root beer.

"I did in the end, walked out of the post office, and offered her a lift home. She turned me down, got into a car with someone, and drove off like a banshee. It was strange. She appeared to be frail, and I would have thought she had dementia, but she seemed to be quite cognitive after she emerged from the post office. She may have flipped me off."

"Beats me. She must have been from out of town. Maybe that's why she couldn't remember her address. May I have the bread, please?" Eric poured more wine.

Terry stared at me. "What address did you finally write on the package?"

"My own. She was holding up a long line. It was supposed to be her wedding ring. Her son wanted it."

Both Terry and Eric shook their heads. Terry did not hold back. "What the hell?"

"You would have done the same thing if you were me." I realized I may have made a colossal mistake.

Terry drained the last of her root beer. "As long as you know for sure the only item in the box was a ring, you'll be fine."

Everyone stared at me as I shook my head. No one said a word. Colin put his hand on my shoulder. "I don't normally do jailhouse visits, but if they have conjugal visits, I might be persuaded."

"You don't think it has anything to do with the threats, do you?" I picked up the plates.

Terry rose to help. "She was in line first, correct?"

"Yep." I hoped she was. *Did I let her in front of me because of her age and frailty?*

"I guess you'll simply have to wait to see if the Federales come for you in the next week."

Both Eric and Terry left after dinner. I finished cleaning the kitchen since there was no sense in irritating the kitchen goddess. Colin was already in bed when I entered the bedroom. He smiled, pulled back the sheets, and patted the bed.

"Invitation acknowledged and accepted. Hey, I was so busy with Terry and Eric. Did you use the Bec Beauty?"

"No, I forgot. Let's take a few with us when we head to Nevada for the wedding."

"When is it? I'm going to do some retail therapy if this is my first official function as Mrs. Colin Chandler."

"Oh, boy, and the drain on my bank account begins now. How many hours have we been married?"

I kicked him under the sheets.

Chapter 25

Colin attended business meetings all morning. He hated Zoom, but he didn't miss the travel. Now that Charlie was not around to provide his private jet, he had to travel with the regulars and, even using first class, he preferred not to interact with strangers. Ninety-nine percent of people were wonderful, but the one percent could make for a tough flight.

Colin rarely ended up sitting in the first-class section. Most of the time, he traded seats with an elderly person, or a returning soldier, so one of them could experience the luxury of sitting with the 'beautiful people,' as I called them.

We sipped our coffee as he outlined his Zoom meetings. "So, darlin', what plans do you have? Will you be kidnapped or assaulted, or search for bad guys today?"

"I'm considering a ride to Saddleback Lake and having a gander to see if the city kids are still around. I need to pick up Luke later and check in on Baxter to find out how his treatment is progressing."

Baxter was still at the vet clinic for his chemo. The vets at Patty's clinic decided it was best if they treated him for a week, and he would come home for two weeks before the infusions were repeated. The chances this course of treatment would work were not high, but we now estimated Baxter was closer to ten years old, and we wished to preserve his beautiful soul for Luke's sake.

"Who will go with you to Saddleback?" Colin didn't even look up from the paper he was reading.

"I think it might be good to break in the newbie. I'll see if Betty Lou could use a break from baby duties."

"Is Betty Lou off maternity leave? I thought she had a few more months." I could see Colin's eyes crease with a smile behind the paper. Betty Lou had been off for just a few weeks. She took the baby wherever she went. She now managed the ranch business these days.

"No, I was taking the baby. She needs to get with the program." I stood to return the dishes to the kitchen.

"Suits me. Just make sure she's armed. I've heard her cry. That alone would make the bad guys run for their lives."

I left for the barn and found Whit Williams had Digger saddled and my fly rod and vest prepared. My waders were strapped onto his saddle, and his shotgun was scabbard and ready for any mischief.

"Thanks, Whit. I'm sorry if I messed up your plans for the day."

"Doc, you're always my plan. A trip into the forest is the frosting on the cake. Do you mind if I take the lead?"

"Lead the way, sir."

After several minutes, Whit held up his hand and stopped his mare. He searched through the dense woods. Digger pawed as we waited for Whit to continue. Finally, Whit quietly reached for his shotgun. He pulled it from the scabbard, placed it across the horn, and quietly searched the surroundings.

Whit signaled for me to remain where I was as he inched forward and continued to survey the forest. Finally, he pointed to a tree where a cougar sat high above us. It waited to pounce. As the cat rose, Whit pulled the trigger and shot into the air. The cat turned, leaped away from us, and was gone. Digger had hardly budged, but Whit's horse spun and nearly knocked Whit out of the saddle.

Without a word, Whit regained his seat and reloaded the empty chamber. We walked on while Whit continued his surveillance of the woods. He finally turned and smiled. "I need to do a little more training on Chicka. She's still green. The good news is I saved your life, and that will make my other boss happy."

"You made this boss happy, too." Any thoughts of riding into the forest without a companion quickly receded. "I'll sit back and let you fish today. You earned it, cowboy."

We smelled the smoke of a campfire as we approached the lake. As we rounded the last bend, we saw the same men with the kids from our wedding day. Instead of boys, several girls seemed to enjoy themselves. *Maybe I had misjudged the program.*

Whit, who greeted the group, wanted to know about current fishing conditions.

Andy Chalmers, the man who came to my cabin searching for the missing boy on my wedding day, stepped forward and said he didn't know. "We don't have poles."

Why were these people in the woods if they weren't learning survival skills? It seemed strange.

"Mr. Chalmers, isn't that your name? What adventures are you having today?" I dismounted. One girl with long blonde hair in pigtails petted Digger's nose.

"What's his name, lady?"

Andy Chalmers quickly pulled the girl back. "You don't know if he's safe, Lucy. When you address someone whom you don't know, you don't say 'lady.' You say 'ma'am' or 'Mrs. Chandler.'" Apparently, Andy knew about my marriage. I didn't remember telling him who my intended was.

"It's Dr. Chandler now. I'm a retired vet." I asked the girl whether she would like to ride Digger. She smiled and nodded, but glanced back at Andy Chalmers and two other men who joined him. I wondered if there were any women counselors.

Andy shrugged. "Just a quick ride. I'm sure these people want to get to the lake."

I adjusted the stirrups after she mounted Digger while Whit watched the others. Whit's hand dangled casually down by the scabbard, and he nodded to me when I glanced in his direction.

"Have you ridden before, Lucy?"

"Yes, ma'am."

"This gelding is a wonderful horse. He needs a light rein, and he responds to leg cues." I stepped back to watch the girl slowly walk forward and turn him to an area that had been cleared, where she could circle and trot.

She knew how to ride. She even cantered in a small circle. Her hands were never out of place as she stopped and backed him. She approached us and dismounted. Her smile was heaven sent.

"Where did you learn to ride, Lucy?"

Her face darkened. "My mother."

"Well, please tell your mother that she's a wonderful teacher. You ride beautifully."

Lucy replied, with no signs of distress. "She's dead."

"I'm so sorry." I was glad to provide the young girl a moment of happiness.

Andy Chalmers placed his hand on her shoulder after she dismounted. "Lucy, that's enough. These people need to be on their way."

Lucy's demeanor changed, and she appeared to shrink as she stepped back to turn to the small group of girls who had gathered around the clearing. The girls watched her retreat to the tents.

"Mr. Chalmers, you have an interesting program. Is there any chance you could visit our ranch, and perhaps the girls could swim? We have a heated pool."

"Thank you, but the girls don't have swimsuits. They're here to learn survival skills, and we don't want to deviate from our goals." Andy Chalmers was nervous. A sweat had broken out on his brow, although it was still cool. He kept glancing back toward the two men who'd been present on the wedding day.

Whit's horse faced away from the men, so they didn't see the shotgun. He suggested we move on. He told the men that we had just run into a cougar and recommended they be on the lookout.

"We heard a gun. Was that you?" One counselor searched the trees.

"Yeah. It's just a suggestion, but I think there are better areas to teach survival skills."

I mounted Digger, and we rode to the opposite shore of Saddleback Lake. I decided not to fish. Whit stood guard while I watched the shoreline near the campsite.

I turned to Whit. "Any thoughts?"

"Yeah. Plenty. None that are good." He cupped his hands for a better view of the area. "Maggie, do you mind if we cut this short?"

My reason for coming was not really to fish. I wanted to see what was going on and if the camp had disbanded. "No need to stay here. Can we return to the ranch from this side of the lake?"

"It's a bit of a hike, but yes." Whit checked the girth on his saddle and tightened mine. He held Digger as I used a boulder to mount.

"Let's ride, cowboy. I might mosey over to the sheriff's office when we get back." *I will definitely mosey on over there.*

Whit sang. "From this valley, they say you are going."

I was shocked. "Hey Whit, you've been holding back on me. Your voice is heavenly."

"Aw, gee, shucks. Thank you, ma'am." Whit had a slight Texan accent, but he could turn it up when he wanted.

"You don't even have to change your name. You could be a classic, country-western star, Whit."

"I actually studied opera." Whit turned and smiled.

"Was that before or after your doctorate?"

"Did the boss tell you about me?" Whit turned to glance back. He pretended to look at me, but I could see he searched behind us in case anyone was following.

"Don't tell me you have a PhD?"

"Uh, no. I studied astrophysics, but when 9-11 hit, you know."

I didn't, but I could guess. "Any regrets?"

"Not a one, Maggie. Not a one."

"Why do you work for my husband? I mean, you could return to school, join an opera, or become a country-western idol—why here?"

"Well, to begin with, it was Luke. Now it's your entire family. My grandfather is a resident in the boss's home for retired actors. When I got out of my Special Forces unit, I was lost. When I went to visit my grandpa, the boss went fishing with the guys that day. My grandfather couldn't go because he'd suffered a stroke. I was sitting with him when Mr. Chandler returned. He came into Grandpa's room to show him the pictures, and we were introduced to each other. You know the drill. One thing led to another, and I was hired to guard Luke. Now I'm here to protect you. You and your dramas keep me guessing, but I'm happy."

When we walked along the trail leading out of the forest, Whit casually glanced back every few minutes. We both knew the next question. "Will you go back to school or pursue any long-range plans?"

"My only plan is to get you safely back to the ranch. After that, everything's up in the air. Right now, I have the best job in the world. I get to play cowboy and shoot the bad guys, and the pay's pretty good. Someday, I'll ride off into the sunset, but for now..." Whit didn't finish the sentence since we both heard a rifle shot.

Whit spun his horse around and pulled the shotgun from the scabbard. He rode his horse alongside me while we both listened. We heard a gun go off again and this time, we could tell it was a great distance from us. We waited and heard a third shot.

"Target practice back at the camp?" I hadn't seen any guns, but that was a reasonable explanation.

Whit sat quietly. "Maybe." He wasn't convinced. "Damn, Doc. You're sure a lot more trouble than Luke is to protect."

I smiled. "Yeah, I try to give you boys something to talk about around the campfire at night. I don't want you all to be bored."

"No, that would take the fun out of this job. Let's head back. I don't want the big boss to be worried."

Chapter 26

We arrived at the barn an hour later. I liked the trail coming from the back of the lake, but it was much longer. Digger was sweaty, and I hosed him. I wasn't comfortable giving the ranch hands the grunt work. It was lunchtime, and I dried Digger and returned him to his stall.

Mrs. Gillard was making soup from some leftovers from our dinner with Eric and Terry. "Hey, Mrs. G. That smells totally delish. Is Colin around?"

"I haven't seen him for a while. He was in his office an hour ago when I took him fresh coffee and a snack. We're almost ready for lunch."

"I'll round him up." I was sweaty and dusty. "Do I have time for a quick shower?"

"Make it fast, Maggie. I must leave in thirty minutes." Since Luke was gone most days, Mrs. Gillard did not need to be around all the time when both Colin and I were at home.

"Yes, ma'am. I'll be quick."

I could hear Colin on the phone, so I slipped into the shower, and as I was rinsing, I heard Colin enter the bathroom. "Can I be of help? My wife is out riding with one of the ranch hands, and I have a few minutes before she returns."

"Oh, and who might you be? I am always up for a back scrub. The problem is my jealous husband. He might catch us, and we could both be kicked out."

"Yeah, there is that. How was your ride? Learn anything?"

"Plenty. You'd better leave. I'm stepping out, and despite what you might think, I have the body of an old lady."

"I could close my eyes." Colin handed me a towel. "Maybe later. I have two more meetings to attend. Would you bring me some food? I won't be finished for at least two more hours. I hate videoconferencing, but it beats flying to California."

Colin was still on the phone when I brought him lunch. I mouthed, "I'm headed into town." I would wait to report what Whit and I saw.

I drove up to the gate to my cabin. It was locked, but there was another little bag with an envelope. I picked up the bag with a small pair of pliers and set it in the car.

I hadn't called ahead, but fortunately Terry was at the station, so I waited for her to call me into her office. I handed her the note, using the pliers, and explained I had stopped at my gate on the way into town.

"It looks like someone is still trying to frighten me. I haven't opened the letter in case you want the DNA or fingerprints."

"Uh, yeah. Well, it seems you have more than that to worry about. I was on the phone with the feds. Your package was stopped from leaving the States. The entire box was lined with a Styrofoam-like substance laced with meth. I've been directed to arrest you."

Terry stared up at me as I swooned and reached for the chair in front of her desk. "Pardon? You're joking?"

"Uh, no. I'm so sorry, Maggie. I have my orders." Terry stood and pulled out handcuffs from her drawer. A deputy sheriff walked in and stood ready, in case there was any resistance on my part.

"Not a joke? Is the note I found on the gate connected? Can you look at the note before this matter goes any further?" I half-laughed. This was so ironic.

"I'm sorry. You're under arrest. Maggie Chandler." Terry read me my rights, but I stopped her.

"Please listen to why I'm here?"

Terry continued to read my rights and her deputy took me into a private room where I was strip-searched and given an orange jumpsuit.

I returned to Terry's office. "The DEA guys should be at your ranch in a minute, and they will begin a search of your property. We felt it was best if we didn't warn you. I'm sure you're innocent, but I have to go by the rules. I'm sorry."

I wasn't going to say anything more, but I remembered the message left on the gate. "Please open the message." I didn't know what the message said, but I hoped it might explain the way I was being targeted.

Terry opened a cabinet and put on gloves. She carefully opened the small bag and folded paper. I waited while she read the note and turned the paper toward me, so I could read it. My heart sank.

Dear Neighbor,

We stopped by to give you information and discuss your relationship with Jesus Christ. We are sorry we could not meet with you. Please call us to arrange a meeting.

Kind regards,

Reverend

Louise Justice

High Mountain Church

My heart sank, but I laughed anyway. "Terry, before the feds arrive, I really came to inform you about the group of campers in the national forest. Young girls have replaced the boys. When I was up there with one of my ranch hands, we didn't see any women counselors. I felt a creepy vibe. Will you follow up on that?"

"I will. Thanks, and sorry this has happened."

"Yeah, and you can forget any more fishing on our property."

"I thought that would be the case. Eric and I will have to locate other spots. I'm sure we'll be fine."

"Fine. Can you call Colin, please?"

"I'm sure he knows by now. I guess the raid is well underway. I can call you a lawyer, though."

"You can't believe I've done anything wrong, Terry. Why would I tell you about it at dinner if I thought I would be arrested?"

"Maggie, a few things come to mind. I would recommend that you not say anything more until you speak to an attorney."

Terry summoned her deputy, and I was escorted to a bathroom where I had to urinate in front of the deputy, who collected a urine sample. I was taken to a small room with only a stainless-steel bench. There was nothing else to do but wait to see what happened.

It was a long wait.

Chapter 27

I could hear a commotion outside my cell. I heard raised voices, and I was sure one was Colin's. "If you don't open this door immediately, I'll break it down."

The door opened, and there he stood. He shook his head and laughed. I could hear him quietly humming the tune, "In the Jailhouse Now."

"What's so funny?" I was less than amused and verging on pissed.

"Darlin', you don't look good in orange." He made a sweeping motion, suggesting I exit the cell.

I rarely cried. However, Colin recognized I was at my breaking point. I was taken to Terry's office, and this time there was a familiar face. The

FBI agent from my abduction and involvement in Charlie McLeod's misadventures was present.

"Hi, Dr. Kincaid. Oops, I mean Chandler. You appear to get involved in things, don't you?"

"Hi, Gloria. Nice to see a familiar face. Has your marital situation changed, as well? Is that a rock I see?"

"Yeah. Looks like we both scored."

"Well, I'm wondering about that at the moment." I stared at Colin, who was admiring pictures of Terry with fish from her previous adventures.

"Mitch and I were married about six months ago, right after your adventure. I switched to the DEA."

Another agent, who cleared his throat and tapped a pen on the desk, interrupted us. "I'm sure you all have a lot to reminisce about, but we need to sort this out. It may all be linked, but it's hard to connect the dots."

I doubted any relation. "The dots. Well, I can't see any connections, but so far, I'm the only common denominator. How could the old lady set me up? Who knew I would be at the post office at that exact moment in time, and how would she know I would help her? Who's sending me threatening letters, and how would all this be related to a questionable kids' survival camp?" The agents took notes, and Gloria's partner shook his head.

Gloria cleared her throat. "Maggie, we've just heard about this from Sheriff Simpson. We need to do some investigations. As far as what you have done regarding the mail fraud, I think we can conclude that no one in their right mind would put their address and name on a package with drugs inside. That was a setup. Who knew you would be at the post office?"

"Colin had received a notice for a package to be picked up. We've been receiving wedding gifts, and usually the ranch hands retrieve the mail and packages, but since I was going into town, I said I would get the mail that day. I can't see that as anything other than pure chance. The only strange thing was this woman's reaction when I left the post office. She was indifferent to me and refused a ride to her house, and then I noticed her speed off in a car with a younger man driving. I worried when no one in town seemed to know her."

Colin leaned forward. "I don't think they're connected, but don't forget, my grandson may be the target of a drug gang from LA. His father is locked up for probable life, but the gang may still want him dead. Also, Charlie's group will go to trial soon for importation of narcotics and Maggie's kidnapping. There is still a trial for the murder of the Calhouns, the former owners of Maggie's cabin. Finally, and God, I hope the last, is her abduction when she confronted Carol Carter about the murder." He stared at me and smiled. "It is the last, isn't it? God, who the hell did I marry?"

"I wonder the same thing, cowboy. My kids are right. This place is a shit show."

Gloria interjected before I could continue, "Uh, Dr. Chandler, do you have any other ideas? Can you think of anything that would tie all this together?"

"Not really. The pre-wedding threats may be a jealous fan. The survival camp has changed from boys to girls and, as unlikely as it sounds, it may be legit."

Terry stepped out of the room to return with a sheet of paper. "The camp is legit. The governor's nephew runs it. My guess is that it's jobs for the boys, and the counselors are untrained friends of the governor's nephew. I sent a deputy to see what's going on. While they are, in all senses of the word, incompetent, they are legit. They have a permit from the forestry service to be there for the month of June."

Gloria watched Colin as he gazed out the window. "Mr. Chandler, have you two planned a honeymoon? Maybe a trip out of town? It might be good to get away for a while?"

"You think the threats are real? We have a second home in New Zealand, but it's winter there, and the entire encampment is under construction. Later this summer, I planned to travel back to where I filmed the *Comstock* series, but we've been invited to a wedding in two weeks, which is near Virginia City. Maybe we could head there. I have to think about my grandson, as well."

It came to me instantly. "Collie, you know Jim Kennedy invited Luke to stay with them this summer. With his Army training." But I was cut off. Colin held up a finger. Instantly, I knew he didn't want to divulge any plans.

"Dr. Chandler, we won't charge you, and we believe that you probably were a victim of circumstances. We think there may be a valid threat to you or your family's well-being. I recommend you either remain at home and place your staff on high alert, or maybe take a vacation out of the local area." Gloria and her associate sat back in their chairs, and I figured they were assessing our reaction.

Colin stood. "We'll consider your suggestions." He motioned for me to follow him. "I'll try to encourage my bride to lie low. I have little hope of her following my directions, but perhaps this will sway her decisions to start our honeymoon sooner than we planned. Thank you all for your diligence and concerns. I hoped for a quiet time because I finally landed the best catch of my life, but it seems I may need to match the hatch and change course directions."

"I'm sorry for putting you through all this. Apparently, since orange is not my color, I'd like to have my clothes back, thanks."

Everyone stood. Despite his age, Colin's voice and stature commanded respect, and no one dared to disagree with him. I sure as heck wasn't going to rock the boat. We left the sheriff's office, and when he opened the car door, Colin raised his finger once again. I glanced quizzically, but knew he had his reasons. He entered my car, took a piece of paper, and wrote "bugged." I cocked my head, and he shrugged. He mouthed the word, "Maybe."

He scribbled a quick, "I only bail my family members out once a year."

This joke made me laugh. He added, "Go home. I'm headed to get Luke. Please stay out of trouble until I get home." I saluted. He laughed, held up his finger once again, and pointed in the ranch's direction.

Colin returned, dropped Luke at the house, and parked the SUV up in the barn. Luke went to his room to pack a travel bag. I didn't know what was taking place. Mrs. Gillard was gone, so just Luke and I were there when Colin returned.

He whispered. "Darlin', we need to leave. I don't know what's going on, but someone in that sheriff's office did not have our best interest at heart. I've never told you this, but since you are chained to Luke and me, you need to know that even when Luke wasn't talking, we both had a 'safe word,' like gelding. Only this word means danger, and in Luke's case, blind obedience. I used it just once before, and that was when you were kidnapped.

"I have Whit and Gabe doing a check on the car. I guess when we were at the sheriff's office, they planted a tracker. Maybe they're the good guys, and possibly they think we're part of the cartel, or who knows what. However, we'll go on our honeymoon and take Luke with us."

"How can we do this if they have a tracker in the car?"

"I had Betty Lou call Doug. If he's available, we'll have him pick us up here to take us to our destination."

"Where?" was all Luke asked.

"In good time. Give me and Maggie a few minutes alone, Luke." Colin's pleading voice was not lost on either of us. "Pack enough stuff for a week or two."

"Luke, bring undies and deodorant. Jump into the shower." I got the look from Luke, which made me smile.

Colin pointed to the bedroom. He went to his desk, pulled out a flip phone, and sent a quick message. He sat down on the bed and pointed to a spot beside him. I dutifully sat down, and he embraced me.

"Who the hell did I marry?" He squeezed my shoulder.

"Yeah, I'm wondering the same thing."

The phone vibrated. Colin opened it. "That was quick. I need some help, Doug."

"Here to serve, Collie. Another fishing trip?"

"Nope. What are your plans for the next few days?"

"Nothing I can't change."

Colin pointed to my suitcase and turned to leave the room. As he left, he remarked. "I'm pretty sure Luke won't mind what I have planned. As for you, darlin', you'll just have to wait."

The next morning, we were packed and waited at the helipad for Doug. He looked at the three of us and shook his head. "Good thing I love you all."

"I'm sure the money doesn't hurt, either. Doug, I'm sorry to be so secretive. Something is rotten in Denmark, and I won't risk the lives of my bride and grandson. We're headed to Nevada. I assume you have a plane for the second leg of our journey. Were you able to get the Cessna Citation?"

"Not the one you think. I got Carol and Hal's. The jet was sold to the Gold Corp guys, who were having financial difficulties. They have leased it out to help make ends meet. They only know it's me who leased it. No questions asked. You could buy it for half price at this stage."

"I'll think about it, Dougy."

"Grandpa, that would make a great high school graduation present since I have to buy my first car." Luke, who was seated in the front, turned to stare at me with a smirk on his face. I shook my head.

Doug revved the copter's engine, and we rose above the property. I saw Digger was out in the paddock near the barn. *Bye-bye, beautiful boy. See you soon. I hope.*

Chapter 28

We landed at the local airport and switched to the jet. We had camping clothes and three fly rods with us. Doug allowed Luke to sit with him in the cockpit. Colin and I sat next to each other. We had to reach across the aisle to hold hands. Colin turned to me as the plane sped down the runway. "Not how I planned this honeymoon, but I know we'll have fun."

"When do I receive an activity program, beautiful boy?" I had my suspicions, but so far, Colin hadn't divulged the week's activities.

"In due time, Maggot. In due time. You'll have to trust me and let me spoil and protect you."

I squeezed his hand. "Just wake me when we land." I was exhausted from worrying about what was happening back home and who was in danger. I thought I'd left all my troubles when I married Colin. I was protected inside a veritable enclave. Many former military men and women living at the ranch would protect me—trapped in paradise.

Sometime later in the afternoon, we landed at the Reno, Nevada airport. Doug directed the plane to a set of buildings away from the major terminal. An older, green, dual-cab truck waited near a private hangar. Doug and Colin threw our bags and rods into the back, and off we went. Doug was headed back as soon as he refueled.

"Want to let an old lady in on where we're headed?" I gazed out the window at the desert and drab buildings near the airport.

"If I see an old lady, I'll let her know. Our first plan is to get new SIM cards. And Luke, you're not to call anyone you know. Am I clear on that?"

"Yes, sir. But how will I know if Baxter's alright?" Luke rolled his eyes and appeared to be dismayed at the surroundings. I wasn't exactly impressed, either.

"We won't know for at least a week. Mrs. G. will pick him up to care for him when he's ready to come home from the vet clinic." We drove for forty-five minutes and turned up a narrow dirt road outside Virginia City to a beautiful log cabin on a hill with a view of the valley below. No one was home, and the door was unlocked. Colin instructed us to remain in the truck while he walked into the house. He emerged from the house and gave a come-on-in wave. He smiled.

"This is Lauren and Jim Kennedy's home. Luke, you'll stay with them for a week while Maggie and I spend a little time alone together. You don't have to stay with them if you would rather be with us." He turned toward me and winked.

"No, Grandpa. I'll suffer alone, as usual." Luke smiled and reacted with a fist pump.

Baby clothes and a stroller were strewn around the living room. "Hmm, I wonder what this means?" I was kidding, yet Luke didn't get it.

"Gee, Maggie, you're a little slow. Obviously, they're having a baby."

"Do ya think, Lukey Boy?" I knew she couldn't be more than a few months along. I noticed nothing suspicious about her at the wedding.

"With Jeff's health scare, they must have told Lauren's parents." Tags on the items read "from Grandma and Grandpa."

"When will they be home? Can you take me to their work?" Luke was eager to see Jim.

"Jim knows we're here. He said he would slip away as soon as possible. That's his truck outside, so he may have to wait for a ride with Lauren. You'll have to wait. Let's see what's in the refrigerator."

Colin opened the fridge door. "Ah, a man after my own heart." Colin pulled out a beer. "The rest of you are on your own." Colin sat down in a recliner, chugged his beer, leaned back, and closed his eyes.

Chapter 29

The room was familiar. It appeared to be a smaller replica of the house on the *Comstock* series. The fireplace was about as authentic as I remembered it when I watched the programs as a child. I had forgotten so much about the Comstock series, but who could forget the fireplace in the great room? Luke sat down to open some veterinary journals that lay on the table in front of the couch. He removed his shoes and propped his feet on the coffee table, and the next thing I observed were my sleeping boys.

I stepped outside to search around. A barn and stable had been recently constructed. There were no horses in the barn, but there was manure. The shelter had hay and even water in the trough. A small room was locked. I guessed Lauren's riding gear was inside the tack room. Colin still had not enlightened me about this adventure. I assumed we would visit Miner's Meadow, but he wanted to surprise me.

Lauren had commented it was a three-hour-horseback ride. Was Colin up for that? I couldn't imagine riding up and staying with all the crowds that Lauren had described. I had to have faith in my husband. He had moved mountains in his time, and I had to pray this would all work out.

I noticed a branding iron hanging in the barn. It was the same brand as was depicted in the *Comstock* television shows. *Where did they get it?*

Jim arrived a few minutes later. He waved and smiled. "Hey, Maggie. We're so glad you could join us. How was the flight?"

I hugged him and described the journey. "Any chance you know what I'm doing this week? My husband has embargoed my itinerary."

Jim smiled and shook his head. "Colin has sworn me to secrecy. I value my life too much to tell you. He is a man of interesting means. Say, I guess our secret is out. Our baby is due in December. Lauren didn't want to say anything when we were at the wedding. She told her dad during his heart scare."

"Of course. Congratulations. Do you know the sex of your child?" I hugged Jim again.

"That is a big no. Lauren doesn't even look at the screen during ultrasounds. I don't care. As long as he's healthy, or she wants to be a vet, I'm good with either."

"Well, this is such good news. I can't wait to talk to Lauren." I considered how excited Becky would have been. I realized Lauren had little affinity for her long-dead mother, and I wouldn't mention it. I was only invited to my daughter's first birth. I already had grandchildren, so it wasn't the emotional experience I expected. I figured Sherry would do the honors.

Luke emerged from the house and was excited to see his hero. "Can we go to the vet clinic to pick up Lauren?"

"No, mate. She won't be home for another hour, at least. She's on call and will bring the vet truck home. I heard we'll work together this week. I have you booked up on vet stuff and some other projects around here. Get ready to rumble." Luke and Jim high-fived each other.

"Oh, Jim. You were right. Baxter has an osteo fibrosarcoma of his jaw. The pathology suggests it was moderately malignant, so we opted for some chemo after removing the mass."

"Yeah, better safe than sorry. I need to clean the grill. We have guests coming for dinner. I hope you don't mind."

"Not at all. Do I know any of them?" I was glad I'd napped on the flight. I hated changing time zones. I hoped this fit into Colin's plans. He wanted us to be anonymous out here, but he had agreed to attend a wedding. I think it was supposed to be in a few weeks, so I guessed we might see the soon-to-be groom and bride. "What can I do to help?"

"Just enjoy yourselves. I'll have to leave to pick up two of the invitees, but otherwise, you are the honored guests tonight. Luke, let me show you how to clean the barbie."

I smiled. Jim had picked up Australian jargon on his trip earlier this year. "Will we eat shrimp on the barbie?" I asked.

"Nope, and no roo either, mate. Or do I say sheila?"

"Only if you have a death wish. I'll check on Colin while you two men bond." I returned to the house to find him with another beer and a bowl of corn chips.

"Is there a party tonight? I see all kinds of dips and chips."

"Yeah. Are you okay with that? Will that blow your plans for secrecy?"

"I guess we'll find out. What time is it?"

I looked at my watch. I'd changed the time when we arrived. "It's six, Collie. Jim's here, but he's leaving to pick up some guests. Lauren's still at work. I should freshen up. Do you know what room we're sleeping in?"

"Not a clue, darlin' girl."

The house had three bedrooms on the first level, but we hadn't explored the downstairs. I took my travel bag into the bathroom. The shower was refreshing, but the hot and cold water was difficult to regulate.

"Darlin', you've taken a long time in there. Do you need some help?" Colin pounded on the locked door.

"Uh, tempting as it is, I think we should delay the festivities, but if you want to tell me what your plan is, I might unlock the door, Collie."

"All will be revealed tomorrow. A car pulled up. This might be Lauren." I heard Colin retreat to the living room. I emerged to follow him.

Two men climbed out of a truck. They were stunning. I touched Colin as we watched them from the window. "Mother of God, step aside, Collie. I am not worthy. I wonder if they're into older women?"

"Just a guess, but it isn't your age that will be the decider." Colin laughed as we watched them. It was plain to see they were a couple.

"Yep, all the good ones are married or gay. Damn. It's a visual delight, anyway." I touched Colin's arm, and he turned to me.

"I wonder if they're into older men?" Colin pinched my bottom, and I swatted him. "Anyway, I've spent my life working with good-looking men and women, and that isn't what turns me on."

"Thankfully, but it doesn't hurt to look. We'd better greet the guests." I pretended to coif and walked toward the front door.

We all met on the veranda. "I'm Maggie, and this is my husband, Colin. We're sorry, but we don't know you. This is all a mystery to us." I shook their hands.

"I'm Rich Reynolds, and this is my partner, Dirk Morgan. We're excited to meet you, Maggie. We've heard so much about you from Lauren." They both hugged me, shook Colin's hand, but otherwise did not fawn over him. Colin didn't appear to mind.

"We'll just put this in the fridge and prepare a few things. I need a beer. Dirk's on call for the fire department tonight, so no alcohol for him. Colin, what are you drinking?"

The two men went to the fridge as if it were their home, returned to the veranda with a tablecloth for the picnic table, and set out glasses and a bottle of wine. Dirk brought out some hors d'oeuvres. They continued to ignore Colin, who clearly thought this was amusing. He sat back on the patio and observed the men without comment. I settled next to him to sip a glass of wine.

Dirk took the lead. He explained he'd moved to Nevada to be with Rich. "I hate snow, but sometimes you need to sacrifice for love."

I laughed. "Tell me about it."

Colin grinned. "Some men are worth it, though, don't you think?"

We heard a vehicle approach. Lauren talked on her phone as she parked the truck. She waved and held up a finger, indicating she would be off the phone soon. I jumped up and went to the truck. It had a traditional vet-pack insert. I was curious about what she could carry.

Lauren emerged and hugged me. She had a tiny abdominal bulge, and her face might have a glow, but I would not have figured she was expecting. "It's a little fancier than what you had in Australia."

"And then some. Can I have a peek?"

Lauren quickly opened the back and released the sliding trays with the drugs, a fridge, and equipment. "Welcome to our little patch of earth. I guess you've heard the big news." She looked down at her abdomen. "Kid Kennedy is a project under development. I've requested him or her not to come out until they are potty trained and can make their own sandwiches."

"Good luck with that one. Will you take much time off?"

"Two hours for labor and two days for settling Jim in. I'm hoping for a Thursday birth. Then I'll have the weekend, too. Any chance you want to renew your vet vows and work for us?"

"You never know. I'd start with Collie. He'd probably love it. I might even make enough to pay for my flies."

"Oh, I forgot the most important update. Dad is great, and he sent me several Bec Beauty flies to give you. He still expects a repeat of our fishing adventure and an invitation to your New Zealand fishing lodge." Lauren put her phone in her pocket and locked the truck.

"Do you know what Collie has planned for our little adventure?"

"If I knew and told you, he'd kill me, so you have to wait. I see you met my protectors. I don't think I told you about everything that's happened to me since graduation. I lived with Rich for a while when my life got a little dicey. He and Dirk kept me safe from a stalker, who made my life miserable when Jim was away with the Reserves."

"Really? Maybe I could use them while I'm here."

"Would Collie object?"

"One can only guess."

"Rich is a schoolteacher, who drives Caterpillars and other heavy machinery in the summer. The rock slide where Becky was killed has a new slide. He currently works up there to help rebuild the trail.

Fortunately, it isn't as bad as when my mom died. The creek didn't sustain damage. Jim and I go up there at least once a year, but with the baby on board, we may not make it this year."

"Hmm, that may make Collie's plans a little different. Does he know?"

"I don't know if Jim told him. I know they talked a few nights ago."

"News to me, but I have married an exceptionally sneaky man." Lauren and I walked toward the house. As we reached the porch, Jim came up the driveway with two elderly people in the truck cab.

Jim parked and went to the other side to assist the couple out of the vehicle. Colin emerged, went straight over, and shook the man's hand. "Henry, it's so nice to see you again. I think this is your old house. I remember coming to advise you about the layout. Did you sell it?"

"I hope to sell it to this wonderful couple. Mary and I plan to live at her house. Let me introduce you to my soon-to-be bride."

I guessed the couple were in their eighties. Henry had a cane, and Mary used a walker. "Mary's excited to meet you and thank you for officiating at our upcoming wedding. We're so grateful." I watched Colin lean over to kiss Mary's cheek. *That's my husband — ever the flirt.*

"Henry and Mary, this is my wife, Maggie. Maggie, this is Henry Davidson, the man I told you about who was part of the Manhattan Project. Mary, I think we're using one of your horses this week. Thank you so much. We appreciate your help." Colin took her arm to guide her to a chair under the veranda.

Mary beamed. "Mr. Chandler, I'm thrilled to be of service. I watched all your television shows and movies."

"It's Collie to my friends. You still want me to do the honors at your wedding? Are you sure?"

"Either that or my funeral." Mary searched for Lauren. "Lauren," she shouted. "I need a drink. And bring one for my bestie. Collie, what are you drinking?"

After dinner, Colin, Rich, Dirk, and Lauren went to the barn to examine the structure. Jim and Luke went downstairs to set up Luke's room. Luke could watch television, but he understood he couldn't use a computer that might give away our location. The had a laptop with Jim's IP address. "No porn, mate. I have it blocked."

I was alone with Mary and her fiancé. I knew Mary was curious about how I knew Lauren. Her only question was, "Okay, Maggie, how do you fit into all this?"

"I know—good question, which needs an answer. My relationship is tangential, at best. I met Collie when I bought the property next to his ranch and his grandson came to ask for a job. It took a while, but eventually Collie and I found each other, and he asked me to marry him after he divorced his wife."

"And how do you know Lauren? She obviously knows you."

"We met in Australia, when she did a locum job there for my old clinic. I was there spelling the new owners, which was part of the sale agreement. We eventually realized Lauren's mother and I were in vet school together. In fact, we lived together until Becky married Lauren's dad. Becky and I both learned to fish when Lauren's father came with us to do some work for Becky's dad in Montana. It's almost incestuous."

"Where were you when Rebecca was killed?"

"I was preparing to leave for Australia. I'm sorry that I wasn't more involved. If there was a formal funeral, I would have attended, but no one seemed to do anything. I know they had to search for her body."

Mary leaned forward and looked both ways. "You know, some of us think she didn't really die. Someone saw her many years later at the grocery store. Everyone discounted the sighting because the woman is afflicted with Down syndrome, but we regulars know she is a savant with names and faces. I guess we'll never know for certain. I just wish Lauren was more interested in the disappearance. She rode all over here with her grandfather when Rebecca went missing."

"I heard about that." I wanted to be polite, but it was ludicrous to think that Becky would willingly abandon her family.

"Well, there's another story. Did you hear about her grandfather's disappearance from an aged-care facility near the time Rebecca was seen in a grocery store?"

Lauren and Colin returned to the patio with the branding iron I'd noticed from the barn. Colin held it up. "Look here. This is from the *Comstock* set. How did you get that, Henry?"

Henry stared at it. "I've never seen that before. It must have belonged to my wife. She bought some items from the auction when they tore down the set a few years ago to make way for the new lodge. My wife purchased a safe downstairs from the sale. She paid a fortune for the damn thing. We could never open it. Remember where it sat behind your desk in the room, across from the fireplace?"

Colin studied the branding iron. "I'm glad someone I know owns it now. Last call for drinks? We oldies need our sleep."

When everyone had departed or gone to bed, Colin spooned me and kissed the back of my neck. "Not gonna happen, my dear husband."

Colin squeezed me. "Thank God. There is no way I could, anyway. You know that branding iron?"

"Yeah?"

"It's not from the *Comstock* set. I have that one back at home. I guess someone else had it made, but it looks older."

"Collie, what do you think about Becky's disappearance? Mary thinks she was alive a few years ago. She told me the woman who thought she saw her at a store was a savant with faces and names. She mentioned something about Becky's dad going missing at about the same time."

"Who knows? But darlin', are you ready for our official honeymoon?"

Chapter 30

"Luke, are you ready? We need to go with Lauren. She'll kick our asses if we don't get out to the truck." Jim had an assortment of food set out on the table. "Help yourselves. Rich will be here in an hour."

I turned to Colin, who was putting on his pants. "Rich is coming? Oh, Collie, you've arranged for me to have a honeymoon with the cat man. You know, men who drive backhoes turn me on."

"You wish. Get up, old girl. Let the honeymoon begin. Are you packed? Remember that you need to bring only the bare minimum, with 'bare' being the important description. Leave the bras."

"In your dreams, old man."

"Honeymoons, where dreams become reality." Colin brought me coffee as I searched through my clothes for warm pajamas and clothes for fishing.

Rich Reynolds pulled up into the driveway with pack saddles and panniers loaded with what looked like sleeping bags and food. His smile would melt a glacier. "Howdy, Maggie. Are you and Colin ready?"

I turned to Colin, who sheepishly shrugged and placed his arm around my shoulder. Colin gazed over at the panniers. "I'm loaded with anti-inflammatories and will hit the whiskey soon. Let's mosey, cowgirl." And we did.

Rich took us to Mary's house, where we loaded four horses into a trailer and headed up into the national forest. Since I couldn't see the road from the backseat, I closed my eyes. I knew a section of the road was along a steep mountainside. It was probably best that I could not observe the edge of the road. I used to tease my kids and shout, "We're all gonna die," when we drove on curvy roads. American mountain roads were a whole different degree of scary.

We arrived at the parking lot, which hikers and horseback riders used as a launching base for Miner's Meadow. I was confused. "I thought there was a rock slide, and the trail was closed. I don't see any cars here. Will we go a different direction?"

Rich explained the trail was off-limits to the public. He'd spent several days constructing a narrow passage, which was used for the men to reach their heavy machinery. They weren't working that day. They'd all been sent to Reno for a safety course. They would return later in the morning. The trail was still closed to the public, but there are always exceptions—again the glacier melting smile. He and Colin fist-bumped.

Colin turned to kiss me. "We have Miner's Meadow to ourselves for six days, care of Mother Nature and the Tahoe-basin, summer-forest crew."

"How many people are aware we're up here alone?" I was worried it might be dangerous if several people thought we were up here by ourselves.

"Just Jim and us. We blacklisted everyone else. Not even Lauren and Mary know where we went. They think we went to Shirley Lake."

"Collie, you must have an angel on your shoulder to pull this off." Rich turned to saddle the last horse. Colin and I stared at each other. We each thought of Colin's first wife, Helen, who'd passed less than a year ago.

"We do." I hugged Colin.

Once the packs were adjusted and we were mounted, Rich raised his arm to shout, "Wagons Ho!"

Colin laughed and quietly mumbled, "Wrong series, but a good one. Ward Bond was a wonderful actor in the *Wagon Train* series. I was invited to do a cameo, but we were too busy with *Comstock,* and the kids were young. If I had time off, I tried to use the time to see the kids and Helen."

"You brought Helen up here in the early days, didn't you? Were there lots of campers at that time?"

"Our production company secured the place for ourselves in those days. We leased the area for summer shoots. For the month of August, the place was accessible only to the crews. We made it popular with our television series. It wasn't well-known back then."

We rode along in silence. When we came to the narrow, rocky passage, I became nervous. "Rich, how sure are you we're safe?"

"Until last week, I'd have said quite sure, but since we've had a second slide, I'm just pretty sure."

We continued on to a fortified area with a guardrail. The plaque I'd heard about was there. Becky and the other woman's name were shown prominently on the brass plate, as was the date.

"A lifetime ago." I swallowed and turned to Colin, who peered down into the creek below.

"Rich, you're down there most days, aren't you?"

"Yep, and I know what you're wondering. There're trout in the creek for sure. The men and I are forbidden to fish as part of our contract, but you're welcome to have at it, Collie."

"No, but we could send Maggie down. I know she'd be game." He glanced back at me.

"I'm keen, and if the fishing's no good in the lake, I might take you up on it. That must have been a hell of a slide." Enormous boulders and gravel were below us. "I don't see why anyone believes Becky could have survived the rock slide."

Both men simultaneously said, "She didn't." End of discussion.

I wasn't going to argue. *Well, some people sure think she did.*

A few minutes later, we arrived at the new slide. The passage was narrow, and I was nervous—extremely nervous. The men negotiated the passage, and I anxiously followed them.

Once we passed the current slide-reconstruction site, I relaxed. The trail was still tapered, and my horse even slipped on a small boulder, but he seemed to catch himself, and we continued up to the mountain crest.

We all gazed over the peak and down to the verdant valley dotted with evergreens and a shimmering lake. It was much larger than I'd imagined from the pictures. Cliffs surrounded the valley below. I felt my heart skip a beat. It had to be one of the prettiest places I'd ever seen.

I immediately remembered Becky and realized she'd never experienced this view. She was only an hour from here when she was killed. I considered all the other things she never saw, including Lauren's graduation and marriage, along with the pending birth of her grandchild. I couldn't think of a better place to honeymoon if we survived the descent into the valley. I was now ahead of Colin. I turned and watched him grimace and shift in the saddle.

I didn't say anything. I knew he was a proud man. He wanted this for me, and he would sacrifice his comfort for my pleasure. *God, I love this man. Just give me one year, but I wouldn't say no to twenty.*

We arrived on the valley floor and crossed several rivulets as we made our way to the mythical cabin, which was built in the late 1800s. It was relatively untouched since the original construction. A wide bed, a wood-burning stove, a cabinet for storing food, and a small table with two chairs were the sole additions to the cabin. Rich told us the story about the rancher from the 1800s, who built the cabin to remind his fiancée of his love for her when she'd left for the future.

"Nice story. I wish it was true." I laughed, wondering where that story came from.

Colin cleared his throat. "You know, it may have come from a *Comstock* episode. Alex Conrad always came up with crazy ideas. I think I remember one like that. We rejected it, but the cast and crew pushed for it because it would make a nice spin-off. Thankfully, saner minds prevailed."

We unloaded the panniers and our duffel bags. Rich suggested we keep a gun. Dangerous creatures were in the woods these days, and they weren't all human. The cougar population was on the rise.

When we'd rested and watered the horses, Colin took a rifle and thanked Rich as he mounted his horse to return to the work site. "I'm only a shout away if you are bored."

I shook my head. "You realize the man I married? Boredom is an unrealized dream." I handed him the lead rope, which was strung to the other three horses.

"Okay, you two, try not to burn the place down. Since I know you're legally married, I won't deliver you a lecture about safe sex, but be careful."

Colin put his arm around my shoulder and pointed to Rich. "Get the hell out of here before I get the gun. I need to fish and..." Colin didn't complete the sentence.

"Yeah, yeah. I got it. I don't want to hear the details from you oldies. See you next week." Rich turned to ride toward the trail leading out of the valley. Colin hummed the tune to "Red River Valley."

I quietly mumbled, "I'll miss those bright eyes and that sweet smile. So good-looking."

Colin chuckled. "Yeah, he ticks all my boxes. Let's hit the lake, darlin'."

Chapter 31

We walked toward the lake and had to skirt around a large tree that had fallen. "I remember Lauren mentioned that. I think it fell when she and her father were up here. Can you imagine if it had fallen on the cabin?" It had to be several feet in diameter. "Collie, did you have any close calls when you filmed *Comstock*?"

"We had them daily. Thankfully, I was kept in cotton wool." Colin peered around and kicked the dirt. "One of the crew members found some old headstones up here. I remember he came into the tent where Alex and I discussed the script for the day, and Alex went to see them."

"Wasn't he a history buff?" It was warm, and I slid out of my jeans and into shorts. "That's how you all got started, wasn't it? Didn't he discover an old diary?"

"I never saw it, but that's what he claimed. He was a strange man. He would disappear for weeks on end and come back with stories and plots that were historically linked to the area and the 1800s. I never knew where the story lines came from half the time. We argued constantly, but we knew we needed each other to make it work. I miss him. After the series ended, we'd get together once a year to talk about old times. He'd have loved you, Maggie. He was a faithful husband, but he always said, it doesn't hurt to look. He sure could bring in the fading stars—the humble and the arrogant pricks. I don't miss kissing women with the worst breath you could imagine."

We kicked the ground as we walked toward the creek. I searched around, trying to think where I'd want to be buried if I was up here. "You know, the clearing near where the fallen tree would be a pleasant spot. I could die happy here."

"Enough of that talk, Mrs. Chandler. Now let's see how the fish are biting."

They weren't, though. We saw a few fish rise to insects, but nothing was as I expected. I watched my beautiful husband change flies. My eyes were getting worse, and here was Colin, with over ten years on me, with remarkable eyesight.

The sun would set soon, and I smiled and pointed to the cabin. I returned to begin dinner before it was too dark. The moon rose above the tall peak. It was almost full. I hadn't realized how close we were to a full moon. There was a window in the cabin. I liked to sleep in the dark. Colin liked to sleep with light. *I will sacrifice my needs for him this week. It's a small gesture. God, I love this man.*

Colin returned as the skillet was hot enough to fry our steaks. I was so sure we would eat trout on our first night. He came up behind me and hugged me. "That's a first. I've never been skunked up here."

"Collie, it's nearly a full moon. Maybe we should try early tomorrow. I can see they're out there." While the phase of the moon could influence the trout-feeding habits, we usually overcame this with fewer catches, but we always caught fish.

"Darlin, I'm going to hit the lake again early. I need mountain trout for breakfast. I want you to sleep in if you'd like. I might keep you up late tonight."

"In your dreams, Collie. In your dreams." *And possibly mine, as well.*

I woke in the morning to bright sunlight and no husband. I stretched and smiled, remembering the evening's activities. I had no qualms about sex outside of marriage, but I didn't want Luke's values to be skewed by mine. There had been a monumental shift in societal norms, but knowing he was raised as a Christian, I thought it was best to at least try to give him some guidance. Of course, Colin and I had stepped outside the boundaries we hoped Luke would use, but if he was responsible, I knew his love life would be far different from ours. He was turning thirteen, and yet Luke was an old soul.

I wrapped a coat around my shoulders and walked to the outhouse. I may have spoken a few swear words when I realized how cold it was. I quickly returned to restart the fire and heat water for the coffee. I knew Colin would love onions for breakfast. I hedged my bets and made sausage. I waited for Colin's return before frying eggs.

I brought a book about wilderness-survival techniques and medicinal plants. I thumbed through it. I would scour the valley to search for some plants for various ailments. There was a first-aid kit in the panniers. It was rudimentary, but I knew our needs would be minimal.

Colin returned with one measly fish. "Your hero returns." His sheepish smile melted my heart. "It's all yours, my beautiful wife."

"Thanks. I made you some sausage, and I'll fry your eggs now." I would not eat the fish. It was Colin's, but it didn't hurt to let him think otherwise.

I prepared two plates, and we took them out onto the porch. I handed him the one without the small trout, and he stared at the plate. I switched and gave him the one with the trout. "Here ya go. Since you're the great white hunter, you get the spoils. Don't count on me to share again, though."

"I saw fresh bear tracks down at the lake. I think we should stick together when we explore." Colin reached over, cupped my chin, and gave me a bite of his trout.

"Delish, and thanks. You know, I'll take the bear compared to all the dramas we left back home."

"If we knew for sure what the hell was going on, I'd feel a lot better. That damn Charlie is still making our lives hell, despite dying twice. He sure fooled me."

"These drug cartels really have a grip on society, don't they? I'll be so glad when it's all done, and someone goes to jail. I know Carol and Hal's trial is supposed to be in September, but are they part of the cartel, and is this all retribution for exposing Carol's role in the murder of my former cabin owners?"

"Darlin' you may be onto something. Would they have access to a computer in jail?"

"That would explain a great deal, you know, but I still think the setup with the post office and my signing for the old lady's drug package was a fluke. Anyway, we're safe up here. Is the rifle in the pannier or under the bed now? Maybe we should get it out and make sure I know how to use it."

"So much to teach you and so little time." Colin pointed to the outhouse while I cleaned up the dishes. "I think we might want to go native today. Don't bother to get dressed."

"In your dreams, Collie."

"Yeah, I thought that might be a long shot."

Chapter 32

Colin, who was saddle sore, decided to just sit by the lake. I took the gun for exploring. I walked out of the woods to approach the cliff base. The valley floor jutted straight up several hundred feet in all directions. I encountered a small cavern, which was recessed less than twenty feet into the cliff wall. I had my flashlight, which I used to scan the cave walls. I did not see any hieroglyphics or other signs of habitation by animals. Some footprints in the dust appeared to be made from boots. I guessed some hikers or climbers may have used this place to sleep and avoid the rain.

I stepped out and walked down the cliff base. I located a smaller cavity and shone my light into the recess. It was taller. Several bats were disturbed and flew out of the cavern. Again, there was nothing of interest inside. I discovered many more cavernous recesses, which I systematically explored. I returned to the cabin to find Colin asleep on the bed. I quietly left him and went to the lake. The sun was now overhead, and it warmed the shallow lake waters. *Perfect for skinny-dipping.*

I disrobed and walked into the warm water and squishy lake basin. I could walk several feet out from the shoreline. I sat down in the water, allowed the muck to settle, and started cupping water over my shoulders to remove the odors from both the ride into the valley and last night's activities.

I was in heaven. I smiled to think that this area was a site of many scenes from the *Comstock* episodes. *Thank heaven for Hank Heaven.* I finally leaned back and let my hair get wet. *Yep, goin' native.* This made me sit up to look around. I glanced toward the area where we'd descended into the valley. *All clear. Phew.*

While I scanned the horizon, I saw no signs of anyone. I thought I heard an airplane, which sounded as if it was coming from the East. I watched, and the sound faded. As I perused the cliff top one more time, I thought I detected movement. I considered it might be a bear and continued to watch the horizon.

I glanced back toward the cabin and woods. I took the gun when I went to the lake. I wasn't afraid of a bear at the top of the cliff, but it reminded me of Colin's warning.

The gun was with my clothes next to the lake's edge. The sun and a few clouds had an ever-changing effect on the color of the lake. The reflection took the lake from blue to green, and back again.

I saw what might be a bear walking along the rim at the top of the cliff. When I gazed up toward the top of the cliff, the bear appeared to be walking upright. This image was strange, and I rubbed my eyes to watch this peculiar vision. *What the hell?*

I sprinted to the lake's edge, snatched my clothes, hurried to the safety of the woods, redressed, and returned to the cabin. Colin presented me with a sandwich and juice. "We'll catch fish tonight if I have to use dynamite." We laughed at the notion. "I believe I saw a bear up on top of the cliff in the opposite direction from where we came in. It was kind of eerie because it rose onto its haunches, looked around, walked a few feet, and dropped back down. Collie, is there any way a bear could come down from the top without coming through the pass that we took?"

"In all the years that I've come up here during the *Comstock* filming, I never saw a bear enter or leave the valley, but I saw a few bears over the years at other locations. How they could enter and leave the valley floor is a mystery." Colin handed me a banana.

"Anything else I should know down here?"

"You're living with a predatory man. Don't worry. He's easily appeased."

"I'm pretty sure his needs have been met." I leaned over and kissed Colin as he sat on the edge of the porch.

We rested and watched insects and birds flit in the grass and tree limbs behind the fallen tree. Colin walked toward the log. He kicked the dirt under the massive trunk.

"I wonder who's buried up here?"

"Are you sure anyone really is?" I had my doubts. The place was so remote, and no evidence existed that any mining occurred.

I returned to the cabin and, after a quick trip to the outhouse, I lay down on the mattress. "Five minutes, and I'll be ready to meet your every wish."

Colin raised his eyebrows twice. "A back tickle?"

"Five minutes, and I'm all yours."

An hour later, I found Colin on the front porch reading and sipping a beer.

"Sleep well? Come here. Darlin', I need you."

"Collie, are you okay?" I was alarmed. It was out of character for him to admit needs.

"Yes, I just have an itch between my shoulders."

"Phew, you scared me for a second." I lifted his shirt and scratched and tickled his back. "What time do you want to head to the lake?"

Before he could reply, the surrounding trees and the porch shook violently. We watched as the trees in the distance continued to sway. Next, we noticed the distant cliff seemed to move, and a couple of boulders tumbled down from above.

<h1 style="text-align:center">Chapter 33</h1>

"Earthquake," we both said at once. I stood to search our immediate surroundings. I felt the earth move once again.

"Another one, Collie. It wouldn't be a volcano, would it?"

"I know tectonic plates are in this area. I'm sure it's an earthquake. I hope it isn't going to change the trip home. If another slide occurs on the trail, we might need to alter our return. I know the worst case would be they would have to helicopter us out. Boy, that was a ripper. Let's hope this shakes up the fish and they bite tonight."

We felt several aftershocks. "I hate to think Luke's not with us. I remember one large quake happened when I was growing up. It was scary."

"Luke'll be fine. He's a Chandler, after all. We're made of sterner stuff, darlin'."

"Let's go over to the cliffs to see if anything changed." I wanted to make sure there was no new pathway into the valley that the bear I saw might use.

"Okay, but we need to stay a safe distance from the cliffs in case there's another big rumble. You're no good to me dead."

We walked out of the woods and could now see a large area of the surrounding cliffs. Several new boulders were there in the morning. We heard and saw a few rocks fall from above. Another aftershock rolled through, and more debris fell from overhead. I was glad that didn't happen when I had explored the caverns before.

We returned to the cabin to prepare to fish. My heart wasn't in it. I was worried about Luke. I tied a grasshopper and a drop nymph onto my line. Colin kept the fly that had caught the single trout he ate for breakfast.

We returned to the lake and stepped into the icy water without waders. Colin was up to his waist in the water. I moved over to an area near where I swam earlier in the day. Since it was shallow, I could get out farther from the shore. I located an abrupt drop-off and without getting as wet as Colin, I could cast into deep water.

We watched for rising trout or a sign of a hatch. Nothing happened, and then Colin pointed to a disturbance on the water surface that showed a small hatch occurring.

He studied it for a moment and retrieved his fly, and I could see he was changing his fly to match the hatch. Curiously, only the rare trout rose to the insects. We continued to cast with no luck, and I changed my flies several times to catch some trout for dinner.

Nothing happened. We didn't even get any strikes. We glanced at each other and shrugged. Were the fish spooked by the earthquake and aftershocks? Did they feel this coming yesterday?

I quietly mentioned I was headed back to the cabin to start dinner. As I neared the shore, I felt another large aftershock and saw a wave shooting across the lake. Colin teetered for a moment and turned to me. He waved and shouted, "Tsunami." The wave was six inches, and I chuckled.

We didn't bring the gun. I emerged from the lake and hurried through the woods to the cabin. I noticed a cup had fallen from a shelf and shattered. I cleaned up the glass. It was the only glass piece in the cabin. Another small rumble passed through, from which I steadied myself by grabbing the oven.

It was getting dark, and the dinner was ready. I cooked pasta and vegetables. I worried about Colin when I heard him leave the outhouse. "I'm so hungry I could eat a bear. The damn fish aren't cooperating. I've seen nothing like it."

"Do you want wine or beer, Collie?" I'd already poured myself a glass of wine.

"I'll join you with the wine. We may be here for longer than we planned. I guess the trail may be compromised, which could put it mildly. I hope you don't mind being up here with me?"

"Food wise, we ought to last another week. How many bullets do we have? We may have to shoot our dinner if the fish don't cooperate." I had gone through the panniers when Colin was still fishing.

"I'm onto them because no fish will outsmart me. I'm headed out in daylight."

A man on a mission. "Have fun. I'll keep the bed warm." I behaved like the wife of a celebrity. This had to end, but damn, it was cold this morning. "Take the gun. You're no good to me dead, you know."

"Actually, according to my lawyers, you're better off than with me alive."

"Collie, don't even think that way. It would kill me if you died. I plan to be the first."

"What would you do if I died tomorrow?"

"Kick your dead ass from here to Christmas. Spend all your money, and take Luke and Digger back to Australia, where only the bad guys have the guns." I handed him a plate of pasta and vegetables. "And I'd take the kitchen goddess along with us."

"Good idea. Luke would be devastated without her."

"You'd better not die. What would you do If I died?" It was unthinkable, but one of us had to be the first.

"I'd go see the sheriff to see if she wanted to go fishing."

I swatted him, and we hugged until we felt another shaker. It was dark, and Colin shined a light toward the rafters. "Looks solid enough. How about we review our individual anatomical variations under the covers?"

"Review away. I'm going to sleep."

Colin smiled. "Yeah, there's that option as well."

As we lay in bed, Colin pulled me into the spooning position. We usually started our nights that way. It was seconds before he was asleep, but I could not sleep because of worrying about Luke and our return on the narrow trail. I felt several aftershocks during the night.

When I woke up, I realized it was daylight, and the bed held no residual warmth. I rose, made coffee, took a quick trip to the nearly icy outhouse, and began breakfast. I made French toast. I knew Colin would bring me fish, which I would cook as soon as he returned.

When he didn't return, I went to get him. I walked out and saw he'd taken the gun. As I stepped off the porch, I heard gunfire. I hesitated, but I heard no more and ran down to the lake. I noticed Colin's rod lying against a partially submerged log.

"Collie?" I shouted. I stopped to listen.

I saw fresh human footprints emerge from the lake near the fishing rod. My heart stopped as I thought I recognized prints from a small bear lead into the water and out again. They were distorted, which confused me.

"Collie?" I shouted again. I felt a minor tremor and peered around the cliff tops. I listened and followed Colin's tracks. A short distance into the woods, I discovered a dead mountain lion. I called again and was met only with a rare chirp of a bird.

I found blood and followed the fresh trail that led on a well-worn path, which circumvented a few fallen logs. A few yards from the clearing where the cabin sat, I found my husband lying in the wet grass.

Chapter 34

"Collie, Collie, Collie. Oh, my God. Please be alive. Please wake up. My darling man, this can't be happening. Oh, God, no, no, no." It was as though I moved in slow motion. I couldn't think. I dropped to my knees beside him. His eyes were closed, and he didn't move. I felt his throat for a pulse and felt a faint throb. I saw blood on his arms, and his waders were shredded. There were no obvious large wounds in his abdomen.

I was in a state of shock, and I couldn't think. I took his hand and felt the warmth. His face was still flushed. I finally realized I needed to act. I felt under his head in case there was a bleeding wound, which might cause him to exsanguinate.

Was it a heart attack? Did the cougar attack him? Since I needed to know, I gently turned him over while I attempted to keep his head and neck straight. Several claw and bite marks were obvious on his neck and back. Under his shirt, I saw one large wound on his forearm. A gash went down his back where the waders had not been pulled up. A second set of bites and gashes were on his lower leg. I heard him moan.

"Collie? Please don't move. Can you hear me?"

I took off my jacket and placed it on the ground so I could roll him over onto his back again. He opened his eyes and smiled. He mumbled, yet I didn't understand what he said. I needed to assess his injuries.

"Can you move your arms and legs?" When he still didn't respond, I took his hand and asked if he could squeeze mine. There was a long pause. "Come on, Collie. Squeeze my hand." Again, there was no response. "Collie, please. Squeeze my hand."

He squeezed, and he spoke well enough that I could understand him. "My rod's in the water. Can you get it?"

I began to cry and laugh. "Yeah, I'll get right on that."

"Kitty trouble. I may have killed him." Colin's voice was weak.

"You did. Can you feel your legs?"

Colin was reviving. "Sadly, yes. I think I've ruined the vacation, darlin'. Worse, I think my waders are ruined, too. I'm sorry. Can you call an ambulance?"

I wasn't sure he was lucid. He smiled and squeezed my hand once again. "Just kidding, ol' girl. I think I'm toast."

I ignored this. I had to figure out a way to get him back to the cabin. There could be more mountain lions out here. "Can you sit up?"

"Maybe. If I had an incentive. I don't suppose you'd be interested in...?" He looked down at his groin. That was the moment I felt he might survive.

"Men." I was exasperated and simultaneously relieved. "Start acting your age, you idiot." I pulled his arms, and he could sit up. He needed my support to maintain the position. We were possibly a hundred yards from the cabin. How could I get him there, up the two steps, and into a bed? How would we get help? No one was expected for at least four more days. I'd consider my options when I got him into the bed inside the cabin.

"Can you stand?" It was a long shot, but how else could I do this?

"Maybe. I'm so cold. Can you get me a blanket?"

I was reluctant to leave him. I searched around and found a large stick that was light enough for him to hold. I covered him with my jacket. Sunlight reached the small clearing, and I didn't feel the cold. "I'll be back in less than a minute. Can you sit on your own?" He fell back. That answered my question. I raced to the cabin and picked up a blanket and a tarp. I quickly returned. I laid the tarp next to him and helped him scoot onto the plastic surface. I detected a small pool of blood where he had lain in the dirt.

"Collie, I need to get you back to the cabin. I'll pull you onto the tarp. If you can use your hands to help, we might get to the cabin to figure out the rest."

A small rope was threaded through the tarp's grommets. I took the rope, and with slow and steady progress, I dragged the tarpaulin and Colin through the wet grass. I rested when we reached the cabin porch.

"I need whiskey, and maybe something for the pain." Colin grimaced.

Colin and I had a stash of ibuprofen and acetaminophen. I administered some with water. "If you're a good boy, and help me get you up the stairs, you can have whiskey."

"I'll be better with whiskey on board."

"Two steps. I'm going to pull the tarp and if you can use your hands to help me get you up the stairs, then you can have a reward."

Our first attempt didn't work. I took some logs, a sleeping bag, and a flat board to facilitate a smoother transition up the porch steps. "Okay, Collie, here we go." I pulled while Colin used his arms and hands to help propel him up the stairs—success.

He lay on the porch. Since the fire in the woodstove was nearly out, and it was warmer on the porch, I rekindled the fire and boiled water. I gave him a sip of whiskey and covered him with the other sleeping bag. I took another one of our towels and, with warm water, cleaned the wounds on the front of Colin's body. I slowly removed his waders, pants, and shirt.

He lay quietly and occasionally winced as I systematically bathed the puncture wounds and lacerations. "Okay, big boy. You must help me roll you over so I can reach the wounds on your back."

Colin was getting stronger and wanted more whiskey. Because I knew the other pain meds were probably not helping to quash the pain, I gave him more. While we were on the porch, another minor trembler rolled through.

I didn't discuss the options with Colin. We both had left our phones with Lauren and Jim. There was no reception up here, anyway. No one would come for several days. I knew the only option was for me to hike out to get help. A helicopter could land in several places. Colin's injuries were not fatal. His age was a significant factor, but sepsis was my chief concern. We did not have any antibiotics.

I felt his pulse for any irregularities, but identified none. His pulse was steady but weak. If I could get him into the bed and stoke the fire, I was convinced I could reach the work site and Rich Reynolds, who could organize a lifeline retrieval for my husband. I was certain

Colin wouldn't survive four more days without significant risk, and he definitely couldn't ride out of here.

I took the mattress off the bed to move it beside the oven. I put water, towels, an old blanket, and his whiskey beside the mattress. If he could reach the handle of the oven, he could replenish the wood. It was warm in the cabin now, but it would be a mistake to let the fire completely go out.

I was sure once I got to the work site, it would take less than an hour for a helicopter to come when Colin could be transported to a hospital. "Collie, can you hear me?" His eyes were closed, but he nodded. "I'm getting help. I'll walk to the work site along the trail. Beautiful boy, I hate to do it, but we can't wait to get you some help. Do you understand?" He nodded again. "I'll move you into the cabin. You must keep the fire going in case there's a delay. Do you understand?"

His only reply was, "Leave the whiskey, Maggot."

I laughed and shook my head. "God, I love you." I kissed him, dragged the tarp into the cabin, and rolled him onto the mattress next to the stove. He could prop himself onto his elbow. I knew he would survive until someone arrived in a few hours.

I placed a cooler with drinks, made a sandwich, and left crackers. I kissed him one more time and told him how much I loved him and that I would see him in several hours.

"Maggot, take the gun. It still has one casing in the barrel. My knife is with my fishing vest. I left it on the shore next to my rod. Please be careful. I'm no good without you, darlin' girl."

I kissed him once again, told him I loved him, and shut the door to the cabin. I shouted, "See you in a few hours, beautiful boy." I retrieved all the gear and set it on the porch. I took my jacket, which was covered with Colin's dried blood, the knife, and the gun, and headed for the trail up over the pass and back to civilization.

Chapter 35

I slipped when jumping across a small rivulet and dropped the knife. I had carried it in case I encountered a second cougar. I tried to run, but my stamina allowed me to run just a short time and then walk again. The trail out of the valley had changed only minimally from the earthquake and aftershocks. Some areas with slippery shale slowed my progress—I moved two steps forward and one step back. I finally arrived at the trail's summit out of the valley. I gazed back and said a prayer. *Please let me reach someone and get him help before the day is done.*

An hour later, I reached the construction site. I was shocked. Two large backhoes were on their sides, and rocks and boulders were everywhere. Several large vehicles were missing. I saw no workers. Was it Sunday? My heart sank, as did my hopes of reaching anyone quickly. The trail was obliterated. There was no way to cross it without going down to the creek. The other side still appeared to be as we left it. *Did they take the other earth- moving vehicles to the city? How much damage had the quake caused near Lake Tahoe?*

I had no options. To get to the trailhead and parking lot would take hours. Even when I got there, the area might be deserted. I could go back, but even if I didn't reach anyone before late tonight, I would still alert a rescue crew, and Colin would be found by morning. I had to press on.

I scaled down to the creek bed. I skipped from one small boulder to the next. It was slow going. I saw fish in the creek, but the stream had changed. Where there had been several small pools, now four large ones would require me to wade through a narrowed area to reach the far side. I knew this was not what I had encountered. I realized this must have been quite a large earthquake. *Was this the epicenter?*

I could traverse the creek pools, but I had to get my feet wet. Fortunately, it hadn't rained, and the water levels were not bad. I was thirsty but hadn't thought to bring water. I knew better than to drink from the creek, which might be contaminated with giardia. *Not going there at a time like this.*

At the final pool, I felt a tremor and turned to look up to ensure no large boulders were dislodged. The tremor went on forever, but was probably only a second. It started a small rockslide, and I had to step back to avoid the oncoming rocks. As I stepped, I knew I'd fallen into a large and deep pool. The water was so cold that I could hardly move.

As I returned to the surface, the water was rushing, which I thought must be from the displacement of the water from the new rock slide.

I was carried downstream. Oh, my God, it was so cold I just couldn't believe how horrific this day was so far. I stood and waded downstream, where I could climb out of the creek bed and continue to the parking lot. I found a place I could climb back up to the trail far from the rock-slide area. I realized I'd dropped the gun when I fell into the water. I didn't want to waste the time to retrieve it.

I was relieved to leave the area where it was so dangerous. The trail wasn't exactly as I remembered it, but that was a few days ago, and I was on horseback at that time. I walked and even ran along the trail, which appeared to have fresh horseshoe marks heading back toward Miner's Meadow. Did I miss someone coming to pick us up? It didn't matter.

I wanted to get back down to the parking lot. I prayed somebody was there, perhaps a truck or even one member of the construction crew, who could radio in our predicament and Colin's need for an airlift.

I had a stitch in my side, and I had to slow down. I finally rounded the bend where the parking lot should be, yet it wasn't there. I was confused. I couldn't comprehend what had happened and how I'd become so far off the track to the trailhead.

I must have come out on another trail. I traced the hoofprints and headed down the mountain. As I emerged down the trail, I could view the valley below. It led to an expansive area where cattle grazed. I was so disoriented. I cursed myself for not bringing my phone.

I finally arrived at a split in the trail. Some idiots had erected a sign that pointed to Virginia City in one direction and the Cattle Creek Ranch in another. *These locals sure love their folklore.*

I walked and ran toward Virginia City. I was disoriented but believed I was heading in the correct direction. I could run more because the path was now downhill out of the mountains. I wondered if I should climb up the hill. *How did I miss the paved road?* I wasn't sure if Lauren's house was closer to me than the city was at this point. I hadn't noticed where we went since I was in the backseat when we drove to the trail head.

I finally entered the edge of a town. It was rough. *Very rough—way too rough.* It must be a tourist town depicting the Old West. I saw people in costumes, ranging from miners to businessmen, who wore clothes reminiscent of the Western television shows I watched as a kid. I stopped an Asian man to ask him where the police station or an emergency room was located.

"Not understand. You need doctor?" he replied to me in broken English.

"No, I need a helicopter to rescue my husband. He requires urgent medical help. A mountain lion attacked him."

The man stared at me and shook his head. "Not help." He pointed to a white building down the city street. Obviously, he was an actor or playing a role for tourists. The building said Virginia City Hospital. "You go there." He pointed again and walked away.

I ran to the building and up the stairs. As I entered the door, I looked at the plaque on the porch, which read, "Virginia City Hospital Constructed for the Citizens of Virginia City." *Nice prop. I wonder why Colin hadn't mentioned this faux-town tourist trap.*

A large woman in a white uniform greeted me. "You've come at a bad time. Do you wish to see Dr. Buchanan? She's away, and our other doctors are in surgery. As you can tell, we're busy." She pointed to the people sitting on benches around the room.

"I need a phone, if that's possible." That request was met with a blank stare.

"We're a hospital, not a general store. That's down the way. I'm not sure what a phone is, but they sell most items you may require. What is a phone? Are you sick or injured?"

I was confused. "My husband is injured. I need help. We're camped up at Miner's Meadow. Is there a rescue unit, or a sheriff I can talk to? It's urgent. A mountain lion attacked him."

"Ma'am, if you can have someone bring him down, we could treat him, but other than that, I'm afraid we're unable to help you. I think you should head to the sheriff's office to see if they can organize a posse to help you retrieve your husband. Where is Miner's Meadow, anyway?"

This woman was a waste of time. "Where's the sheriff's office? This is an emergency. I don't have any time to waste."

She pointed up the street and wished me good luck. *Not a clue. This place is off the planet. Or is it me? Am I hallucinating? It's not a dream—or is it?*

I left the medical center and walked down the street. Something was familiar about the Western-themed buildings—something extremely familiar. I couldn't recall where I had seen this before, but it gave me such a déjà vu feeling. It was a cheerful atmosphere. I observed the townsfolk dressed in their faux Old West outfits, and even a couple of horses were tied outside a saloon. This had to be a movie or television-film set.

I raced to the sheriff's office and entered. I recognized the two men seated at a desk. I didn't know where I'd met them, but I knew them. My head was swirling, and I was becoming faint. I stared at them without even speaking. They played checkers. *Checkers? Who were these people?*

"Excuse me. I'm in desperate need of help. A mountain lion has attacked my husband up in the mountains at Miner's Meadow. I must get him to a hospital. I know about the earthquake. The trail is gone, but I wonder where I can receive some help to get him out—maybe a helicopter?"

The men looked at me as if I were from another planet. The younger man turned to the older one. "Ray? Do you know what she's talkin' about? Ma'am, I'm not sure where Miner's Meadow is, and I've never heard of a 'helicopter'."

The older man stood and pulled out a chair for me. "You look like you've been in a bit of difficulty. Glenn, fix her something to drink."

"Yes, but my husband is in terrible strife. Please, may I use your phone? I should contact the authorities?" *These men were so out of their depth. They must be deputies or cleaners.*

"Do you mean a telegraph?" They insisted I sit down to drink some water. The older man handed me a cup of coffee. I took a sip and could barely drink it. It was like drinking old coffee grounds.

"I'm not sure what's going on here, but I have to return to my husband. He needs pain meds and antibiotics. I can see you're not going to help me. Please, just point me to a telephone."

As I stood, the door opened, and in walked another familiar face. I failed to make a connection, but I recognized the face. He stared at the checkerboard.

"Gentlemen, I see you're in the thick of the daily battle to fight crime. Maybe I should come back when you aren't so busy."

"Hey, Danny. Maybe you can help us. This woman..." The older man paused. "Ma'am, have I missed your name?"

"Maggie Chandler. My husband is Colin Chandler. Perhaps you've heard of him? A mountain lion has attacked him. Please, I can't waste any more time. I need a phone and a helicopter. I want to get him out of the national forest. We were camping up at Miner's Meadow, and he may die if I don't get him some help." *Danny? He was so familiar.* "I'm sorry, sir. You look familiar. What's your last name?"

"Buchanan. Dan Buchanan. Where did you say your husband was?"

"Miner's Meadow. Everyone knows where it is. Can you help me?" It hit me like a bullet. This guy was the actor who played Danny on the *Comstock* television series. The older man was the town sheriff, and the younger man was the deputy. They should all be dead by now. They had all aged. How did they locate people to remake the program? *Does Colin know about this?*

Dan took my arm to escort me to the door. "I know where she's talking about. Glenn, I'll take her back to the Cattle Creek Ranch and organize to get her husband. I'll bring him back here, if it isn't too late. Becky and Pa are up near there now, and I'm sure your husband is in excellent hands. Their paths must have crossed."

The two men watched us leave and bid me encouraging goodbyes. The actor took me to what was a livery stable and ordered two horses. One was the paint horse that the *Comstock* series used, and one was a bay gelding.

"I'm sorry, but I think we need a helicopter." I firmly waited.

Dan stared at me and smiled with dazzling teeth. His curly brown hair had grayed, but he still was fit and remarkably dashing. "Ma'am, can you ride? I should get you out of town. I'll explain when we're out of Virginia City."

I used a mounting block, and we walked to the edge of town in seconds. Danny turned to me. "Mrs. Chandler? I think I know what's going on. Only a handful of people would understand where you come from. Will you trust me? I need to get you back up to my father and Becky."

"Who's Becky?"

"She's my father's wife. She's a doctor. If you don't think this is too rude, when were you born?"

I told him, and he smiled. "Why does it matter?"

"Oh, it matters. And everything you said happened today?"

"We're wasting time. Please, maybe just take me back to this movie set. I must get some actual help. What's your real name? I need a helicopter. This is a genuine emergency." I was apoplectic. I wouldn't deal with actors and people who couldn't help me. I needed to get back to civilization—now.

"There aren't any helicopters here in Nevada. You're gonna have to trust me."

I remember this sensitive, caring young man from the television series. "Okay, where are we going?"

"To the place you call Miner's Meadow."

Chapter 36

We rode up the same trail I'd traveled down an hour ago. Storm clouds had gathered. I knew the weather report was for beautiful, clear weather when Colin and I were up at Miner's Meadow. I hadn't noticed until then that the sky was different. I left a cloudless meadow.

I was confused and saw the same sign pointing to town and the Cattle Creek Ranch. We covered the distance quickly. I knew we'd have to dismount to go to the creek to pass the area of the rockslide.

As we approached the cliff and the area of the rockslide, I realized the trail was easily passable and in better shape than when Colin and I had crossed it two days previously. I looked down at a beautiful creek. I didn't see any trout, but we were moving at such a fast pace that I didn't stop to do more than glance. As desperate as I was, I realized Colin would ask me that. He was like that. I smiled, but then the tears came. I tried to hide them, but the Danny actor turned and saw me. He stopped.

"Do you want a break? I'm sorry about all this. I'm sure Becky and my pa can help."

When I asked for his real name, he replied, "Daniel Buchanan." Since I didn't want to anger him, I played along.

An hour after passing the area of the rockslide, we were at the peak of the pass leading down to the valley. Miner's Meadow appeared essentially the same as when Colin, Rich Reynolds, and I arrived a few days ago. I saw smoke coming from the trees that surrounded the cabin. The cumulus clouds were now gathering, and shadows danced across the lake.

"Smoke." I pointed, and the actor smiled and nodded. He pulled out his pistol and fired a shot into the air.

"That's a warning shot. Becky likes to go native when she's up here, and my pa always asks us to fire a warning shot, so we don't catch her in a compromising situation."

"I don't understand how they got past me. There must be more than one trail into the valley." *This whole saga is beyond bizarre. Who the hell are these people? Is this a cult?*

"Only one trail, ma'am. They've been here for three days. I'll let my pa and Becky explain. You wouldn't believe me, anyway."

"Please, let's hurry. My husband needs medical attention ASAP."

The actor turned to me and cocked his head. "Yes, I understand. What does ASAP mean?"

"As soon as possible." I responded, wondering how someone as famous and probably as worldly as this man was didn't know the term. Or was he pretending? The idea of a cult was growing.

When we arrived at the valley floor, I noticed the grass had dried significantly, and small bushes that had dotted the valley floor earlier in the day had disappeared. I recognized things were different, but my need to get to Colin made me dismiss this anomaly.

We approached the cabin, which was uninhabited. I dismounted, ran into the hut, and found it deserted as well. I almost fainted when I realized that someone had already collected Colin. There was no way he could have left on his own. I turned to the actor, who shrugged. "I don't see the horses, but the fire's still going. They must be down here. We'll wait, and if they don't show up in a few minutes, we can ride over to the other side of the lake."

Dan opened the woodstove, which differed from what I remembered. I glanced around the room. The bed was smaller than I remembered it. The table was altered, and the panniers were not there. This was not the same place. The exterior of the cabin was identical.

"Excuse me, Dan. This isn't the cabin I left. Are two cabins located down here?"

As I peered around the room, I heard the voice of someone approaching. "Dan, what's wrong? Is Hannah alright? Is it the children?"

The voice was familiar, but I didn't know how I knew the man. I ran to the door and almost fainted. It was Colin who appeared healthy and upright.

I quickly realized this man must also be an actor and somehow, he appeared as a cloned version of my husband. His hair was slightly longer, and he appeared to be broader across the chest, but he fooled me for a second.

"What the hell is going on?" The older actor shouted.

"Pa, this is Maggie Chandler. She talks like Becky. I think she may have suffered the same fate as our Becky. Where's Bec?"

The older actor turned to the woods and whistled. "She's coming. What's this all about?" He stared at me. Or was it my clothing?

"I need help. My husband's up here at Miner's Meadow, where a mountain lion has attacked him. He needs to be rescued. I need a helicopter. I thought he was here, but I'm obviously lost. I need your horse. I must get to a phone. Is this a waste of time?"

Neither man said a word. They only stared and waited. The younger man looked out the single window, searching for the mysterious Becky.

"May I take your horse? I can leave it wherever you want. My husband's in dire condition. I've got to take him to a hospital." I heard footsteps on the porch. I turned as my classmate and my long-dead friend raced into the cabin. She'd aged and had significant gray hair, but it was her. I could hardly breathe. "Becky?"

"Maggie?" Becky blushed and took the older man's arm when I noticed her tears.

Chapter 37

"What the hell, Becky? I guess you know the trouble and pain you've caused your family. I don't have time to give you the kick up the ass you deserve. I must return to my husband and get him some help." I turned to go.

"Maggie, hear me out. I don't know how you got here, but my guess is you haven't got a clue what you've done and where you are. You need to listen to me. If you're lost, we're probably the only people in the world who can help you. First of all, do you know where you are and what time it is?"

The actor called Dan blocked the door. The older man took me by my shoulder and forced me to sit on one of two chairs. Becky sat down on the other. The two men remained standing. The older man placed an ancient coffeepot on the stovetop, approached Becky, and rested his arm on her shoulder. It was at that point I noticed the rings. *They must be married, but isn't bigamy illegal?*

"My husband's been critically injured. I don't have time for a story. I need to find him some help. He's alone in a cabin somewhere near here. If you can't help me, please just let me go." I was furious and beyond desperate.

"Your husband is probably right here, but he's not here now. He's in the future. I'll ask one question. Did you fall in the creek along the trail?" They stared without moving to wait for an answer.

"What's that got to do with this? The trail back to the parking lot is impassable. Another rock slide occurred, and yesterday there was an earthquake with aftershocks. I couldn't pass, so I walked down to the creek. A mountain lion attacked Colin early this morning. I hiked out for help, but I must have taken a wrong turn. I ended up on a movie or television set, or is it a cult?"

Becky sat forward. "Nope, on all accounts. You're exactly where you were this morning, except you're about 125 years earlier. Maggie, you're in the 1800s. You've time traveled. I should introduce you to my husband and stepson. Sam Buchanan and Dan are the ones who eventually found me when I had my accident back in the future. I was in a rock slide in the 1980s, right after our graduation. I tried to get back to get help for Julie Smyth and me, but I walked into the creek and traveled back to the 1850s. The same thing's happened to you."

"Bullshit, Becky. You guys are in a cult of crazies. I don't know what you think, but I don't have time, and I need to go and get real help." I stood, but Dan blocked the door and folded his arms.

"Ma'am, you need to believe her. We're the only ones who know about this situation. Becky took my son to the future a few years ago, when a rabid dog bit him, but he recalls only a few things from that time because he was just two years old. He likes red trucks. I've never seen a red truck except his pictures." The man who resembled the actor from the *Comstock* series was quite sincere. I could read the anguish on his face.

"I figure you can understand why this is so unbelievable. First, you look and talk like the actors in *Comstock*, and yet you're all dead except for my husband. Do you all remember my husband, Colin Chandler?" I received blank stares with no sense of recognition.

"You have a town with other characters who resemble the actors on the *Comstock* television program, but it has been gone for forty or more years. Mr. Buchanan, you look so much like my husband, who played Sam Buchanan in the series. Can you understand my confusion? How do I return to him to get some help? It's late. If you can't help me, I need to leave to locate paramedics or a retrieval team. How do I get back to my husband?" *These people appear extremely real and very off the planet. As if I believe what I see...*

The man who portrayed Sam Buchanan appeared confused. "I'm not sure what this television program is about. Becky told me about the box with moving pictures, but I don't know about anything called *Comstock*, other than that people call our silver-mining reserve the Comstock Lode."

Becky stood. She glanced at Dan and Sam Buchanan. "I have more to tell you. I may have more insight into your history than I've let on, but for now, it sounds like we need to get Maggie back to the portal. Dan, your father and I are the only ones who know where it is. I think it's best if we show you now. I should probably go with her."

I didn't understand what they were talking about. Becky's husband put both hands on her shoulders. "Not alone this time, darling. I'm going, too. Dan, you'll have to take over the Cattle Creek Ranch while I'm gone."

Dan walked out to the horses. "What if you don't return? And what's a television show? And how do I tell Hannah and Gee Ling?"

Becky appeared apprehensive and bit her lower lip. "Yeah, I guess it's time I did some explaining."

Hearing the name Gee Ling brought it all back. I'd heard Colin speak about the actor who played Gee Ling on the program. Apparently, he was quite a jokester. These people were acting as if it was all real. The problem was that they appeared to look and talk like older versions of the television actors. The resemblance of Colin to the older male actor was uncanny. They were identical twins. It had to be a cult.

"You know, after graduation, I came up to the Tahoe area to check out the vet practice that Jeff and I planned to buy, and as you probably know, I went up to Miner's Meadow with Julie Smyth. I can tell you more while we ride to the portal, so you can get back to your husband."

While I needed to return to Colin, I realized I had to understand where I was. I turned and noticed the large tree that had fallen was still standing. "Everyone thinks you were killed with the Smyth lady, but your body was never located. Did you know your father spent years riding around the area with Lauren, trying to find your remains, or to discover that perhaps you had survived the rock slide?"

"Yeah, I'm aware of all that, and of many things that have happened since I disappeared. I've traveled back on three occasions. Yes, I was spotted at a store several years ago. When I first time traveled to the past, I tried for nearly twenty years to learn a way back. I was desperate to return to Jeff and Lauren. I traveled all over the States, attempting to identify a portal to get back. When I did, I discovered Jeff had married my sister. I knew Lauren was at Auburn. I was engaged to Sam, and when we finally found the portal through another time traveler, Sam insisted I go back to see Lauren."

"Do you realize Lauren's been affected by all she's been through?" I could not conceive that Becky had turned her back on her own daughter and chosen to live in a different world. Or could I? I thought of my children living in Australia while I was living the life of a queen here in America. *Or was I in America? Where was I? Who the hell are these people? Is this real, or am I dead?*

"You know Lauren? Is she okay?" I could hear the desperation in her voice.

"Yes, we met in Australia, and she attended my wedding. She lives near Virginia City and works at a vet clinic. She's married to a wonderful man."

I studied Becky's face. I could tell she wanted to ask a question. "What?"

"Is she pregnant?"

In an instant, I realized she'd met her daughter and the implications. "Did she come here? And where the hell is here? I need to return. My husband desperately needs help, and I must get back to him." I turned to the horse I'd ridden into the valley.

Becky watched me, waiting for a reply. I was still so furious with her and this mythical, time travel nonsense that I didn't want to give her the satisfaction of telling her she would be a grandmother. *Why would she ask that question?*

Both men had saddled the horses and checked and tightened the cinches. We all mounted to head out of the valley. The clouds were now threatening.

"Maggie, please tell me that Jim and Lauren are alright."

Lauren knew about her mother? Why has she kept this to herself? Did they meet regularly? Does this explain her indifference to the notion that her mother was dead? Did Lauren know Becky was living in the cult? Was she okay with it?

"Lauren and Jim are familiar with the portal, and they visit every summer. The last time they came, they said it might be their last. We all felt it unwise to time travel during a pregnancy. Unless something terrible has happened to them, we're hoping she's pregnant."

I was almost faint with anxiety and disbelief. "Just get me to your portal or whatever, and I'll find help for Colin. You guys can stay here in your stupid fantasy."

As we climbed out of the valley, I took more stock of my surroundings. There were not any signs or steps along the trail that were present when Colin and I descended into the valley. There was more vegetation, and there were more trees than I recalled. I watched the lake, and while it appeared to be the same, I saw more water than I remembered, which changed the shoreline. No evidence of a recent earthquake existed. Then the clouds were so different.

Dan led the way. "What's television, Bec?"

Becky, who was ahead of me, seemed anxious. "I swore I'd die with this knowledge, but I guess I should explain. Sam, do you remember the man who once said, 'Hail Mary'?"

"Yeah. What does that have to do with television?"

"I think I may have told you he might be a fellow time traveler like Frank Lash?"

"You mean Alex Conrad? Go on." I could hear the authoritative voice, which was so much like Colin's. Alex Conrad, who was Colin's partner, was the man who actually came up with the concept for the television series. *Is this where he got the idea?*

Becky reluctantly continued. "Apparently, he discovered a way to travel from the 1900s to the 1800s. Alex Conrad met you and the boys and developed a television show based on your family."

Dan stood up in the saddle and adjusted his scabbard. "Bear scat." He pointed to feces next to the trail.

"Do you have grizzly bears up here?" I knew they'd been mostly eliminated during the gold rush.

"A few are left around here. Don't worry, we won't let one get you." Sam Buchanan had hardly spoken since I'd arrived. "We only shoot them if they're about to attack. Becky's told me about conservation and the need to protect all kinds of animals, even ones that are dangerous."

It was hard to look at the man whom I remembered only as a younger version of the television star, but then again, who was I talking about? He was the spitting image of Colin. We rode for another thirty minutes and joined the creek below the cliff face and trail where we traveled. We followed it for a mile or so. I was nervous about a rock slide, but the others seemed unconcerned.

Becky finally showed the area where she said I had to cross to return to my husband. The idea was ridiculous, but I was desperate. However, I realized there were no large earthmovers down where she pointed. How were they removed so quickly? It was now about four in the afternoon, and in the high mountains, the shadows were increasing.

"I must get back to him before dark. I doubt I can return to the town to rent a helicopter today. How do we get down there, anyway?"

"We will pass the area where the original rock slide occurred, and then we will get into the water. I'll show you when we're next to the water. It will take another forty minutes."

Sam Buchanan pointed to a specific pool of water. "It's that pool right there."

The entire creek differed from what I remembered this morning. After I fell into and emerged from the stream, I hadn't noticed the difference. I did now.

Chapter 38

We rode past the cliff face and dismounted. We had to climb down to the creek and walk upstream until we came to the large pool. I recognized this, but the terrain surrounding the pool was different. It was not as close to the cliff face, and the bushes were more abundant. When I walked out of the pool earlier in the day, I was in such a hurry to get help I didn't pay much attention, but I noticed a fishing fly that had fallen out of my pocket. It was a Bec Beauty.

Becky saw it, too, and picked it up. "I must have dropped this. How did that happen? I wasn't even down here."

"It's from me. Jeff made some for me." I searched her face for a reaction.

Becky wistfully smiled and shook her head. "Yeah, I've used them for years."

A gusty wind blew, making the creek pool hard to see. "If this is true, and I return to my time, I can't see why you could help. I'll walk out and head straight for the town. I won't get there until late, but I don't think you can help."

"Maggie, I'm a doctor now. When I couldn't get back home, I didn't make enough money as a vet, and since I knew modern medicine, I was way above the average doctor for this time. I went to medical school, and I work at the clinic in Virginia City. My partners and I care for the people all over the area. When we cross, if it's like you say, Sam and I can go back to the cabin to care for Colin, and you can go to town. It'll be the same time of day."

"That makes sense. Okay, how do we do this?" *What the hell am I doing, asking these people for directions?*

"We just jump in the deep area, and when we emerge, we're in the same time zone and day, but in the future, or in your case, the past. To be honest, I leave my clothes on. Was it cold when you fell in?"

"No. It was warmer, and there were no clouds. It was cold when I emerged, though." *Could what they are telling me be true?* "I can't see how you can help if you don't have any antibiotics." I wanted to be rid of these nutters. I hoped Becky would come alone. I would love to take her back to civilization. *Of course, this is all a nightmare, and none of this is real.*

"Lauren brings antibiotics and buries them. We have a place where she leaves some by the creek at least once a year. If I'm desperate, I can time travel and get what I need. I know where to look, so we're coming." Becky turned to Sam. "Ready to meet the future, darling?"

I could tell that Sam was nervous. "I've been waiting years for this moment. Will I see the box with the moving pictures?"

"No. We're just going back to Hank Heaven to help the man who plays you on television." Becky hugged Dan.

Sam seemed disappointed. "Dan, you know if we don't return, and unless Clint returns, it's up to you to carry on. The Cattle Creek Ranch rests in your most capable hands."

"Right, Pa." They shook hands. Modern people would hug. These people took their roles seriously. My memories of the Comstock series were returning. I did laugh, thinking back about how the character on *Comstock*, who played Danny, always said, 'Right, Pa.' I saw Becky laugh as well.

"Danny, please tell Hannah how much we love her. I never want her to know about this. She has a long and wonderful life ahead of her." Becky gazed wistfully at her surroundings. "Okay, I think it's best if we go together. Let's hold hands and jump. It'll be cold, so get ready." Becky took my hand and then Sam's hand. "On three."

Yet after she said "one," they pulled me into the icy water, and we all three hit the bottom and resurfaced. We were over our heads when we hit the bottom, but as we resurfaced, we could see Dan watching us. We hadn't time traveled. Becky was shocked, and she once again took our hands and pulled us down, yet we didn't go any farther than the bottom of the pool.

When we surfaced again, she walked out of the water. She stared up and down the creek. "What the hell?" She then said she would go alone and for us to follow her. She went back into the water and submerged herself several times. Becky resurfaced each time.

"This is the hole that I know takes us back and forth. Right, Sam?"

Sam pursed his lips. "I spent three weeks removing the boulder that blocked the passage, so Lauren could return to her time. The remnant of that boulder is over there." He pointed to a large boulder which was the size of a golf cart.

Becky studied the water. "I'll try another one. I'm not sure what's happened." She walked down to the next pool. Becky's hands were almost icy blue, and she weakly smiled at Sam.

Dan, or the actor, stood behind me and rubbed my shoulders and arms. I shook violently by now. It was probably more from my anxiety, but damn, I was cold. We watched as Becky plunged into the hole upstream from the pool where I knew I had emerged. She next went to the pool on the downstream side. Since this pool wasn't deep enough to bury her, Becky sat down, clutched her knees, and went underwater.

Because this approach didn't work either, she returned to the original hole to try again several times. She emerged again and again. The last time Sam went into the water and forcefully pulled her out. "Enough. It's not working. Bec, you need to stop. I don't know why it's not working, but it isn't."

Becky was blue and exhausted. She cried. I was on the verge, but I was so confused. My teeth chattered as I asked them to take me back to town. One good thing was that my credit card was in my jacket pocket.

Sam tried to warm Becky. He held her and stroked her hair and back. "No, you can't go back there. We'll take you back to the Cattle Creek Ranch. There's no other way. No one in town can help, and we don't want to stir up anything."

I was distraught. "I think I'll go back to the cabin. If I return there, at least I'll be near Colin. You can do what you like, but I'm not wasting time."

"Maggie?" Becky stared at me.

"Yeah?" I glared back, realizing how awful my situation had become.

"I know how you feel. I've been in your shoes. You have an advantage since you and I know what is happening. I didn't know when I first crossed in time. Please, let's go to the ranch. We can find you some dry clothes. I'll explain and if you want to leave, I'll help you. Please, just tonight. We can try again tomorrow. I don't understand the reason the portal doesn't work."

I was fighting tears and exhaustion. My throat was sore, and I had chills. I felt guilty that I hadn't found help for my husband, who might be dead by now. I felt powerless and confused. The idea of time travel was ludicrous. I had fallen into a cult. Why did Becky try so diligently, however, and risk so much to get me back to Colin? *What was happening? What was real?*

Chapter 39

We mounted our horses and began an hour's ride to Becky's home. Dan led the way, and I followed. Becky and her husband, if I could think of him as her husband, rode behind me. The horse I rode was well trained and comfortable. He made a sorrowful trip nearly tolerable. He wasn't my beautiful horse, Digger.

I thought about my friends and family. I was separated by this preposterous barrier of time. I was alone. Becky and I'd been the best of friends even though she'd married early in our vet-school years, but now that I knew she left Jeff and Lauren to live with these pretend people, I realized she was no longer my friend. It was becoming dark, and as we rode around a barn, I recognized I was now at the film set of the *Comstock* ranch house.

The structure was a perfect rendition from the television show I'd watched as a child. Even an old rose bush climbed up on the first-story roof. The porch was exactly as I remembered it. There was a lantern lit inside the house.

Dan took the horses. He would put them up, feed them, and then go to his own house down the way. "Ma'am, I'm so sorry we can't help you. I'm sure you're confused, but Becky and my pa know what they're talking about. They are the only ones who can help you. Please listen to what they say."

"Thanks for all your help, Danny. I'm sorry, but this is all new to me, and I simply don't know what's real and what's fantasy." *Am I talking to an actor, a cult member, or a real person?*

"Becky and my pa are real." We both turned to see an older Chinese man come out from the kitchen door and break into a ramble in Cantonese. Dan shrugged. "You'll find out that Gee Ling can be riled when he has unexpected mouths to feed. I'm going home. I have four children and a wife waiting for me. Good evening, ma'am."

Becky beckoned me into the main house, which appeared to be a clone of the 1950s television series. She took me to a room with a trunk of clothes. I was much taller than Becky was and would not fit into her clothes, but the trunk contained dresses of all sizes. Dresses were not my go-to clothing. "It's only until your clothes dry. Sam will start a fire, so we can dry them quickly. I guess you realize there's no electricity. Sam and Gee Ling will light lanterns. When you're dressed, come downstairs. We'll have a bite to eat, and we can discuss how to return you to your time and husband." She set out three dresses from which to choose. I was still wet and cold, and I stripped down, used one dress to dry myself, and put another one on.

It was June, but in the mountains, it was still cool at night. A steady rain had begun and the moon, which was so prominent at the cabin, was hidden. As desperate as I considered this situation, I laughed and wondered if the moon phases were the same if the ridiculously wacky idea of time travel was true. I was exhausted, and the bed was very inviting. If I took a power nap, I doubt they would even notice.

A knock on the door startled me. It was the cook. "Missy need food. Come down now before food cold."

I jumped up and realized I must have slept a few minutes longer. I had a watch under my long-sleeved dress, which I held up to the gas lamp. It had moisture under the glass but was still working. I'd slept for more than an hour. I opened the door, and the cook was gone. When I descended the stairs, I tripped on the hem of the dress. I fell down the stairs and hit my shoulder on the railing. I swore and then realized this was offensive to the man who called himself Sam Buchanan, but it made Becky laugh.

After they helped me up, Becky examined my arm and shoulder. "I don't think it's broken. Can you move your arm?"

I moved it and was sure I was okay. "Well, that was embarrassing. Sorry to be so late."

I glanced over at the familiar dinner table, where there was only one place setting. "We already ate. Sit down, Maggie, and we'll bring you some food." Sam placed his arm against my back and guided me to the table. Becky sat across from me, while the Gee Ling character brought out ham and biscuits.

"Gee Ling not ready for guests. Mr. Sam not tell Gee Ling. He bad man. So sorry, missy."

The front door opened, and a stunning, tall girl with dark hair entered. "Ma, what's going on? Dan said you'd returned early with a friend."

Becky immediately stood to hug the young woman. She looked back at me, and there was no mistake about her intention. There'd be no discussion of how and where I came from in this girl's presence. "Maggie, this is our daughter, Hannah. Hannah, this is my medical- school classmate, Dr. Maggie Chandler. We weren't expecting her, but here she is. It's late, and you have school tomorrow, darling, so go to bed."

The lovely girl was far too young to be Becky's biological daughter. Was Hannah Sam's daughter or adopted? I didn't know what was going on. I wasn't sure I could believe them, anyway. She had shiny, thick, braided black hair. With high cheekbones and beautiful brown eyes, she was stunning.

She hugged both parents and shook my hand. She entered the kitchen, where I could hear her tell the cook good night, after which she screamed.

I heard the cook tell her to take her hands off the dough and to get to bed. As she walked back through the dining area and up the stairs, she was holding her bottom. "Ma, I don't know why you allow Gee Ling to punish me."

Becky rolled her eyes. "Because you deserve it. Don't have us choose between you and Gee Ling, darling. You will be out on the street in a heartbeat."

I watched Sam nod as he offered me brandy. "Yes, thank you." I pointed to my shoulder. "For medicinal properties only." Both Sam and Becky nodded as Sam poured a rather large amount.

"A medicinal quantity, then." Sam poured a similar amount for himself, but only half for Becky. "My wife is what you might describe as a 'lightweight' in your time."

After I finished my ham and biscuit, we all went over to the couch, which was in front of the great fireplace. I examined the hearth, which appeared to be a replica of the one that was in Lauren and Jim's house. This brought all the confusing aspects of my current situation to the forefront.

Becky took the lead. "First, we'll go back to the portal pool in the morning. I don't know why it didn't allow us to pass. There was only one time it didn't work, and that was following a tremendous rainfall, and the large boulder that Sam mentioned filled most of the pool. Sam worked for weeks to remove it. However, we know the pool is clear now. Lauren and Jim have come twice during the last few years. They had no issues except waiting until the area was free from wondering eyes.

"Lauren came three years ago when she met a fellow time traveler who knew me. Frank Lash helped me return to the future after over twenty years of trying. That's when I went back, or forward, and found Jeff had remarried and had two more children. I was engaged to Sam when we discovered the portal pool with the help of Frank Lash. Your husband is Colin Chandler, who played Sam in the television series, right?"

I nodded and waited for more of the story.

"His partner and coproducer was Alex Conrad, who had the original inspiration for the *Comstock* series. Alex was also a time traveler, and he would come during the summers for years before and during the series. Obviously, he's dead, but I met him when I traveled to the future and found Jeff married and Lauren in vet school. And, yes, I broke my father out of the care facility to take him up to his cabin in the mountains. He asked me to write his story to give it to his grandchildren. We stayed up there for weeks until he passed, and I buried him next to my mother, whose body was secretly moved to their cabin.

"You see, if I had discovered a way to return when I first arrived here in the 1850s, I would have gone back in a heartbeat. It took me so long to find a way back, though, that I felt it wasn't fair. The truth is, I'd fallen in love with this wonderful man, and I was committed to him. Becky and Sam glanced at each other. There was no mistaking the bond they had for one another.

"When I arrived, the Buchanans were much younger than in the television series, and all three boys were younger versions of themselves. I stayed with them and eventually told Sam I came from the future. That was ugly and resulted in my moving to the East to earn a medical degree, serve as a medic and doctor during the Civil War, and work for over ten years in a Baltimore hospital, where Sam located me once again."

I'd ask her later about why she said ugly. I recalled the ring that Jeff had found in the Gettysburg Museum. I'd wait to ask her about that, as well. There were so many questions. "What happened to Hank? How did that work?"

"Alex must have come and known that Hank died unexpectedly. I think it was pure chance that the actor who played Hank passed away, as well. You know, he didn't have to follow the real life of my family."

Sam looked away, and I saw his hand shake. He had to be approaching the same age as my husband, but like Colin, he was ageless. "While you were sleeping, Becky told me about the television series. I would love to meet your husband. I hope we can go tomorrow. We think the initial plan is good. Once we arrive, head to town for your friends while

Becky and I will go to the cabin to tend to your husband until he's rescued."

This approach sounded reasonable. I was convinced Colin would still be alive the next morning because he had food, water, and pain meds. My biggest concern was the possibility of shock and sepsis. He needed care and antibiotics. "If what you say is true, why isn't the portal working?"

Becky stood up. "I've thought about it. I recall you described an earthquake, but it hadn't damaged the pool when you accidentally fell in and traveled to us. Didn't you say aftershocks happened? Maybe the pool is temporarily blocked?"

I remembered an aftershock that caused me to lose my equilibrium. "Yeah, that's how I lost my balance and fell into the pool. Are you suggesting the other side may be blocked? How can we open it so I can get back tomorrow? I can't be gone any longer than a day. Please tell me that isn't true." *Oh, God. Am I stuck here? How am I going to get help for Colin? Is there another portal?* "Do you know any other time travelers who didn't use this portal to arrive here?"

"I know of one who arrived somewhere back East, but she didn't know how since she was injured and delirious. She's dead, anyway. Her name was Pam Wilkins, who migrated out here, was one of the town's matriarchs, and was one of my most admired friends."

This must be a nightmare, and I'll wake up in the cabin with Colin making coffee. I recognized I was being sucked into this concept of time travel. *So ridiculous.* We said good night, with Sam saying, "pleasant dreams," which I remembered from the *Comstock* programs. I was surprised how the memories of the television program flooded back to me.

Becky showed me the water closet. "It came after the series ended. We're a very modern household, you know."

I laughed. "Yeah, I can see that." I made my way to the bedroom. The lamp was lit, and fresh water was in a jug with a bowl on a small table with a mirror on the wall above.

I glimpsed in the mirror and wondered about the identity of the woman who stared back at me. Did she live in the present or the past? I realized sleep would be elusive.

Chapter 40

Becky knocked on the door. "Maggot?"

This name made me laugh. She and my sister had always called me that. "Yeah?" I was trying to sleep in the dress Becky had provided.

Becky opened the door to bring me a nightgown. It looked like the one I'd seen Danny wear in the early *Comstock* episodes. It was musty, but clean and dry. I guess sleep will be tough for you tonight. "Care to talk?"

I wanted to slap her. I didn't ever want to see her again. I still couldn't believe I was in the 1800s. It had to be a cult. Local places must exist where nut jobs, who were raised with *Comstock,* didn't want to leave the past. How could she fall for this fantasy?

"I can't imagine anything you could say that would justify your actions, but knock yourself out."

I listened as Becky described the rock slide, her means of survival, and her eventual arrival in the town of Virginia City. "It was a new town, and the mines were the primary reason the town existed. By chance, when I went back to the rock slide site, I met a very young Sam and Gee Ling and spent a few nights here at the Cattle Creek Ranch. They invited me to stay, but my sole goal was to return to Jeff and Lauren. I left the Buchanans to travel out west to Sacramento and San Francisco, where I felt I had a better chance of learning how to time travel."

"Go on." I didn't believe her, but I wanted to hear her out.

"I was arrested for thievery and sent to prison. That's a story in itself. Anyway, I had no means to get out and was certain I would see my time out in jail. Fortunately, young Clint Buchanan, who was on his way to college, discovered me in the San Francisco prison and had me released after the charges were determined to be false. I returned to Virginia City with no clue how to cross back into the 1900s."

"Out of curiosity, the Clint actor quit the television program. What happened to the Clint who lived in this century?" *As if the actor's story and the 1800s Clint had to match...*

"Clint is alive and lives in Australia with his wife and family. Sam and I were going there to visit him this year."

"As I said, I eventually moved back East to become a doctor. By that point in time, I was sure I would never find a way back to Jeff and Lauren, but I continued to search and hope."

"Why didn't you stay here, or return when you received your degree?" My nap had erased any need for sleep.

"When I eventually told Sam the truth, I showed him my only picture of Jeff and Lauren. He went crazy, and I knew I had to leave.

It wasn't that he didn't believe I was from another time, but it was because he knew I was married, and he had no hope for any further relationship."

"Didn't he see your ring?" I then remembered the picture of the ring that Jeff had shown me after my wedding. Knowing it was probably in the collection of the Gettysburg Museum among the Civil War artifacts, this is how I could either verify Becky's claim of time travel or confirm my belief that she was in a cult. "Becky, where's your ring?"

Becky held out her hand. She had a quite elegant wedding band and an engagement ring. They were beautiful and probably worth a fortune. "Nice, aren't they?"

"No, I mean the one Jeff gave you."

Becky looked down and didn't say anything for a moment. She stared out the window. "I lost it during the Civil War. You know, cleanliness wasn't fashionable at that time. I'd met Oliver Wendell Holmes Sr. while I was in medical school. He was Oliver Wendell Holmes Jr.'s father. The Supreme Court guy? By the way, I know him, too."

"Prove it. Get him on the phone." I smirked inwardly.

Becky ignored my suggestion. "Anyway, did you know he lectured about germs and cleanliness? Holmes Sr. was a doctor. I always removed my ring when I performed surgery. It must have fallen through a hole in my pocket when we were attending to casualties. That's when I gave up on ever seeing Jeff and Lauren again."

I didn't want to tell her that Jeff had found the ring. It hit me like a rock. I realized she probably did time travel, and I was traveling as well. "Becky?"

"Yeah?" She turned to face me and took my hands.

"I'm sorry. Jesus H. Christ, I think you're right."

"Yeah. Been there, done that." She smiled.

"Got the T-shirt." I replied.

A puzzled look crossed her face. I understood she had not heard the phrase.

"Been there, done that, got the T-shirt? Maybe that was an Australian phrase?"

"The last time I spoke with you, you were moving to Australia. What happened?"

"Stayed in Oz all my career, had three wonderful children, kicked lover boy to the curb, retired, and moved back to the States to fish and write cozy mysteries about vets. I found the love of my life. He was my neighbor, his grandson lives with him, and that's how we met. Luke will turn thirteen, but he is so mature and smart. His mother was Colin's daughter, who Luke's father murdered.

"I ran into a bit of strife with some unsavory characters along the way, who appeared to be resurfacing. Colin decided we should get away, and he always loved Miner's Meadow. We recently held a small wedding at Colin's ranch, and I guess I should tell you that Jeff and Sherry were there, as were Lauren and Jim. As you can probably guess, Lauren's pregnant. She won't travel soon. Becky, when I moved back home from Australia, I left my kids and even grandkids. I have no business telling you what you should have done. I'm having a difficult time with this time travel idea, but I can't explain it otherwise. Tell me about your daughter."

"Hannah came to us a few years ago. She was taken from a wagon train by Indians and lived with them for several years. I think you can see she could pass for a..." Becky paused. "I think I should say indigenous or native American? Anyway, we adopted her and are raising her. Sounds a great deal like your grandson. We think she's fifteen, and she's already committed to a boy who is at engineering college. Unless there's an appreciable change, I suspect they'll be married when he finishes his education. I hoped she would become a doctor, but she shows no interest in that career."

"Yeah, the modern terms used now are indigenous or Native American. Did you search for her family? She's a stunner."

"She wasn't when we took her in. Hannah was thin, she had contracted lice, and I thought she was a boy. It took a while to get Sam's consent to adopt her, but they're inseparable now. She has a way with young horses. Hannah trained my mare, which she gave to me as a surprise birthday gift. How about we both try to get some sleep, and we'll leave for the pool in the midmorning when the temperature is warmer? I don't think the rain will affect the water level."

Becky hugged me and left. I cried. I was alone and in a different world, and the prospects of returning to Colin seemed to be miniscule at best. I lay awake for hours, but finally I slept. I heard a knock on the door. "Ma'am, it's me, Hannah. Ma says you need to wake up and get ready. I'm leaving for school soon. I hope you're here when I return."

Not me. I was headed to the future, come hell or high water. I hoped.

Chapter 41

I barely heard a knock on my door several minutes later. "Ma'am, my ma wants you to come down to the table. She said to put on these clothes, and Gee Ling will wash your regular clothes." I opened the door where Hannah stood holding the garments. "Thank you, Hannah. I hear you have quite a story."

"I'm not sure what you mean, ma'am." She presented me with the bundle.

I wondered if I had mentioned unpleasant memories. "Your life before you came here?"

"Oh, I thought you meant my school story. It's due today, and I have to leave to get to school. Ma let me wait so I could see you one more time. It's a two-hour ride, so may I be excused?"

"Two hours? Is that each way?" I was surprised.

"Yes, but I don't mind. I plan to be a doctor like my mother someday, and I know I need to study." Hannah covered her mouth. "Oh, dagnabbit. I didn't mean to tell you. Please don't tell my ma."

"Scout's honor." I watched her quizzical look.

"Ma'am, did you live with Indians, too?" She backed away from the door, and I could tell she was trying to end the conversation.

"No. I was in the Girl Scouts." I realized the Girl Scouts may not have started yet. "It's a club back East for young girls. Nice to meet you, Hannah."

"Yes, ma'am." She turned to run down the stairs. I heard her father admonish her for running down the stairs and a door slam. *OMG, she's a knockout.*

I donned old-fashioned pants with buttons and a tan man's shirt. I used my bra and panties I'd washed in the basin in the room. My socks were nearly dry. I descended to the great room. Becky and Sam were seated at the table, where the Gee Ling character served coffee and platters of food.

Dan, or Danny as I remember him, walked in and wanted to know whether we were ready to have another go at the creek. He asked Gee Ling if he wanted trout for supper. I guessed Gee Ling didn't know the family secret. "Yes, Danny. Gee Ling cook fancy trout for our guest?"

"Uh, not tonight, Gee Ling. We won't be back until late, and we may all stay up at Hank Heaven. Why don't you visit your cousins in town?" Danny patted Gee Ling's shoulder as I witnessed both Sam and Becky cringe.

"Big secret in this house, and no one tell Gee Ling. I stay here to guard the Cattle Creek Ranch. You have fun without Gee Ling. Humph." Off he went into another Cantonese litany.

Sam shook his head. "Are the horses saddled?"

Dan whispered. "Yeah. I can stay for a while to see you off. I have a meeting with an Eastern buyer, who's interested in a couple of hundred head of cattle if we can drive them to Salt Lake."

"Maybe you should head to Virginia City, and we can turn the horses loose. Think of an excuse, so they don't send a posse out for us, Dan."

"Right, Pa." Becky and I stared at each other, attempting to suppress a laugh.

"What?" Dan saw the interaction.

"In the, shall we say, future, you say 'Right, Pa' a lot on the television series."

The men looked at us and shrugged.

Sam gazed at Becky, who was almost convulsing while she tried hard to stifle a laugh. "It must be funny, but, you know, a little more 'Right, Sam' from you would be nice."

Becky didn't even glance up. "And when you're right, I will be the first to acknowledge you. Don't sit by the telegraph, darling."

I appreciated the humor, but then I realized my husband was in dire condition, lying on the cabin floor, waiting for me. I stood up and pronounced, "I need to go now."

We all progressed toward the front door. Gee Ling came from the kitchen to hand Becky a saddlebag filled with food. "Don't worry, big missy. Gee Ling here for little missy when she come back from school."

"Thank you, my dear friend." Becky hugged Gee Ling, walked toward the door, and beckoned us all. She quietly leaned toward me and whispered, "Let's get the heck out of Dodge."

Dan returned from the barn. He insisted on joining us because he wanted to watch as we disappeared into the water. "If Jenny is any more annoyed with me, I may have to join you."

Danny explained Jenny cared for the two girls and two boys. He often took Little Hank with him to lighten her burden. We rode to the cliff face once again. They wanted to examine the pool from above. It didn't seem to be any different from the previous day, but it varied from when Colin and I rode past. There was no sign a rock slide had ever occurred. The sun was out, and the water appeared aqua and calm.

Becky pointed out the exact spot where the plaque for both her and the other woman would be displayed. The small, flat granite boulder showed no signs of a plaque.

"No plaque." She turned to me and shrugged her shoulders.

I responded to her in kind. I didn't think she'd go to all the trouble if she wasn't convinced she was in the past, and this approach was the only way back to the future. My anxiety increased. What if it didn't work today? If Colin didn't receive some treatment quickly, I wasn't sure he would make it.

Both she and Sam peered down, and after what seemed like a lifetime, Sam cleared his throat. "No evidence that the rain did anything. I can see several trout, and it looks the same as always. Let's give it a go."

We turned back to the place where we slid down to the creek. Dan stayed up on the trail and took the horses. Becky approached bushes above the creek, but well off the trail, and dug out a large plastic bag. Sam commented he still could not get over the idea of 'movable, transparent glass.' They had fresh clothes, took mine, wrapped them inside, and walked to the water's edge.

Becky turned to Sam. "Let me go first this time, darling."

Sam shook his head. With his 'take no prisoners' voice, Sam quietly took command. "All or none, Bec. Not a chance in Hades that I'm letting you go alone."

I wished to get back first. "Please, let me go first and, if I don't break through, I'll let you two decide. If I get through, I'll wait an hour before I head to the parking lot. The men should work on the trail today. When I left, two large, overturned trucks lay near the water's edge. We must be careful to get out and get away without letting them know the way we arrived."

"All or none, ladies." There was no other way. It was eerie how similar Sam's voice was to Colin's. I laughed as I wondered if it had been me who time traveled so many years ago. Would I be married to this man?

"What?" Becky wanted to know what was so funny.

"Nothing. It's a nervous laugh. I'm ready. Shall we hold hands?" I dreaded the cold I was about to experience. "On three?"

Sam held the bag in one hand and Becky's hand with his other. I grasped Becky's hand, but leaned down to check the water temperature. It felt even colder than before. "Damn, it's freezing." Becky laughed when I remembered the *Comstock* characters didn't swear. "Well, it is." I blushed but heard a "three," and was pulled into the water with Sam and Becky.

We emerged after pushing off from the bottom. We gazed around and quickly knew we hadn't traveled. We held hands and dropped underwater once again. This time, I experienced a pull, but when I emerged, I realized we had not journeyed. I was distraught, not to mention cold.

Becky turned to Sam. "Maybe the pool accommodates only two. Let Maggie and me go, and you come after." She grabbed the bag of clothes, and the two of us stepped forward to the deepest area and submerged ourselves. Again, there was Sam, standing in shallow water when we resurfaced.

"Okay, just me this time." I could tell Becky was nearly as frantic as I was. This portal pool was her lifeline to her other family. Even though she opted not to use it, she had understood she could time travel if necessary.

Once again, she submerged herself and resurfaced. "I can feel the water pulling me, but I can't seem to transition. Something must be wrong on the other side."

"Let me try." Sam leaped into the water, creating an enormous splash. For an instant, we couldn't see him in the swirling sand and bubbles. I had hope until I spied his gray hair plastered onto his forehead as he rose from the water.

"My turn." I would stay down and hold my breath. I retrieved a large rock that could weigh me down. Both Becky and Sam stood by the creek as I turned and smiled at Dan, who was holding the horses.

I cannon balled into the water to force myself to drop and stay for what seemed like a lifetime. My arms and legs ached from the bitter cold. I was possibly three or fewer feet below the surface, but I peered up and thought the surface was lighter. I pushed off the bottom with my feet and turned toward the opposite shoreline. Yes, it was different, or so I thought. I spun in the water and saw Sam extending his hand toward me. Becky covered her mouth with her hands and shook her head.

Sam helped me to the edge of the water, where I sat down and buried my face in my knees. I was cold and shaking, but I didn't cry. I lifted my face to see Becky again, who tried the different pools with no success. She returned to sit down alongside me. We hugged each other to warm ourselves up. "Maggie, did you feel the pull toward the bottom of the pool? I experienced it in the portal pool, and not at all in the others. I think the problem is with the other side of time. I believe the creek may have changed from the earthquake and aftershocks. It had to occur after you traveled here. I'm so, so sorry."

My throat hurt because of the shock of my situation and the hopelessness I felt. I wanted to cry, but I didn't go over the edge. I stared at the water and shook my head. This could not be happening. I must find a way back home. If Colin didn't receive any help soon, he would most likely die. Then what is the point? I then remembered Luke. Even if Colin died, I still needed to care for Luke. I cried. It was a few brief sobs, but no one missed them.

Sam lifted me to a standing position. We were all wet and cold. He wrapped his arms around me and held me. "When Lauren arrived here, I promised Becky I would move heaven and earth to fix the stream, so Lauren could return to the future. I don't think this one is up to me, but I know Lauren will know what has happened and will have the men open the passageway with their gigantic machines. It may take a few days for anyone to realize what's taken place, but I am sure she and Jim will repair the damage."

We each took the time to change from our wet clothes into the dry ones in the plastic bag. We ascended the creek bank to the trail, where Dan stood with the horses. He helped us mount. We turned toward the Cattle Creek Ranch.

Becky had been silent. "Are you okay, Maggie?"

Suck it up, sister. "Never better. I'm living my *Comstock* childhood dream. I'm riding the trails with the Buchanans." I wiped my tears as we mounted our horses.

Before we'd parted at the portal pool, Becky suggested what they might say to Gee Ling and Hannah. "Our plans changed. It's simple. Maggie will be with us for a few days more. We don't need to elaborate. The only person who will wonder is Hannah. Darling, you can deal with her."

I didn't want to return to the Cattle Creek Ranch. As a young girl, I dreamed of living with the Buchanans, but now I wanted anything but that. "Do you mind if I return to Miner's Meadow? I want to revisit it and..." But what was the 'and'?

"It's not there. Nothing is there from the future, Maggie. We can go, but this is where I go to travel." Becky pointed to the creek.

"How about if I go on my own?" I needed to be alone.

"You can't go by yourself. I mean, it's not safe, and you aren't experienced enough to be up here on your own." Becky studied Sam's face.

Sam squared his shoulders. "I'll take her. We'll be back by supper."

Chapter 42

We rode for the first hour in silence. I imagined Colin lying on the cabin floor, wondering when I would bring him help. If the earthquake had been strong enough to obliterate the creek portal pool, I expected the damage in the Tahoe area would be significant. The truck-and-machinery drivers would be called to the populated areas to repair damaged infrastructure.

I knew Lauren and Jim would be concerned about us. They might try to get some help for us sooner than the four days before we were due to be picked up. I guessed, instead of riding out, they might send a helicopter. There was one sizable area where helicopters could land in the meadow by the cabin.

I imagined they would locate Colin, and if he was coherent, would ask about me. If he wasn't able to communicate, or dead, they would wonder where I was. They might think I'd been eaten by the mountain lion. If Colin could talk and tell them the mountain lion was dead, perhaps they might think I was crushed in another rock fall near the creek.

I could just see the headlines in the national news. This time, it would be all over the world. "Colin Chandler's bride is killed in a rock slide that had claimed the life of another woman over two decades ago."

Would Lauren and Jim consider I had time traveled and was now caught in the past without a viable means of return? Or would they believe I had perished in the rock fall? How many weeks would pass before they could allocate machinery to dig into the rubble and realize I did not die in the slide? What would happen to Luke? Would one of Colin's sons come for Luke? Would he return to the ranch? What would my children think?

I followed Sam as we traveled on horseback to Hank Heaven. Ever the gentleman, Sam hesitantly asked how Colin and I met and what the television series was like. "Did many people watch it? Did it show all my sons and Hannah?"

I explained the program ran only a few years after the actor who played Hank died. Colin and Alex recognized this would be the initial sign the series had peaked and lost some ratings.

"What are ratings?" Sam pointed down to the valley when we reached the summit.

"Television is big business. Most of it is free, or people pay a fee to access literally hundreds of programs. Advertisers put their commercials into the program every few minutes to pay the networks that own the television series. The networks vie for audience numbers.

Back in the time of *Comstock*, just four or five channels existed. In the 1950s, the programs that depicted the Old West were popular, but by the mid-sixties, other programs overtook the Westerns, and the audiences no longer watched them. The sponsors who advertised during commercials withdrew their support, and *Comstock*'s days were numbered."

I clarified that the actors who played the roles of his sons, even the townsfolk, and Gee Ling, all either retired or moved on to other programs. The actor who played Danny was remarkably successful and enjoyed several hit shows he produced and acted in after that. "Sam, all those television shows are now what are called reruns, which is how they make money called residuals. For example, my husband receives money every time the old show is played anywhere in the world. Colin is an extremely wealthy man because he wanted the rights to the program and declined the quick money for his acting role. He's a lot like you, if what I saw on television is true. I think you took your profits to either purchase more land or cattle or plant more trees, rather than using the money to live a lavish life. I can see why Becky's attracted to you."

We descended to the valley floor, and I rode around the lakefront and along the cliff faces. Not much had changed. The grass was greener than I remembered it, and the rivulets were running more compared to when I arrived with Colin. A few things were different that I hadn't noticed yesterday. The lavatory was missing, and the porch was smaller than the one in the future. The tree stands were thicker, while campsites I saw when Colin and I arrived several days ago were not there. I smiled and shook my head at the notion of 'days ago,' when, in fact, it must be more than a hundred years from now.

Sam stopped to point out Hank's grave to me. I didn't want to tell him in the future a tree would cover Hank's grave.

"I heard there are other graves up I the valley. Do other family members want to be buried up in Hank Heaven?" I didn't say what I knew.

"Becky and I plan to be buried next to Hank. Are our tombstones still there?"

I lied. "Yes, but since the markers are partially buried, most people never see them." I didn't add they'd been covered by the tree and essentially obliterated from history.

I performed a quick search inside the cabin for any signs that Colin had been there or had been rescued. I knew it was ridiculous. *Almost as ridiculous as time travel.*

I remounted, using the porch as a mounting block. Sam easily mounted from the ground. I could tell he considered my need for a mounting block amusing.

"Are you sure I can't stay here? I don't want to be a bother to your family."

"You and Becky are cut from the same stone. I should tell you what happened when I took Becky up here when she first arrived in our time."

Sam described misbranded cattle up here and how Becky returned against Sam's wishes and a cattle wrestler nearly killed her. "She's lucky to be alive. If she'd been mine, I would have thrashed her, but then, one of our vows was no physical punishment. I can't tell you how many times I've regretted that promise."

I laughed. "Sam, you would have hit her only once, since she would have been on the next bus outta here."

"Bus?"

"It's a long car that carries many people at one time, kinda like a long stagecoach."

We quickly returned up over the pass and back to the Cattle Creek Ranch. As we approached the ranch house, Becky emerged from a small structure near the barn. I asked to go up to the room I'd been assigned. I had a headache that verged on a migraine.

"Maggie, we won't give up hope. We can test the water every day. We know how much you're worried about your husband. We'll do anything in our power. You must have faith."

"Yeah, it took you only twenty-plus years, Bec. I'm sure I'll eventually find my way back, but what will be there when I return?"

Chapter 43

As we tied up our horses, Gee Ling exited the kitchen door. "Gee Ling happy to see Mrs. Chandler. You miss Gee Ling?"

"Dr. Chandler's not feeling well, Gee Ling. She will go up to her room. Will you help me fix some food to take to her in her bedroom?"

I had no desire to eat or talk. "No, thanks. I'm going to sleep for a while. I need to consider my options."

Becky leaned toward me and whispered, "You have no options. You are Gee Ling's prisoner. He won't take no for an option. Prepare to be spoiled."

I smiled politely. "Is this how they treated you when you first arrived in the past?"

"Yep. The men were all starved for female companionship. In those days, Sam and his boys were younger than they were on the television show. The boys were so cute and polite. Clint was out of school and was getting ready to head east for college. He went by ship to Panama and crossed the Isthmus of Panama on land. That's how he found me in a jail in San Francisco. He rescued me. I would probably still be in jail if he hadn't noticed my horse tethered outside a house where I'd lived for many months. I need to tell you about my horse, Penny, but why don't you try to get some sleep? I'll make you some tea to help with your headache. Maggie, I'm so sorry this has happened to you. I'll do anything to get you back with your husband."

"Thanks, Bec. I just wish I knew Colin was alive and receiving medical attention. He's such a robust man for his age, but the injuries were horrific. Give me an hour. I want to shake this headache, and then I should be fine."

Becky returned with an awful-tasting hot drink. She wouldn't leave until I finished it and told me to rest as long as I liked. "You know, we aren't even born yet. We have time to save your husband. We need to find a way to travel back there."

"I guess I don't understand. Are we in parallel times? One hour here, and one hour there? Or is it different?"

"As far as I can explain, we're in parallel times, but staggered. So if you stayed here for five days, when you return, it would be five days later there as well."

"Most likely, Colin's lying on the cabin floor, waiting for help that isn't coming. I don't think he can stand, and I left enough water for possibly a little more than a day, but definitely not enough for four days."

Becky pulled a quilt over me and asked me not to think about it—as if. I didn't, though. I drifted off immediately and didn't wake until the evening, when someone knocked lightly on the bedroom door. "Ma'am, would you like some supper? Ma says you can come down, or I can bring you some food."

"Hannah, is that you?" I was groggy, which I suspected was from the tea. She must have put a narcotic in the drink.

"Yes, ma'am."

"I'll be down in a minute. What time is it?" I'd left my watch hidden in my room, but the sun was low.

"It's almost seven, ma'am. I'll ask Gee Ling to wait for supper. I'd advise you to hurry. Gee Ling doesn't like to wait."

I smiled, remembering the younger version of these men from the television show. If I wasn't so concerned about my husband, I could easily enjoy this escape. I now realized what Becky endured. She was here with no one in whom to confide. She was separated in time from her husband and family. She didn't know how she arrived or the way back. I'd accepted the ridiculous time travel concept, but at least I had some idea that it could be a two-way notion.

I came down to dinner in my own clothes. I was surprised to see Becky in a dress. She smiled and cocked her head. "In the remote chance that you're with us for a few days, we will definitely find you some clothes. I hope your headache is better, and you're able to eat some of the delicious food that my wonderful friend has prepared for us. Why don't you sit at the other end of the table? Would you like some wine? Hannah, please help Gee Ling serve dinner." Becky was so formal. She had changed from the fun-loving vet student I'd known. I guessed I'd changed, as well. *How many years?*

Sam held out a chair for me and poured us wine. Hannah was given what looked like full-cream milk. She and Gee Ling brought several dishes of meat, potatoes, onions, carrots, and gravy. Despite my receding headache, I realized I was famished. I knew we couldn't discuss today's adventure in front of Hannah or Gee Ling.

Hannah was enthralled by my story. Becky explained I was from Kentucky. I'd traveled to visit relatives in Oakland, California and surprised her. Becky knew I'd been in town and had told the sheriff I'd been up at Hank Heaven. We didn't mention I'd requested help for my husband when I came to town. The Buchanans had briefly discussed the anomaly in my presence. They knew the older man, who played the part of the sheriff on the *Comstock* television series, would visit soon. They would cross that bridge only when Ray Thompson arrived. Maybe I would be gone before such time.

After we finished dinner, Sam would go down to talk with Danny and his wife, Jenny. Hannah helped Gee Ling and wanted to visit the foreman's wife, Mrs. Little, for some help with her new essay.

"What's it about?" I was curious about what the school was teaching.

"The future, ma'am. We're supposed to write about what life will be one hundred years from now. I should consult Little Hank. That boy sure has an imagination."

Sam, who glanced up at Hannah, attempted to hide a smirk. Becky could not keep from laughing. "Be back and in your room in an hour, or there will be consequences."

"Yes, ma'am." From the door, I noticed Hannah stick out her tongue at her mother.

Becky responded. "I saw that. I expect you to show a little more respect in front of guests."

I knew Becky didn't see it and simply guessed. I shook my head. "So much like my kids. My grandson, Luke, tests the limits as well."

Sam excused himself. He wanted to check the horses.

Becky glanced at Sam, knowing he was giving us a chance to talk alone. "Tell me about your life, Maggot."

"The quick version is that I married the Australian, and we moved to his homeland. We divorced many years ago, but we had three children who are now grown with families of their own. I had full custody as they grew up, and eventually they all married and moved interstate. I retired and moved back to the States, where I bought a cabin in the mountains. I began writing books and wanted to live alone, fish, and ride. Since I needed time to adjust to a quiet life from the routine of my practice, I abandoned my family. I know you didn't choose to do that now, so I forgive you. Who am I to talk?"

Becky went to a cabinet to pour two small glasses of port. She looked over her shoulder to ensure we were alone. "And how did you meet the television-star version of Sam? That must be a story. Colin Chandler was married when I vanished, wasn't he? I'd discussed this with the owners of the vet clinic when I came out to interview for the job."

"Yep. When I moved into the cabin, a young boy came over from the neighbors' property. He appeared to be a deaf-mute, and he wanted a job. He was Colin's grandson, but I didn't know that when I met the boy. His father, or associates of his father, had murdered Luke's mother. He was in hiding since he was a witness. I realized Luke could hear, and he faked it, although I didn't know it at first. Or I should say it was his way of protecting himself after witnessing such a horrific scene. After he became sure of our friendship, and he was secure in my presence, I got him to talk, and we became friends. I still didn't know he was Colin Chandler's grandson. Anyway, I finally met Luke's grandfather.

We had some adventures, Colin discovered I loved to fish, and all the rest is recent history. I've been married less than two weeks."

"Oh, Maggie, I'm so sorry. Were you on your honeymoon up at Hank Heaven?"

"Yeah, kind of. You probably wouldn't realize it, but marriage to a celebrity does not always mean good times. Some people want you dead or use you to get to your spouse."

Becky roared. "You don't think Sam is famous? Oh, my God, Mag Wheel, it sounds like we are living parallel lives. I've been kidnapped and held for ransom. I almost died. I should tell you about Mrs. Gardiner."

I understood the story must be funny by her reaction. "Bec, let's just say Colin and I are on the lam to hide out from multiple issues. It was only for a week or two. Colin planned a second place after Miner's. I mean Hank Heaven. We all had changed our phone SIM cards, and we could not be contacted, so certain individuals could not locate us."

"SIM cards? Maggie, you realize those individuals aren't even born yet. I think it's safe to name names." As Becky said this, in walked both Sam and Hannah. *How do I explain cell phones?*

Hannah asked if we wanted to hear her story. Sam rolled his eyes but encouraged her to read it. Becky and I had to stifle a laugh.

"Go on, darling. Don't pay attention to them." We got the look.

"Okay. The Future of the United States, by Hannah Buchanan. I am sorry to report that all Indians are dead. The territories are now all states. There are forty-two. My pa was the governor, and currently his grandson is the president of the country.

"Homes have wires running into them, and with a button, we can turn on a light. You can now travel by cart without horses, although horses are still preferred. You can even use machines that fly like birds, and you can sit in a bird machine to move from one place to another.

"The best part is that girls can vote and can be governor or even a senator. Girls are emancipated when they are thirteen and can marry."

"Hannah Buchanan, you will not read that in class. Change that immediately. Do you want the school board to think we even allow such thoughts? Rewrite it now, and I want to see it in the morning." Sam tried not to laugh as he directed her to make the changes.

Hannah turned to us. "I know it's true. I can see into the future. You would not understand what the future is like. You're all too old."

I shook my head, trying to hold back a laugh. It took me a second to realize I didn't know what would happen. When will I know if Colin survived? Would I ever know?

Chapter 44

"Let's ride, Maggot. I want to give the portal a go before everyone is up. Bring some clothes and prepare to freeze." Becky walked into my room without even knocking. She threw back the blanket and shook me.

I was groggy from the medication and alcohol the previous night. We'd talked for another hour after Sam had gone to bed. Becky wanted to know what was new in the world. She wasn't interested in politics or the social aspects of life. She wanted to know about the advancement of science and medicine.

Becky inquired about some of our mutual friends and classmates. She was interested in my estimation of Lauren and Jim when we met in Australia and worked together for a short time. I explained the only classmate I knew about was John Mitchell. I sat on a plane with his associate. He's doing well. I told her about Lauren's competency and how well suited she and Jim were. I told her Lauren's due date, and that they didn't want to know the baby's sex beforehand.

"And Jeff?"

"I hate to say it, but he experienced a mild heart attack and had angioplasty."

"Is he alright now?"

I described what they'd done, using stents to increase the circulation in his heart muscle. "His cognitive capabilities are fine, and while he was still a little weak when we parted, he received the best of care. This treatment should increase his stamina for fishing, which we planned to do again next summer." I paused, realizing it would be Colin, and not Jeff, who might not be fishing again. If I can't return, it might be both of us who are gone.

I had to stop thinking that way. We each took a biscuit with ham and saddled the horses. Becky's horse was a beautiful chestnut mare, which she said was a descendant of her first horse when she arrived in the 1800s and the black stallion she'd saved at birth on her first visit to the Cattle Creek Ranch.

"What do you call her?"

Becky grinned. "I'm afraid our family is a little short on imagination. I tried to call this mare several names, but I was outvoted. Once one horse dies, or is sent to the paddock, they reuse the names. Sam's horses lasted the longest, but when he finally switches horses, the next one gets the same name. Aside from a few changes, my horses will always be called Penny, and Sam's will always be Cash. I prefer sorrels. I had one named Jack and one called Copper. They're all related to the original

Penny, and this one is a gift from Hannah. I was outvoted with regard to names, and Penny was long dead."

Becky quietly saddled the mare. "Do you remember the black horse with an unusual triangular snip on his nose that was prominent in many *Comstock* episodes? I helped him at birth, and he became the lead sire of the Cattle Creek Ranch herd. He played in many of the *Comstock* episodes. Apparently, Alex Conrad thought to duplicate him, as well as the cast, to mirror what he found here."

I didn't remember the stallion, but Becky watched more of the television programs than I did when we were younger. Hannah trained the mare that she gave Becky a few years ago after Becky and Sam were married, and they had adopted Hannah. Becky told me about the horses she'd ridden over the years. Her favorite was Penny. She described a racing mule that Danny and Gee Ling had conspired to buy for Sam's birthday. The mule would respond only to women, and she rode the mule until his untimely death from a snake bite.

"He saved my life. A group of former Civil War soldiers, turned rustlers, kidnapped me and held me hostage for several days. Spit, as we called him, kicked the man and broke his leg. My captor bled to death from the femoral artery. As you can see, it's not as easy living in the past as you might imagine."

"Apparently not." We approached the portal pool. I would wait to tell her about my kidnapping incident, but it was amazing how our lives were so dramatic, and yet similar, despite living a century apart.

Becky tethered her horse to a tree, and I tied mine to hers. Becky said she would try alone. If she was successful, I should untether the horses and join her. She had her 'magic' plastic bag with dry clothes. It was amusing to think that these baggies, which actually had not been invented yet, were so interesting to Sam and Danny. We slid down an embankment to reach the pool once again. There was no change from the prior day. I felt the water. "Bloody hell, it's cold."

Becky removed her boots to leave them by the pool. "It only shows you how much I love you. I've been back three times, and I vowed I'd never do it again. By the way, I know 'bloody' is a swear word. I hate to admit it, but just as you saw on television, we don't swear.

As a doctor, I know there are different standards, and people in the 1800s are not all angels, but in our family, we adhere to the more refined societal norms. Women are considered chattel in marriage, and the husband is the head of the household. Of course, Sam and I have a unique arrangement, and he knows I have my boundaries. I try to limit my swearing to when it's really needed. I restrict myself to one swear word a day unless I forget—like now."

"Jesus Christ, it's colder than a witch's..." I didn't hear the ending since she was underwater. It seemed like forever. I counted to ten before I saw her emerge. She treaded water and dropped back into the pool several times without success. I finally could see she was becoming exhausted. I grabbed her hand to pull her out of the water.

"Enough. It's not working. What the hell am I going to do?"

Becky grimaced and shook her head. "I'm sure the pool is blocked from the other side. Let me change my clothes and warm up. I need to think." We crossed the creek, which was low in several areas. Becky easily made a fire with a flint.

"Is it okay to start a fire in a national forest?"

Becky chuckled. "I don't know, but this is the property of the Cattle Creek Ranch, and I can start a fire wherever I like."

"You and Sam own all this land? You own Miner's Meadow?"

"Hank Heaven, you mean? Yep, both Sam and I will be buried up there with Hank someday. Did you notice how much Jim looks like

Hank?" Becky added more sticks to the fire. "You know, women are second-class citizens, and I don't own any of this, in the eyes of the law, but I'm considered an equal partner with Dan, Jenny, and Sam."

"Maggie, it'll be three days now? If Colin's alive, there's a chance he'll be rescued. If he tells Lauren that you went for help, she'll surely consider you've time traveled, and she'll see the portal pool has been damaged. I'll bet the ranch that Lauren will get Rich to dig out the portal pool for her."

What Becky didn't say was if they found Colin dead, and could tell his injuries came from a mountain lion, they might assume the lion killed me, too.

"Who's familiar with time travel on the other side of time?" I had no idea.

"As far as I know, only Lauren, Jim, and Frank Lash. Rich didn't know, although Lauren was living with him when she came to us a few years ago."

"I can't believe she did that. She's hidden it from everyone." I guessed that is why she preferred not to talk about her mother.

"There may be others. When I returned to see Lauren after I was engaged to marry Sam, I attempted to return to Sam and the past. I selected the wrong pool. A ranger who caught me mentioned a story about the area having a portal pool. He admonished me to reconsider my life, probably thinking I was trying to run away from my current problems.

"He didn't know, but obviously somebody had passed on the myth about this pool or area being magical with a way for people to escape from their problems. That was tricky, but I waited until he left and jumped into the pool that he thought was the correct one. Was he a time traveler? I don't know." Becky was dry and warm from the fire. She dressed in the riding clothes she wore around the ranch. She laughed as she claimed the men hated these clothes and would scold her for looking like a male ranch hand, when she was really the queen of the Cattle Creek Ranch.

"Anyway, it worked then. I did it again when I needed to know whether Sam died when he was in Cuba, trying to rescue Clint from a work prison. It's a long story. I was certain he would be buried up at Hank Heaven, so I time traveled and went to the graves to find his date of death, except I couldn't see whether it was an eight or a nine. That told me he'll pass in either the 1880s or 1890s, and he was still alive. Of course, my gravestone is right beside it. All I could see was the beginning of my name, and I didn't want to look, so I didn't proceed any farther."

"You saw your own grave marker? Creep city. Who's Frank Lash?"

"He was the man who showed me the way to return to the future. He was a history professor, and like Alex Conrad, he knew about the portal pool. That's how I returned the first time. He showed Lauren how to use the pool as well. There was my friend Pam, but she passed away from breast cancer. I'm sure there are others, but I don't know them. I was afraid to tell people about where I came from. I was worried they'd put me in an asylum. Since I heard Frank playing a Nat King Cole tune in a saloon, I knew he was from the future. Maggie, if you can't return, I'll..."

I stopped her. "Don't go there, Harper—I mean, Buchanan. I have a grandson. When I married Collie, I knew he would probably pass before me. It was worth it. If he's gone, I have no regrets. How about you? You're much younger than Sam. What happens when he dies? Do you stay or go?"

"Hannah. She's the little girl I never got to see grow up. I know right now she's a pain in the ass, but she's my responsibility, and I can't wait to see her mature, get married, and have grandchildren. I mean children.”

"Do you feel like Dan's children are yours?"

"When I don't, they remind me by asking me to babysit."

"Lizzy is a bright little girl. She loves the more feminine things in life. Little Hank is all boy and draws pictures of cars. We hope he forgets about his trip to the future, but so far, he still remembers cars and airplanes. Little Elaine is too young to categorize, but she loves animals and the baby. Sam Jr. is only four months old. I hope they stop at this point, but who knows? At least Sam has his dynasty. No, I'm here for life."

Becky picked up some rocks and tossed them into the water. "I wish there was a way to test the pool without getting so goddam wet." Since she looked around, I could tell she was nervous about swearing. She uproariously laughed. "Kind of liberating to swear out loud."

"My turn tomorrow, sister." Becky was too tired to argue.

Chapter 45

Back at the ranch, it was obvious Sam was annoyed that we sneaked around without him. There was no mistake that this would not occur again if he had anything to say about it. When Hannah left for school, he set down his paper on the dining table and stared at Becky, who pretended to ignore him and reached for the bacon. Sam caught her arm and said, "Not going to happen again. Am I clear?"

Becky whispered, "No, not really. If we all leave every morning and then return, the ranch hands and Gee Ling will become suspicious. I'll take a fishing rod tomorrow. I plan to test the waters every day. Am I clear?" There was no threat or resentment in her matter-of-fact voice.

My concern was I had to wait another twenty-four hours. This was killing me. I wanted to search for another portal. Had these people ever considered there may be one? Could there be a hidden cave or another pool in another creek? I wanted to explore the area. Would this be a geographically significant region where many portals existed? Maybe a mine shaft might lead me back home. Sitting at the ranch was a waste of time.

"Do you know of anyone who has gone missing around the area? Miners or prospectors?"

"Of course. It happens all the time. Are you thinking there may be others who time travel?" Becky sipped her coffee.

"Yeah, well, maybe that pool isn't the only portal. Possibly, this is an area with many portals," I whispered, so Gee Ling didn't hear our conversation.

I could see Becky was considering the idea. "What if there were some, but they took us to another time?"

Gee Ling entered the dining area. "You want more food, Mr. Sam? I take plate?" He waited while Sam handed him his plate. "Everyone happy?" Gee Ling was no fool. He observed the tension. "I make roast beef for dinner tonight. That make everyone happy?"

"That sounds wonderful, old friend. What can I do to help?" Becky attempted to diffuse the disharmony. "I must go to town and the clinic today. I thought maybe you and Maggie might take a ride to see some of the views on the Cattle Creek Ranch, darling."

I was uncomfortable with Sam. He was gracious and curious, but I sensed he didn't trust me. I'd obviously made him aware of the television show based on his life. Clearly, Becky had never informed him about the fame of his historical character. "I don't want to be a bother.

I'd like to go into town. I wouldn't mind a look around in case any other time travelers are lurking about."

Becky shook her head. "If you don't mind, Maggie. I think it's best to keep you away from anyone until we know it's going to be a longer visit. In the interim, it's time you met Jenny and the children. She'll have a dress or two that will fit you. Is that okay, darling?" Becky took Sam's hand and brought it to her cheek in a gesture of compromise.

Sam relaxed. "I'd planned to ride up to see how the breakers are doing. Maybe we can get Maggie to look at a few of the horses and later head to the upper meadow to check the cattle."

"Wonderful, darling. I'll take the buggy into town. I'll make a list of anything that we may need. I won't be long, but I have a women's birthing clinic, and I think only a few ladies are coming for checkups."

Becky left the table to go upstairs to her room. Sam followed her, and I could hear a muffled discussion—trouble in paradise.

I turned to Gee Ling, who was clearing the table. I rose and gathered the plates. He smiled and thanked me. "You come to Cattle Creek to see Gee Ling any time, missy."

"Who knows? I may be here for a while." Hearing myself say that was disheartening. *Was I giving up too soon?*

A bay gelding was tied to the hitching rail next to the classic *Comstock* buckskin, which was the riding horse for the television series. The two horses were saddled and ready. Each horse had saddlebags. Sam's horse had a scabbard with a shotgun on board. I'd already heard Sam call him Cash, which is the name of the horse on the television program.

I prepared to tour some of the ranch with Sam. I pretended to observe his stock, but my actual purpose was to seek another gateway to the future. My clothes were unusual for the times, but they weren't too conspicuous. I noticed no one had zippers, but my pants zipper was hidden. I had a buttoned shirt. Sam came out to the barn to hand me a jacket that hid most of my clothes and chaps to cover my jeans, which I suspected he thought were too tight and provocative. He gave me a wide-brimmed hat. "I can give you a bonnet, but my guess is this hat is what you would prefer. It's Bec's hat."

"No, this is fine." The chaps were long, and I knew they weren't Becky's—no zippers here, either, but just leather straps. I smiled, thinking of the term Colin and I frequently used. I was being dressed for the 1800s.

"Sam, have you ever heard the expression 'match the hatch'?"

"No. What does it mean?"

"When Colin and I are fishing, we use flies to match the current insects that are present in the streams and lakes."

"I figure I've done that most of my life without knowing the term. It is interesting that the lake up at Hank Heaven has its own particular fly. Most of the time, we match the hatch, as you say. It just doesn't work sometimes. That's when we use one Becky likes. She showed me how to tie it. She said her former husband named it after her. She calls it a 'Bec Beauty.' I've struggled to locate the material to replicate it because it's pink, but I've finally found a source for the pink. It's quite successful when we can't match the hatch, as you say."

I'd forgotten to try that when we were fishing up at Miner's Meadow. "Yeah, Lauren showed me. It's a fish magnet, isn't it?"

"You modern women have the strangest sayings. Let's ride, cowgirl. If I'm not being too modern." Sam easily mounted with no help. I took my horse over to the mounting block I'd used before. I saw Sam smile as he watched me mount.

"What?" Did he find my need for a mounting block amusing?

"Are your pants too tight? Can you lope? Are you sore from all your riding?"

"Sam, I ride most days back home. I have a wonderful horse on our property. And no, these pants stretch. Next to electricity, stretch pants may be the most significant invention of the twentieth century."

Sam's lips twitched as he suppressed a smile. "Possibly a little too inventive for now. Tell me about your horses."

I described Digger and how Colin had lent him to me in exchange for assisting with his grandson. I explained our modern-day barn with heated stalls and a covered arena. I talked about the mountains, the terrain, and the house we lived in. He'd learned about electricity from Becky, but several things were new to him, such as security cameras and electric gates. He mentioned he would like to see some heavy equipment that could move boulders the size of an elephant. This reminded me of the *Comstock* episode, when Hank and Danny took on an elephant. Did that really happen in his life?

"Did you ride an elephant once?" *Did everything I watched on* Comstock *really happen, or were some stories fabricated for the television series?*

"Maybe. Has Rebecca been telling tales?"

"Possibly, but that was on an episode of *Comstock*. She didn't mention an elephant."

"Tell me about another one you watched." Sam seemed relaxed, but I noticed his right hand was down on his thigh, and he kept tapping his middle finger against his thigh. Colin did the same thing when he was agitated.

When I thought back about the shows, the one episode I recalled was the one in which Hank thought he'd seen leprechauns. "Did a troop of dwarfs come to Virginia City once?"

Sam pulled up on his reins and stopped dead. I could see he remembered something and was reminded that this story involved his deceased son, Hank. He couldn't suppress the smile. "And?"

"Hank thought they were leprechauns."

Sam glanced upward. "We laughed about that for years." Sam was silent. I guessed he was thinking about Hank. "That son of a gun. He stole stories from my life. I'd love to get a hold of him."

"Alex Conrad's deceased. The series has been over for years. There are no more episodes. You're safe now."

Sam's voice softened. "Did they show any romantic episodes? Is Rebecca in them?"

"Yes, there were plenty of love scenes and romantic encounters. That's how I know what I call Miner's Meadow is really 'Hank Heaven.' Hank described the valley in an episode when a woman he loved was dying. He told her he wanted to take her to his magical place, which he called Hank Heaven."

Sam looked away. "And Rebecca?"

"No, the programs began about the time Rebecca left for the East to pursue her medical degree. *Comstock* ended before she returned to Virginia City. She never received a mention. Time travel was too futuristic for Alex Conrad. Maybe it was too close to the bone. I think he and Colin discussed a time travel episode, but Colin was against it. I may be wrong about that."

Sam pointed to a lean-to where several men were working. I saw a man who rode a bronc. I had to remember horse whispering wasn't invented. It was rough, but in their own way, these bronc riders seemed to get the job done. The horse I rode was well trained.

I realized Sam could sense my thoughts. "Becky says her father did things differently, but we have a contract with the Army to supply one hundred eighty horses in three months. As a result, we use our old methods. Becky and Hannah take a few to finish them. Becky's father taught her to train horses. I think you met him?"

"Old Jack. Yep, tough on family and gentle on horses. He was a master. I spent a week at his place twice when we were in vet school. That's where I learned to fly-fish."

"Is there much fly-fishing in Australia? According to Clint, he's never heard of trout over there."

"There are trout now, but lots of people fly-fish for saltwater species. It's hard work, which is why I came back to the States after I retired."

At the corral, I met the men and watched young bronc riders saddle and mount several horses. The bucking varied from a few crow-hops to horses that would make the cut to the National Finals Rodeo. Two horses had more than one rider, but so far, all the horses eventually settled down. Once the buck was out of them, the horses were moved to a second corral where they rode in circles and continued the training. We watched and conversed with the men for an hour. Sam introduced me as Becky's medical-school classmate from Montana.

The men were curious, but they were under pressure to get several horses started, and only greeted me before they resumed their business. The foreman stopped to talk to Sam. Merv Little was possibly five or more years younger than Sam was. He limped, and I suspected he could benefit from a hip replacement. I wouldn't discuss this with either Sam or anyone besides Becky. It was wishful thinking.

He and Sam chatted as Sam observed the men riding. Sam pointed to one man. "Fire him, Merv."

"Huh, why?"

"Too good-looking. I don't want him around Hannah."

They chuckled. "No chance, Sam. A saloon girl in town is driving him insane."

We finally moved on. I asked if Hannah was dating. "At what age are girls allowed to court?" I grinned, realizing I was already using the vernacular I remembered from the *Comstock* series. I could see Sam consider his reply.

"I guess you know about first and second base?"

"Yeah?" *Is that a thing now?*

"Becky caught Hannah with a boy at second base."

"Is that bad?" I didn't know what acceptable behavior was in the 1800s. Second base was fairly common when I was Hannah's age.

"We sent him away." Sam grinned and couldn't stop chuckling to himself.

"That's harsh. Was he a ranch hand?"

"No. He lived with Merv and Cassie Little when his father died during an influenza outbreak. Alexander Thistlewaite attends engineering school. If they're both still in love when he graduates, they'll probably marry. Becky wants Hannah to become either a teacher or even a doctor. She says that education will give her freedom of choice. So far, she shows no interest in anything except breaking horses. At least she isn't interested in her first beau."

"What was wrong with him?" I knew they didn't have an actual birth date for Hannah.

"He was a gadabout. He was the son of Becky's friend. He was older, and I could tell he would ruin Hannah. Thankfully, he left to go to Georgetown, California. I may have made an error. I hear he's turned out to be the foreman of a lumber mill."

I'd heard the term gadabout, but not in actual conversation. "A gadabout. Sheesh, that would have been a disaster." I couldn't stop laughing.

"What do you say in your time?" Sam continued up a steep rise.

"Was he handsome or just trouble?" I followed Sam as I searched for more creeks or rocky outcrops that might hide a cavern.

"I suppose people would say he was good-looking. Becky said he resembled a famous vocalist. His name was Elvis. I don't remember his last name."

Oh, my God. "Presley?"

"Something like that." Sam stopped and turned to look back down on the pastures and crops of trees.

"Eye candy." This was too funny.

"What?"

"In today's world, one term, and it isn't the only one but a popular term, for a good-looking person, is eye candy." I explained the term and how it often means someone who is attractive on a superficial level. "The man, or woman, is good-looking but has no other qualities. Parents of teenagers in the early days might have considered Elvis to be eye candy, but the man could sing. He was not just eye candy. Neither is your bronc rider down at the corrals. He can ride a bronc. He could be a rodeo star in modern times and make millions in the bronc-riding industry."

"What will the world come to? I'm not a fan of education for the sake of education, but Alexander will garner a reasonable wage after he completes his mining engineering degree. But in modern times, will a bronc rider make millions of dollars?" Sam shook his head.

"Here's the sad part. Teachers are an important factor in the evolution of society, and yet they still only scratch a living in my time, you know, the future. Those who invent silly children's games and toys can make millions. I think a guy who sold pet rocks made millions. It was sold as a smooth, painted rock in a box."

"And people bought them? I've never wanted to leave my time, but it would be nice to see a plane fly." Sam gazed up at the sky.

"Couldn't Lauren bring her phone to show you movie clips? You know, she could even bring you some scenes from the *Comstock* series."

"She brought us pictures of herself and Jim and a wedding picture, but we agreed to keep our lives and times to ourselves. I only planned to time travel with Bec simply to protect her. A gun is buried in a secret place and, when we arrive at the other side of time, we can dig it up. I know Lauren knows where it is, but I could do it again if I needed to protect Bec or myself."

We reached the summit of a steep and long trail. A herd of mixed-breed cattle grazed in a large valley as far as the eye could see. The grass was still green and high. "Do they stay up here for the summer, or do you move them up into the higher elevations?"

"This is a staging area. The boys will drive them up into the mountains, where they will eat the grass in the Eastern Sierras for the summer. They'll be brought back down out of the mountains in early fall. A large portion will be driven either north or south, depending on the availability of feed along the ranges and trails where they will eventually be bought by the cavalry, or back East for the folks in larger cities.

"Becky says several television programs and movies show the romantic side of cattle drives. In truth, it's a hard journey. One year, she and Lauren took the cattle south when I was ill with pneumonia. You see, Bec has taught me modern medical terms. Some people call it the old man's friend. Death from pneumonia can be a blessing, compared with some diseases."

"Interesting. So Lauren stayed with you for several months?" She sure fooled me.

"Initially, it wasn't by choice. Time travel is a dangerous business. She arrived during the biggest storm we've ever encountered. She almost drowned and, a few hours after she arrived, a large boulder either came down from the cliff face or rolled down from above. It blocked the portal pool, which lodged in the creek until we moved the rock. I did it slowly, so I wouldn't disturb the portal.

"When she was ready to leave, we received a telegram that our cattle had to be sent to a facility on short notice, and we'd also had a dreadful influenza outbreak in our town. Since many of our regular ranch hands were ill, Lauren, Becky, and Dan went on the cattle drive. When they returned, it was winter. I ordered a diving suit from Scotland. Realizing it could be treacherous on the other side, Lauren used the diving suit to travel back to her time in winter. We never thought we'd see her again, and we knew she was betrothed to Jim. We never expected to meet him. We knew Lauren would cease to visit us when she was with child, for that very reason.

"Becky thought she'd never reunite with Lauren again, and it was a blessing when she and Jim showed up two years ago. Maggie, we'll do everything in our power to get you home, but I have a feeling this is a problem that can be solved only on the future side of the portal. We're not aware of any other portals, but we suspect they exist. We simply don't know."

"Too bad Alex Conrad died. Maybe he could have helped Becky get home. It sounds like their paths almost crossed."

Sam stared at me without smiling. "Thankfully, he showed up while Bec was back East. My three previous wives passed away before I met Becky. I could not bear to lose her. We've experienced our separations.

When I learned she was married and devoted to her husband and child, I eventually courted other women, but none of them ever matched my Rebecca."

I agreed. "Yeah, love is a torturous emotion. I thought I was in love with another man when I met Colin, but I was foolish, lonely, and swayed by what he offered me. He was married, anyway. My track record for choosing men is dismal. Fortunately, my sister checks them out for me."

"I think I understand. We've all been fooled. My mistakes are probably in that foolish television series."

"Uh, yep. There were a few, if you can believe what they broadcast on *Comstock*."

"I can't believe they named the series *Comstock* after Old Pancake. Now, there's a gadabout. Anyway, he's gone from these parts. He's from Canada. Maybe he's gone back there."

"I think I looked it up, and he's dead and buried in Montana. Might have been suicide."

"I'm not surprised. Maggie, shall we stop and have something to eat? A nice creek is located down behind those rocks."

"Sure. Need to lighten my load, anyway."

Sam turned to show he didn't understand. When I pointed to the afflicted area below my belt, he blushed.

Clouds gathered, and we heard a rumble of distant thunder. "I think we're in for an afternoon storm. A large cave is in the cliff face. Do you want to see it?" Sam pointed to an outcropping of rocks across the valley floor.

"Sounds like a plan."

"Another modern phrase?"

"Hm, maybe." *Oh, please let this have a portal.*

Chapter 46

When we dismounted, Sam found a long tree branch with a few leaves on the end. He lit it and took my arm as we entered the cavern, from which several bats flew out. Sam stopped and stared down at noticeable fresh footprints. He extended his arm to guide me to walk behind him and put his finger to his lips.

We quietly walked farther into the cave. I saw Sam had a revolver in his hand. He held it out and cocked his head to listen. I heard nothing except a drip of water. Sam found a lamp, lit it, discarded the branch, and continued. The cavern was big enough that we could both stand. He still didn't say anything as we slowly advanced. I recalled the time that Charlie McLeod's associates took me hostage and left me to die when the cave flooded.

I whispered, "Maybe we should retreat?"

He shook his head. He turned a corner, where we found a makeshift table and chairs. There was a bed next to the table. Sam smiled. An oil lamp rested on the table, and Sam quickly lit it and smiled. "That old codger."

"Old codger? You know who he is?" I felt like I could relax. "Want to tell me what's happening?"

"Maggie, you claim to have watched several life stories on the television box. Did you see one in which my former ranch foreman and I were held hostage?"

"Oh, yeah. Your sons even held a funeral for you. Wasn't that eccentric guy killed?"

"No, he wasn't. He was imprisoned for a few years, and we never heard from him. He should have been hanged, but I intervened to make sure he survived. He must be hiding up in the cave. See the carving on the table?"

The beautifully carved scene depicted a man and a bear who faced each other. Under this were the initials *N* and *G*. "He's up here somewhere."

"I'm right here." The man, who resembled the actor who played him on the *Comstock* set, rounded the corner. He pointed his pistol at me. "Mr. Buchanan, it's been a while. Who's your friend?"

"Hello, Ned. Up to your old tricks?"

Sam stood between the man and me. *What old tricks?*

"Now, Sam. I'm a reformed man, who is too old to seek any further revenge. Maybe your friend might make a good hostage, though. I need a grubstake, so I can restart my life. You know, they work you like a dog in prison, and they don't pay you a dime. I'm considering heading to South America. My cousin lives down there, and he says it's a good place to live with lots of beer and scarlet ladies."

"You'd be better off to get a job right here. I can always use some help. If you come back to the Cattle Creek Ranch, you can stay in the bunkhouse and start some work tomorrow. How about it?"

I still stood behind Sam, who was the same charitable man portrayed in the *Comstock* series. I remembered many episodes when Sam gave down-and-out cowboys jobs with varying outcomes. Some became upstanding citizens, but frequently they betrayed the Buchanans. I nearly laughed to think this encounter would make a great episode in the series.

"Nah, Sam. That sounds like work. I done enough of that in prison. Now you know if I shoot you, the bullet will go straight through you, and the old lady behind you will get it, too. I'd suggest you put down your gun and let's talk. She your wife Sam? I heard you got married again."

Both men had their firearms cocked and ready. "No, Ned, that won't happen. You won't even feel your finger squeeze the trigger if you don't put yours down now."

What the hell? This fantasy is not what I envisioned. "Hey, guys. How about you both put down your guns and talk like friends?" Many conflicting thoughts surfaced. *Old lady? If Colin was dead, and I died, maybe we'd be reunited in death. I needed a reality check, but then again, where the hell was I?*

"Sam, I ain't got long to live. I got a son back in St. Louis. I want to give him something, so he doesn't think I was a wastrel. Step aside, and no one will get hurt."

Sam, ever the gentleman and hero of so many television episodes, quietly shook his head. "You know I can't do that, Ned. How much money would it take to make your son happy?"

"Five thousand dollars." Ned stood to adjust his gun.

Sam roared. "She isn't worth five hundred dollars, Ned. You're dreaming."

"She isn't? How about the five hundred?"

"Ned, I guess you realize I don't pay ransom money. Never have, and never will. She's only my wife's friend. You know, if you'd picked my wife, I'd be more interested in a ransom, but frankly, she isn't that important to me. How about we have a drink and talk about old times?"

Fortunately, I still stood behind Sam, and Ned couldn't see me laugh. *What a dream.* I tapped him on the shoulder and whispered, "I'll tell Becky."

What I thought was a dangerous and potentially lethal situation had now become a comical one. Would this trend continue?

I could see Ned waver. "Sam, I'd do that, but I ain't got no whiskey."

"I have some in my saddlebag. I can send the lady for some if you like."

"I weren't born yesterday, Sam. She'd ride away, you and I'd be here alone in another cave, and we both know how that turned out last time."

"Sir, I promise I'll bring it back. If you let me get the whiskey, I'll be back in a flash."

"What does a flash mean?" Apparently, Ned was considering releasing me. I prayed there was something in the saddlebag that would help us overpower the man. He was old, and his hand shook. His face was red, and he had bruises over his exposed skin. I could see he required medical aid.

Ned reconsidered. "Sam, I sure could use a drink."

"Maggie, will you get the whiskey? It's in the saddlebag on my horse."

"Will you be okay?" *Would he have a shoot-out when I left?*

"Get the whiskey and, if there's any grub, get that, too. Ned looks like he could use some food. Take my lantern, or give her a candle."

Ned had a candle, which he lit. I took it and eased past him toward the horses. I saw Ned's mule tied near our mounts. I found the whiskey in one saddlebag and some crude sandwiches in the other. I noticed a vial of white powder along with the sandwiches. It was not labeled, but I hoped it was a narcotic of some sort. I couldn't decide what to do. *Should I put it in a sandwich or whiskey?* I decided the sandwich was safer. I tipped the vial to my tongue. There was a faint, bitter taste. I changed my mind and dumped the entire vial into the whiskey flask. I'd let Sam and Ned drink it, while I would remain awake and alert.

The candle had blown out, and I could not light it. I stumbled into the dark and dropped the flask and sandwiches. Nothing broke, but a small amount of sand entered the pack with the sandwiches. I eased along the wall of the cavern to rejoin the men.

I handed the flask and sandwiches to Sam, who immediately offered them to Ned. He showed no hesitancy in offering both. "Ladies first." He handed me the flask and tore a small sandwich in half.

I declined the alcohol. "I don't drink, Mr. Buchanan. Where I come from, we think alcohol is an abomination." I knew Sam would take this false confession as a warning that the potential drugs were in the whiskey. Sam shifted, put the flask to his lips, and appeared to drink heartily. He offered the flask to Ned, who did the same. He next gave

Ned a sandwich, and we consumed the food. I continued to stand and watch the two men. Both had guns at their side.

After a minute and a few more swigs on the flask, both men seemed drowsy. "So, Ned. How about we make a deal? If you let the lady go, I can be your hostage again. How does that sound?"

"Sam, you take me for a fool. She stays, and you go get some money." The effect of the drink became apparent. He closed his eyes for a brief second. I said nothing and watched to find out if the powder had also affected Sam.

"Ned, you know I can't do that. She isn't worth much, but I have a reputation, and I won't leave her. You'll have to keep us here and try to find someone to pay you for us both. It's a fool's errand, my friend. Dan is well schooled on the idea of paying for a hostage. He won't."

It was a slow process for Ned to drink the whiskey. He was a sipper. Sam appeared to be chugging. I could foresee this going in the wrong direction. After several minutes, Ned closed his eyes and laid his gun on his lap. Sam still didn't move. Was he as intoxicated as Ned was? I sat behind Sam and leaned forward. Sam's eyes were closed, too. I felt Sam slowly put his hand on my forearm and push me back.

I waited for several minutes while he sat without moving. Ned finally slumped over. Sam quietly and steadily reached forward to grab the gun. This action startled Ned, who lurched for the revolver as well. Following a brief tussle for the firearm, Sam easily overpowered Ned—game over. Sam stood up to point the gun at Ned, who drifted in and out of consciousness. Sam tied his hands and reached for more of the bread.

"He's too big and drunk to move. What was the weather like when you retrieved the whiskey?"

"There were thunderclouds, but it wasn't raining." On cue, we heard a roll of thunder.

"We may be here awhile. Maggie, I want you to hold the gun. Don't trust him and if you have to, shoot. Aim for his chest. I need to see what's happening outside. Will you be okay?"

"Sure." But I wasn't. I was distraught. I'm not going to die, and my husband may die or already be dead. I may be forced to shoot a man, and I was cold and thirsty. I wanted out of this nightmare.

By the time Ned was awake enough to get on his mule, it was too dark. The thunder and lightning finally diminished, and the rain was light. Ned was docile. I figured he realized he was headed for prison once again.

His first incarceration was a case of mistaken identity. He should never have gone to jail and Sam was on the jury that convicted him. Once Sam realized his error, he worked to get Ned released. Ned was no saint. Ned had been to prison for robbery and other transgressions. His second incarceration was from holding Sam and his foreman hostage. This one, if he survived, would probably be his last.

He was jaundiced and thin. I suspected liver disease. Sam said the vial contained laudanum, which makes a normal person sleepy, but with Ned's debilitated state, it might have even killed him. Sam mentioned he was not traveling well himself and would need to sleep soon.

I was supposed to watch Ned while Sam slept for a few hours. I was not under the influence of anything, and it was easy for me to watch the men while they slept. Toward daylight, Sam woke. I went out to relieve my bladder and returned. My eyes had grown accustomed to the dim light from the small candle. I didn't need the lantern. The rain had cleared, but there was a light dusting of snow. I hoped the snow was only in the higher elevation and not down at the portal pool of the creek.

It was still warm in the cave. I told Sam, who helped Ned stand and moved him out toward the opening. Ned had a warm jacket, but Sam and I had only light ones. We quickly re-saddled, mounted our horses and Ned's mule, and began our journey down the mountain. When we reached the plateau, Ned lurched forward in the saddle and slumped to the side. He would have fallen off, except Sam had tied his hands to the saddle horn.

Sam quickly dismounted and caught Ned, who was unconscious. He lifted him back on the saddle but realized Ned was dead. "Maggie, help me untie him."

I was in shock. *Did I kill him with the laudanum?* "Is he dead?" I dismounted and held Ned's hands as Sam untied them from the horn. We both lowered him onto the ground. I felt for a pulse and put my ear to his chest. There was no mistake about the smells emanating from his body. Excrement and vomit oozed from him. I was gagging. Death wasn't as clean as the movies or even the *Comstock* television series had depicted.

With great effort, we watched him for several minutes to confirm the obvious and pulled Ned's body up over the mule. Sam strapped him onto the saddle for the trek back to the ranch, and probably Virginia City. I rode behind the mule that Sam led and constantly looked for signs that Ned had revived. The smell was awful. I even retched twice as I followed the dead man's mule. Sam and I were cold, and at our slow pace, we had little chance of warming up until we left the mountain.

Chapter 47

We arrived back at the corrals where rain had fallen, but no snow. The temperature had dropped. Even so, I didn't relish jumping into the portal pool at this temperature. Sam asked one man to take the body to town. He explained why he hadn't returned. I sensed he wanted to protect my reputation. There was no joking about our time together alone in the wilderness, as likely would be in the future. He escorted me back to the ranch house. Becky, Dan, and his family were at the main house. Everyone had prepared to ride out to find us. I was introduced to Dan's entire family. The children were inside with Gee Ling and Hannah.

Danny's children were all young. The baby was only a few months old. They named him after Sam. Lizzy, the oldest one, doted on the infant. Little Hank was becoming more and more like his father in image and actions. Elaine was nearly two, and I could tell the terrible twos were not a recent invention.

Dan was off to the corrals to help with the horses. Jenny took the children back to their house, but she said they would return for dinner.

Becky recognized my distress. We went to my room, where she presented me with more clothes. "I hope we won't need these, but who knows what will happen?"

"If I somehow just knew Colin was safe and being cared for, I wouldn't mind this adventure, but it's the not knowing that's killing me." I eased onto the bed. "I've hardly slept, but can we try the portal pool again?"

Becky understood what I wanted. I needed to test the portal pool. By now, I was confident Lauren would be suspicious that I'd time traveled by accident, and she would probably figure the earthquake had damaged the pool. How would she explain this to her friend Rich? If Colin was dead, she might decide the risk of telling another person was not worth risking her reputation. Actual time travel was possibly the biggest discovery known to date. What if everyone knew you could use a portal pool to go back and forth in time? The movie *Back to the Future* would move from the fantasy category to general fiction.

"Let's have a bite of food, and when everyone's gone, we'll head back to the portal pool." She suggested I lie down for a quick rest, and she would call me when lunch was ready.

"Don't let me sleep over twenty minutes. I want to get back to the future in daylight." Becky's stare told me she knew more than she was admitting. "Bec, how do you know about that movie?"

"When Little Hank had been exposed to rabies, and we stayed while he received treatment. I saw the movie at Lauren's insistence." Becky appeared to be embarrassed.

"Huh? How did you escape detection?"

"I was discovered the first time I returned from the 1800s. The Smyths' daughter saw me in a store, but the second time, I stayed with Lauren and her friend, Rich, and he didn't know who I was. Then, Lauren's fiancé returned from deployment, and Jim knows the secret. I never planned to go again, but I'll risk it to help you save your husband. I guess he's currently in a hospital, wondering where you are."

After lunch, Sam, Becky, and I headed for the portal pool. This time, Sam wanted to be the first. He made several attempts and described a pull as he went underwater but could not get all the way through. "I feel a swirling motion that reaches my waist, but that's it."

Becky went before I tried. We all felt the downward pull. Becky suggested maybe it was the people on the other side working in the pool. "If they are, Colin is probably alive, or could at least communicate that you tried to get help and were not another victim of the cougar."

Sam wrapped Becky in a blanket and vigorously rubbed her to dry and warm her. "I didn't feel that pull the last time. I'm sure it's different. I would never have believed this if I hadn't watched Lauren disappear into the water a few years ago."

"We need to try again tomorrow. I'm so sorry, Maggie. I wish I could do something." Becky leaned into Sam.

"I know you've done all you can. Have you done anything to change history? Did you really see Lincoln? Why didn't you tell him about his pending assassination?"

"I decided against doing anything that might change history too much. What if it changed my, or my parents' life and maybe I wouldn't have Lauren? Maybe I wouldn't have been born. You know one sperm wiggle in the wrong direction, and Lauren might be Lawrence?" Becky covered Sam's ears with her hands. "Maggot, we don't discuss sperm or semen in mixed company in the 1800s."

Sam's face reddened. "Rebecca, I like to think of myself as a modern man. I have my limits, but I'm not bothered by the word sperm. Don't forget you showed me the seeds in your microscope once."

I tested his resolve. "If I told you I made part of my living collecting semen from stallions, freezing it, and inseminating mares with it, that's not off-limits?"

Becky shook her head. "You froze semen? You could get live foals from frozen semen? I thought it didn't work with stallions. That's an advance."

"Sure could. I did it myself."

"Wow." Becky, who appeared intrigued, was about to request additional details.

This time, Sam shook his head and placed his hand over Becky's mouth. "You haven't said 'wow' for a while. Spare me the details."

We returned to the ranch house, and Becky took me to her infirmary. I was astonished that she had this on the Cattle Creek Ranch. "How many people work for the Buchanans?"

"We have about thirty full-time people and over two hundred in the spring and through the fall. I see the men for injuries and ailments, but about a dozen wives are in various stages of pregnancy. We even have a small school that Cassie Little manages. Did you meet her husband, Merv, up at the corrals?"

"Yeah, the man with the limp. Too bad he can't get a hip replacement. They're so common now."

"Merv broke his tibia three weeks ago. I can't radiograph it, but I'm sure it's a hairline. This is his second fracture. He's a tough man and, despite my insistence that he rest his leg, he refuses to take time off."

"Are you kidding?"

"Nope. It's a tough life out here. There's no insurance, sick leave, or government subsidy for time off. Of course, Sam would pay his full wage even if he was home resting his leg, but Merv's a proud man."

When we finally returned to the house, Dan's family had arrived. Sam rested in his traditional chair in front of the fireplace. The baby was in his arms, and his eyes were closed. Hannah was with Elaine, while the older children were in the kitchen with Gee Ling.

Jenny brought a couple of dresses and a traditional riding outfit with culottes and a leather vest. I thanked her and suggested that I'd only borrow the wardrobe for a few days. We went upstairs to my room where we could talk. She was aware of the time traveling concept from Little Hank's rabies scare. She wanted to know about pregnancy prevention and whether anything was new that Becky would not know about.

I laughed and said that I hadn't considered it for quite some time. "Abstinence?"

"Well, that isn't going to happen, although with four children in the house, it's harder."

"I guess your best chance is to continue to breast-feed?"

"Yeah, Becky suggested that as well."

"I guess Becky's given you all the information that will work these days. In modern times, we have a pill. If Lauren ever returns, maybe she could bring you some."

There was a knock on the door, and Hannah entered. "Jenny, I'm all done in. If you have any more kids, I'll run away."

I tried to stifle a smile, but I failed, which made Jenny laugh. Hannah was no fool. She assumed our conversation was like her thoughts. Since Hannah and Gee Ling were the only two adults who didn't know about the future, we quickly shut down the conversation.

Dinner was announced. I said I would dress and join them shortly. Jenny and Hannah left when I decided on the gold dress. As I put on the dress, I snagged my fingernail. I peered at my finger and remembered Colin's raised finger as a sign he'd reached his limit on whatever I had said or done. I tried to hold back, but it was impossible. *Gelding, Collie. I'm trying. Please hold on. Please.*

After I composed myself, I went down to dinner. Becky must have realized I'd just had a moment since she squeezed my arm as we sat together. I couldn't be too sad with all the chaos that ensued. Little Hank and Lizzy were barely restrained. They were separated, yet they still threw food at each other. Dan took Lizzy outside and when they returned, she was tearful and apologized to Sam and Becky. She sat in Sam's lap, and I saw her stick out her tongue to Little Hank when Gee Ling entered the room with dessert.

I was finally excused from the festivities. I reminded them I'd been up most of the night, guarding the man in the cave. I said I wanted some fresh air first and left for the barn. By the light of a lantern, I watched the gelding I'd ridden over the last two days. I walked into the stall, wrapped my arms around his well-muscled, glossy neck, and sobbed. I finally stopped and realized Sam stood in the doorway.

He was embarrassed to be found watching me. "I came to turn out the lantern for the evening. I didn't mean to scare you. I understand how you feel. Becky and I sometimes have been separated for a long time and wondered if the other was alive or dead. I know what you're going through. Those are not just words. I understand. As I said, I've lost three wives. I knew there was no hope each time, but when it was Becky who was missing, or even me, I didn't know if we'd be reunited. I'm doing everything I can, but we must wait and pray that the people on the other side of the transporting pool free up whatever is stopping you from crossing."

Despite the social norms against a married man embracing a woman married to someone else, Sam took me in his arms and allowed me to cry. He felt like Colin. He smelled differently. While Colin occasionally had cigars, Sam smelled like pipe tobacco. It was so familiar and yet different.

When I heard the door of the ranch house open, we parted. I thanked Sam and turned when Becky entered the barn. "I leave you two for a moment, and I find you together in the barn."

Sam quickly replied, "No baseball, Bec." We all laughed,

"I should hope not." Becky turned to the main house. "Maggie, we'll try as long as it's safe."

"I'm sorry. I should be happy to be here and know that you're alive, but my joy is tempered with not knowing whether Colin has survived, and if he didn't, how devastated Luke must feel to have lost his family."

"I'm familiar with the feeling. Not knowing what the future brings once you've gone to the past is the killer." Becky held my hands. "It's been just a few days. Luke will be reunited with you shortly, but I know Colin's life hangs in the balance. We'll make an attempt every day until we're successful in getting you back to your time."

As we walked back to the house, I saw lightning in the distance. Dan and Jenny prepared the children for an early departure. Gee Ling and Hannah were in the kitchen, arguing about who would wash and who would dry. I don't think anyone noticed I'd been crying, but I quickly escaped upstairs to my room.

Chapter 48

The distant lightning had moved over the ranch early in the morning. It was intense. I could detect the first signs of daylight in the East. Clouds obscured the sunrise. I heard rain when I returned from the water closet to my room.

The rain increased as I sat in bed, waiting for the others to rise. Hannah knocked on my door and requested permission to enter. She would stay home that day. She wanted to show me the story she'd written about the future.

She'd even used the word 'car.'

Whoa, that's a bit close to reality. "Where'd you get that word?"

"Little Hank says it all the time. He and Ma went back East for treatment when his puppy bit him, and Ma thought he might get hydrophobia. Did you know that's a disease that kills you, and it also means a fear of water? I guess you do, don't you? How was medical school? Did you work with Dr. Blackwell? Ma said she was the first lady doctor. I still want to be a doctor, but I don't tell anyone in case I get married. I have a beau, you know."

Hannah continued talking until we heard a tremendous crash. Lightning struck a tree or something close to the house. We heard an ear-piercing roll of thunder. Hannah and I ran to the window. The barn was on fire. I met Sam and Becky in the hall. Becky and I were in our sleeping gowns, but Sam had on his pants and an unbuttoned shirt. We descended the stairs and left by the front door. Hannah was told to remain in the house. "No, I want to help."

Sam shouted, "All right, but if you step into the barn, you may as well head to the woodshed right after."

The hayloft was ablaze above the horses. Sam shouted to two nearby men to help get the horses out of the barn. Becky and I both ran into the barn, and we tried to get the horses to leave, but they wouldn't. We had to put ropes around their necks and lead them out to Hannah, who took them to a corral far from the barn.

Since the last three horses' manes and tails were smoldering, we smothered the flames with wet gunnysacks. Sam was still inside the barn, trying to get a trunk from a small room off the tack room. Becky yelled for him to come out.

The loft collapsed, and he was trapped. Becky screamed and attempted to get into the barn, but it was too hot, and burning hay bales blocked the passageway. The men held Becky back from the raging fire.

Hannah clung to me and screamed for her father after her return from the corral.

As we all looked on in horror, Sam came around the corner of the barn. His hands were burned, and his hair and clothes were singed. He was engulfed by Becky and Hannah who tried to pull him from the burning structure.. The men formed a brigade to extinguish the fire with buckets of water. Sam finally yelled to them to stop. "Let it burn."

Dan galloped up, dismounted, and ran to his father. He stood helplessly by as he watched their beloved barn burn. Becky tried to get Sam to go to the infirmary, but the lightning still struck close to the house and bunkhouses. All the ranch hands along with their spouses stood by, watching in horror. I wanted to crawl away. When lightning hit a tree about a hundred yards away, we all hurried into the main ranch house.

There must have been forty or more people in the house. I dressed in the riding outfit that had been suggested. When I emerged, Becky wanted me to assist with the horses. We returned to the corral. The last three horses that were removed from the blazing barn had burns along their backs. One was breathing rapidly and appeared to be in shock.

My experience with burns in Australia made me the expert, but no one knew. I was certain the last horse would not make it. While Becky tended to Sam and the ranch hands with minor burns and affected by smoke inhalation, I offered to manage the horses.

Hannah accompanied me to raid Gee Ling's pantry for honey. I would have preferred to start the horses with anti-inflammatories, tetanus vaccine, and burn cream. I used what was available. The lightning moved away, while the rain came in spurts. As we examined the last horse, I received the shock of my life. Jim Kennedy walked up the road. He was soaked, and his clothes were torn.

As Jim walked toward us, he gave me a private wink. I searched his face, and he nodded. Mindful that he was in unfamiliar company, he spoke with measured words. "Hi, I'm passing through. I was searching for someone, but I can see you have your hands full. My partner is fairly busted up, but I'm sure he'll survive, and I was looking for somebody to help me." The smoldering remnants of the barn were behind Hannah and me. "I see the storm has caused considerable damage. May I help?"

Hannah inspected the stranger. I knew Jim had traveled back to this time at least twice. Becky and Sam would know him, but obviously, Hannah didn't know. "Hannah, will you please get your mother? Perhaps we could help this man and his friend."

I waited for Hannah to leave, stared at Jim, and waited to hear more.

"He'll be okay, Maggie. He's in the hospital in Reno. His only concern is you. He told us you'd gone for help. It was about the time of another big shaker. The portal pool was filled with debris and rocks. I asked Rich to check under the debris. If you weren't there, Lauren and I thought perhaps you'd time traveled. I had to take a chance and try to come to rescue you."

I was crying. I finally gulped out, "And Luke?"

"When he knows you're okay, he'll be fine. Only Lauren knows where I am. Colin is beside himself. I tried to persuade him you might be alive. Who here knows about you and where you come from, or I mean when?"

"Sam, Becky, Dan, and his wife know, but no one else. That was Hannah, who is Sam and Becky's adopted daughter." I tried to pull myself together. I realized I would leave when the Buchanans needed help. I was consumed with both joy and guilt. Colin was alive. I would soon be with him. How could I leave Becky? I hated to leave her with all the drama from the fire, but I had to get back to both Colin and Luke.

I recalled the stress that I experienced when my parents were dying, and I lived very far away. I felt helpless and hated myself, but my children needed me even more, and my mother was so forgiving. She insisted I stay in Australia to care for my family. "I don't want to hear you talk about guilt again." They were the last words I heard from her.

"How was the water? Can we go back now?" I hugged Jim and quickly pulled away as I heard people coming.

Becky ran up to us and stared at Jim. Hannah and two of the ranch hands assisted with the horses. Becky pretended not to know Jim. "May we help you?"

Jim smiled and stood away from Becky. "I'm not sure. I need some help with my friend. He's injured, and I know he'll survive, but it would be nice to get him some help. This woman seems to be knowledgeable about doctoring. May I borrow her? My partner's a day's ride away, but I can assure her safety."

"Maggie, do you trust this man? Do you want to go with him? I can send someone with you if you're worried."

"I'm sure I'll be alright. He seems friendly and safe." I smiled at Jim.

Becky searched Jim's face. I knew she wanted to ask him about Lauren. "Hannah, will you go back to tell your father we have a visitor? I'll return to the house in a moment?" Becky's voice was sharp and direct. I was sure Hannah would understand this was a delicate situation.

"Yes, ma'am." Hannah was confused and didn't want to leave.

"After that, I want you to cut linen strips so we can make bandages." Becky pointed to the house. "Now."

As Hannah sprinted toward the main house, a single clap of thunder rocked the area. When Hannah was out of sight, Dan ran down to the corral. Jim, Becky, and I moved under a shelter. Dan turned and saw Jim. It was obvious they'd never met. I saw the shock on his face and knew the reason. Seeing Jim was like seeing his long-dead brother. Jim looked so much like the actor who played Hank on the television series. Since the other actors were almost dead ringers, I guess Hank was, as well.

"Want to tell me what's going on?" He stared at Becky.

I could tell she was deciding how to approach the moment. "Dan, this is Jim Kennedy. He's Lauren's husband from the future. He's here to search for Maggie. It's complex. Maggie's husband's alive, and Jim crossed from the future in the same pool we showed you, so he could find Maggie to take her back home." Becky turned to Jim. "Jim, this is Dan Buchanan. He's Sam's son and my son-in-law. He's Little Hank's father."

Dan looked at Jim as though he'd seen a ghost. Jim understood Dan's shock and disbelief. Jim put out his hand. "I guess I'm your brother-in-law. I'm Lauren's husband."

Dan shook Jim's hand. Dan didn't respond, but continued to stare at Jim without a reply. Dan turned as he heard his father approach. Sam's hands were bandaged, and his clothes were scorched. As Sam walked toward us, he realized Dan was looking at a man who resembled his long-dead brother, Hank. "I guess you've met. Hi, Jim. Have you come to collect Maggie? Is the portal open again?"

"Hello, Sam. Yes. Maggie is needed in the future. Her husband was alive, but we weren't sure whether a mountain lion had attacked her or if she'd time traveled. Of course, there are only a handful of us who know that time travel is a possibility. I should take her now. The weather is fine on our side, but we've sustained several tremors since the first earthquake, and I want to get her back before another rock slide could block the pool."

Becky finally asked about Lauren after making sure they were still alone. Jim smiled. "Due in six months. Everything's great, and she's working like a trouper. We still live near here, and we couldn't be happier."

Becky hugged Jim and thanked him for coming. "You two must go now. Don't wait a minute longer. The rain will soon raise the water level of the creek on our end, which could trap you here for days." Becky hugged both Jim and me and returned to the horses. They were ready to decide on the severely burned gelding, but the others would hopefully live. Their personal horses were saved first and were not injured. I saw Penny in the distance. Next to Digger, she was a wonderful horse.

"Becky, I don't know what to say. You're an incredible woman. I can see the reason you've chosen to stay. I'm sorry to leave you with all this, but my husband and Luke need me. Who am I kidding? I need them."

Sam laughed. "June is always a good time to visit. We spend it up at Hank Heaven. The weather is usually pleasant, and the water is nice. So nice to meet you, Maggot." He made everyone laugh. I hugged them both before Jim and I walked back to the trail to Hank Heaven and the portal pool. I looked down and realized I was dressed in an 1800s riding outfit.

"Jim?" I pointed to my clothes, and he grinned.

"Your choice, Maggie. I buried your clothes along the creek. No one will be there. The entire trail to Miner's Meadow is closed. I don't know when it will reopen. Rich is in the process of working on other repairs in town."

Dan said to take the outfit because Jenny had more than enough clothes. "She won't miss it, but we'll miss you, Miss Maggot. Safe travels."

Since there were no saddles, we traveled by foot. Jim hugged me when we were out of sight of the ranch hands. "Thank God, Maggie. Colin's beside himself with worry."

Chapter 49

We arrived at the portal pool before noon. The water was still calm, and the clarity was perfect. Jim pointed to the exact spot where we'd already unsuccessfully tried several times.

"Lauren and I like to hold hands, so we aren't separated. You ready?" Jim took my hand.

"Your clothes are torn. Is that because of the time travel?"

Jim looked down. "No, that's from catching them on one machine still down at the pool. With everything that's happening in the Tahoe area, I couldn't ask Rich to come up to move a few boulders, so I did it myself."

"You did? Boy, Lauren is lucky to have you." *A total renaissance man.*

"Yeah, when you're a horse vet, it helps to know someone who drives a backhoe. Lauren mentioned that was what attracted her to Rich before she knew he was gay. I figure I needed to meet that need in her life and several months ago, Rich taught me the finer art of driving heavy machinery. Ready?"

"I hate leaving them in so much strife, but yes. I need to get back to Colin and Luke. Let's go swimming."

We held hands, and he said, "On three."

Once again, I was shocked by the cold. It was still overcast, and I swear the water was ten degrees colder. When we emerged, the sun was shining, and the water level was higher because of the redirection in water flow from the many granite boulders that had fallen down from above. I noticed a remnant of the old barricade where Becky's commemorative plaque had been drilled into the cliff face. Several large vehicles looked like I remembered them when I fell in the water and crossed into the past.

I was on the other side of time. I knew it was my time. *Welcome to the future.* I recalled Hannah's class assignment. It was summer and, with the fire at the Cattle Creek Ranch, I wondered if she would ever present this assignment to her teacher, or worse yet, her class. The paper was too close to the truth.

We changed our clothes and buried my riding outfit. Jim took my hand as we climbed along the initial path down by the creek. Progress was slow. We finally walked past the cliff face and began our climb up to the main trail. The slippery shale made the ascent difficult. Jim pulled me up, and we eventually saw the truck. *Oh, to sit down.* The parking lot had a locked gate. Jim had Rich's key.

I commented, "Nice to have friends in high places."

"Thankfully, Rich and Dirk have a puppy with issues." Jim and I started for Reno. When we were down in the valley, he called Lauren to say that he had the goods and was headed for the hospital. She said she would meet us there. "Beware. The press is out in the hospital's foyer. Remember the access door we used when Rocky was a patient?"

Jim nodded. "Good idea."

I closed my eyes as we drove into the desert. "Any major damage from the earthquake? Any deaths?"

"There were three, but one was just found." Jim stared at me.

"Shite. I was on the casualty list? Should we call someone? Have they searched for my body?"

"I was kidding. Well, not really. You were listed, but they thought you had been attacked by another mountain lion. With all the damage, they didn't look for you. Since Colin doesn't know we found you yet, let's reunite the two of you before we tell the world about your resurrection. I guess you don't want this to be a media frenzy. Correct?"

I nodded. "You know, if the world thought I was dead, maybe my other troubles might end, as well. I'll let Colin decide. I like your thinking, Jim Bob."

"Ha. That's what Lauren calls me."

I closed my eyes and once again, time was suspended. When I felt the truck cross a speed bump, I realized we must be in the hospital parking lot. We saw Lauren and Luke at the back door of the hospital. Luke hugged me as I slipped to the ground from Jim's truck. He tried not to cry. I held him and rocked back and forth inside the hospital door. He hummed "Walk Likea Man," which made me cry, as well. Lauren put her hand on his shoulder. "Hey, mate. Let's let Maggie see your grandpa."

"Oh, sure." Luke wiped his eyes and wanted me to follow him. There were no hospital personnel to see us. We entered an elevator, which stopped on the second floor. An older Hispanic man entered, and we traveled up to the fourth floor, where we walked down a long corridor.

We finally stopped, and Lauren looked through the window. She put her finger over her lips. "He's asleep." Jim placed his arm on Luke's shoulder. "How about we go grab a couple of cool ones and let your grandparents have a moment alone with each other?"

Luke looked at me, turned to Jim, and shrugged. "I guess. See you in a while, Mag Wheel."

"Love you, Lukey Boy. I will reinstate back tickling. You're no longer under punishment."

"Oh, man, Luke. Is there anything better?" Jim knew what we were talking about.

Luke glanced at Jim and shook his head. "Such a dweeb. Lauren, what do you see in the guy?"

"The moon, Luke. I see the moon, the stars, and the sky. March, mister. Let these two old codgers become reacquainted."

I quietly opened the door. Colin was pale. He had an intravenous line, while electrodes recorded his heart rate and oxygen levels. He didn't move when I bent over to peer into his bruised face. I couldn't see his lacerations below the blanket. I sat down in the chair to watch the monitor and his breathing. I wanted to hold his hand, but I wanted him to sleep.

Several minutes later, I realized I'd fallen asleep and was stirred by him touching my face. "Darlin' girl. Where've you been? You scared me."

"Went to get help, but I got lost. How are you, beautiful boy?" I stood and kissed him.

"Better now. I guess I'll cancel the Tinder account."

"Nice try, Collie. You can't lose me that easily." We both cried. Despite his stature, Colin was a crier. I was not. Well, that was until I felt I had something to lose.

"Darlin' girl, what happened?"

"Yeah. I guess we need to talk. You won't believe me."

"Try me."

"I don't know where to begin. Probably the best way to start is with your partner and coproducer, Alex Conrad."

"What's Alex got to do with it? He's been dead for a long time." When Colin reached for his water, I put the cup and straw up to his lips. He struggled to sit up. He'd aged in the last few days.

"Did you ever discuss the way Alex created the idea of the storyline for your television series?"

"He claimed he discovered an ancient trunk with several old journals from a rancher who'd come from the East and settled in the foothills and eastern slopes of the Sierras."

"Did you ever see the journals?"

Colin took another sip before he leaned back on his pillow. "I was in the process of finishing a movie at the time and simply took his word for it. I knew he had an interest in the Old West and the mythical cowboys-and-Indian stories. He also liked to mine for gold and silver. Why?"

"Those people were real. The Buchanans existed. Alex didn't make them up." I stared at Colin's face, which didn't register surprise.

"Darlin' girl, seriously. Where've you been?"

I hesitated. I wondered how he would take this. I knew Lauren and Jim would back me up, but Colin's life was precarious. *Would my admission cause him to have a heart attack?* He held my hand as he waited for my reply.

Just as I jumped so many times into the frigid water, I took the plunge. "The past, Collie, I've been to the past. I met the actual Buchanans, and I stayed with them. If someone had asked me about time travel a week ago, I figure you know what I'd have thought. It's real, beautiful boy. Becky Harper lives there. She married Sam Buchanan. I have a great deal more to tell you."

A buxom, blonde doctor, who then knocked on the door, wanted to know how Colin was feeling. "We noticed on your monitor at the nurse's station that your blood pressure went up. I think you need some rest. Your friend should probably go. We should change your bandages, anyway."

Colin stared at me. Seconds passed before he spoke, but it seemed like an eternity. What would his response be? Would he introduce me as his wife or ask me to leave?

Chapter 50

"Mel, I hate to admit it, but this is my loony wife. Despite what I told you about being single and on the market, I'm hitched to this nut job for life."

The doctor acted as if she was devastated. "Mr. Chandler, you sure know how to break a heart. My girlfriend will be happy, though. I told her I was going straight."

The doctor shook my hand. "So nice to see you're alive. You had this old geezer so worried." She turned to Colin and cocked her head. "Stay or go?"

"You can stay, Mel."

Mel smiled and shook her head as a nurse wheeled in a cart with bandages and bottles of saline. "It's always the oldies that give us the most lip."

"My bride is with me for life. You know, she's a vet. She has lots of experience with wounds. Maybe she could take over, and I can get the heck outta here?"

"Not today, Mr. Chandler. You have two more days of intravenous antibiotics."

"I'm Maggie. Don't listen to anything he says. I'm retired and, as much as I'd like to bust him out, I need about forty-eight hours of sleep. You can have him."

Luke, Lauren, and Jim knocked on the door and walked into the room. Luke hugged me again. "Where's your wallet, Grandpa?"

Colin shook his head. "Not again?"

"Yep, I'm back in the fold. Back tickling, here I come."

I smirked. "Collie, when are you going to learn about betting with your grandson? We can't afford to lose money like that. I need a shower. How about if I return to Lauren and Jim's place, grab some fresh clothes, and come back?" I turned to Mel. "Is it all right if I spend the night?"

"There'll be no"—she paused—"fooling around?" Mel turned toward Luke, whose face reddened and cringed.

"Doctor, I can assure you, we'll behave like nuns." I gave a single nod in Colin's direction.

Colin crossed himself. "Darlin' girl, don't promise anything over which you have no control. There are movies about wayward nuns."

Mel pointed to the ceiling, where a camera must hide in a globe. "FYI, we don't turn the camera on without notice. Consider this your notice, kids."

Lauren and Jim chuckled, and Jim placed Luke in a headlock. Lauren hugged Mel to thank her for everything. "Mel, if you want me to play this week, you'd better be nicer to our friends."

"You guys are friends?" *Small world.*

"Lauren's our pathetic right fielder." Mel rolled the tray with the bandages to Colin's bed.

"I got on base last week. That's a PB."

"You walked. I saw it, Maggie. You could have stolen second base, but you didn't even try." Luke shook his head.

"Luke, I thought we were a team. No more vet-truck days for you, little man. If you recall, we had an aftershock when the next batter was up." Lauren pinched Luke's ear. "Where do you plan to sleep tonight cause it ain't under my roof?"

Luke looked at Lauren, who was now beginning to show her advancing pregnancy. "On the other hand, are you sure you're expecting? I'd never guess by looking at you."

Jim and Lauren caught the drift. "Okay, Lukey, one night's lodging. No more talk about my softball skills. Pretending I'm not becoming a whale will work for only so long."

I turned to Colin. "I'll be back within the hour, cowboy. Do not leave Dodge."

I could tell his pain level had climbed. I kissed him, and we all left the room.

"We can try to sneak out the back way, but there are reporters at both entrances." Lauren cocked her head, waiting for a reply.

"Lead the way. We might as well get it over with. I think honesty is the best policy when you know subterfuge will catch up with you in the end."

On the way out of the hospital, the press was waiting. Several reporters held up their phones to take photos. "Is it true you're now Mrs. Chandler? How is Colin doing? Can you confirm it was a mountain lion, and you ran away to get help but got lost? How did you find your way back? Aren't you scheduled to testify in an upcoming trial with drug smugglers?" The questions continued. I was disappointed to hear a mention of the drug cartel. Our cover was blown out of the water. *We might as well go home.*

"I can neither confirm nor deny any of this. Mr. Chandler is recovering. Thank you all for your interest." I tucked my head and walked through the small group of reporters.

When we reached Jim's truck, Jim told us to sit in the back, where the tinted glass obliterated any view of Luke and me. He and Lauren were careful not to mention where I'd been for the last few days in Luke's presence. They told me about Mel and their other friend, Cary, who were both ER docs. "They were short staffed here, so Mel volunteered to work in Reno for a few weeks. It suited her because her new girlfriend lived in Reno."

Jim had to return to work. We dropped Luke and Jim off at the clinic and headed for home. When Lauren and I were finally alone, Lauren turned to me. "On a scale of one to ten."

I interrupted her. "Were you about to ask how mad I am that you didn't tell me about your double life?"

"Well, something like that. Seriously, how are they?"

"Who are you referring to?" *Just a little test to make sure I didn't dream it all up.*

"My mom and Sam? Are they healthy? Did Dan and Jenny have another baby? They had three the last time I was there. Is there another one on the way? How's Hannah?"

I didn't say anything for several seconds, and I shook my head. "Everyone's fine. Your mother and Sam are ageless. Jenny has a new little boy, who's been named after Sam. Hannah is quite the stunner. She wrote a story about the future for a class assignment. Becky and Sam asked about you. Why the hell didn't you tell me? Never mind, I know the reason. The whole idea is ridiculous. I told them you weren't coming this summer, and they were happy that you must be with child. Do you know what your father has found?" I finally stopped my rant.

"No, what did my father find?" She turned into the driveway.

"He and your mom, I mean Sherry, found your mother's wedding ring in a museum associated with Gettysburg. He didn't want to upset you, but he mentioned that discovering the ring, as well as an unlikely picture of your mother attending the injured in a Gettysburg hospital, tipped him over the edge and possibly caused his heart attack."

"What would you have done if you were me?" Lauren attempted to defend herself.

I considered this question and shrugged. "I would have done exactly what you've done. Do you have to go back to work? I want to shower and dress. Can you take me back to the hospital?"

"Sure, but may I take a baby nap? This pregnancy is killing me. You've been there. When do you catch up on your sleep?"

"I think I caught up when the youngest was about thirteen, but when they received their driver's licenses, there was another kind of sleep deprivation. Would you like me to wake you up in an hour?"

"Or three?" Lauren went to her room and closed the door. I was about to step into the bathroom when Lauren stuck her head out of her bedroom. "Going back?"

"I don't plan to, but now that I know about your mother and her life, I don't know."

"You tell Collie?" Lauren held her abdomen and stretched her back.

"Briefly. He's pretty drugged up. I'm sure I could deny the conversation."

"Maybe." Her voice sounded doubtful.

I filled the bathtub, and after a minute, I was asleep as well. My nap was short, and the cooling water in the bathtub roused me. I forgot to ask her if Rich knew about the portal pool.

Chapter 51

I let Lauren sleep for an extra thirty minutes. She was on her feet instantly when she woke up. "Let's ride, cowgirl. I still have to see a man about a horse."

Lauren discussed her current cases with me, along with her plans to take the last six weeks off before the birth. She wanted to return to work as soon as possible. I told her even if I wanted to stop working after my first one, we needed the money. I had no options but to work throughout my pregnancies. It suited me, anyway. My ex was a horrible husband, yet he was a good father in the early days.

As we pulled into the parking lot of the hospital, we noticed three sheriff's vehicles parked at the front. Lauren drove to the back again, and no reporters were present this time around. She dropped me, and I quickly entered the hospital. Colin's doctor, Mel, was on her way out.

"Hi, Maggie. I'm glad to catch up with you. Your husband asked me to give you an update. The wounds are all healing nicely. His vitals are good, and we even helped him to the bathroom. Are you certain about his age? I swear those wounds would have killed someone half his age."

I was so relieved. I turned and clenched my fists. Mel put her hand on my shoulder. "Hey, he's going to be fine. I'm so sorry for what you went through. How did you find your way back? You must have been scared to death."

"You can't imagine what I went through. I can't thank you enough. The epicenter of the earthquake must have been close to where we stayed. I still haven't been told when he was picked up."

"We think it was the day after his injury. He was vague about when you'd gone for help. He said you'd left, but that was all. He kept asking for you, but he was confused. We can't believe he survived."

"Thanks again. We have some problems back home. However, we'd planned to come out anyway for a wedding. I thought nothing like this would happen. Hopefully, we'll be out of your way in a few days."

"Maggie, your husband is delightful. He's such a gentleman and never a bother. His only worry during the last few days was you." She opened the back door and held up a finger. "Remind him the monitoring camera is on tonight in case he gets frisky." She left without turning back to see me shake my head.

Colin was reading a paper when I arrived. He set it down, smiled, and patted the side of the bed. "Come here, darlin' girl. I want to hear more. I'm hoping it's true, but tell me, did you fall and possibly hit your head?"

I expected such a response and reaction. I considered lying and admitting I had, and that I was confused, but I was convinced Lauren and Jim would back me up. "I wish I could say I concocted it, but I can't. I saw Becky. I met the real Sam Buchanan. You're twins. Alex found cast members who were exactly like the real people I met. Lauren knows. She and Jim have been there."

Colin lay back, and I lowered the bed. He held my hand, and I began my story. I wasn't sure when he'd stopped listening and had fallen asleep, but it was dark outside. I closed the drapes on the window and moved to a recliner. Nurses who entered the room interrupted my sleep several times that night. The lights and the occasional beeping from the machines awakened me a few more times, but I fitfully slept. I woke when a tray was brought to the room with Colin's breakfast.

I was instantly famished, since I had skipped dinner. I wanted coffee, which reminded me of the coffee that Gee Ling served. Even hospital coffee was better than what the Buchanans drank.

I assisted Colin with his food and helped him walk to the bathroom. A new doctor entered. He was a Middle Eastern or Indian man with a confident, winning smile. "Ah, Mr. Chandler. I see your wife has been found. You must be overjoyed."

He placed his hand on Colin's arm and squeezed it. "Sit up, please. I want to auscultate your chest."

He introduced himself as Dhanesh. "Many people call me Dr. D."

"That's your first name? Is everyone here on a first-name basis?"

"Maggie, Dhanesh is my primary-care doctor. His last name is Vachin. He writes books, as well. He's read me part of the book he's currently writing. He's pretty good."

"Mr. Colin, I'm good at putting you to sleep. Let's be truthful. Very nice to meet you, but today is my last day in Reno. I will fly to Chicago tomorrow to attend a conference on trauma. Then I fly to India to see my father, who is ailing."

Colin thanked him for his help and asked him to send him the book when it was published. "Maybe it will inspire my wife to resume her writing career."

The antibiotics started as a slow intravenous drip. Once again, Colin patted the bed and wanted me to sit with him.

When we were finally alone, he whispered, "Tell me more, darlin'. What is it like on the other side of time? Start from when you arrived on the other side. You said you fell in the creek below the rockfall where Becky Harper and the other woman died? I think I met the older woman once in the drugstore. She was a bit of a character. Platinum blonde and a take- no-nonsense attitude."

I began from the time I rose from the freezing water, lost the trail, and couldn't find the parking lot. I explained the signs pointing to Virginia City or the Cattle Creek Ranch. "Collie, there's an actual ranch with the exact name of the one in your television series. The Cattle Creek Ranch exists. I mean, it existed."

Colin smiled, reclined his bed, and folded his hands on his abdomen as I continued. I described the encounter with the people in Virginia City, the hospital staff, and the sheriff's office. "Again, they're all doppelgangers, Collie."

When he didn't comment, I related my introduction to Danny Buchanan. I said he has the exact features of the actor who played him in real life. I laughed. "What the hell is real, anyway?"

I recounted the ride from Virginia City to Miner's Meadow, or Hank Heaven, and my shock when I met the actual Sam Buchanan. "Collie, he's so similar. His smell is different from yours, but he's your twin."

I looked over at Colin, who was asleep. I quietly left the room in search of food and met Jim and Luke in the hallway. Luke told me about attending a calving with Lauren and performing a cruciate repair with Jim. He was in heaven. He looked inside Colin's room and closed the door. "Are you sure he's going to be okay?" I could tell Luke was frightened.

"No one lives forever, but I don't think your grandfather will kark it this time. He's counting on fishing with you one more time, Lukey. He's sleeping. Wake him at your peril."

Luke was visibly relieved. Jim said he would take Luke back to the clinic and they would return tonight. "Any word on when they'll release him?"

"Maybe tomorrow. Do you mind if we hang out at your place for a few days before we head home?"

"We'd be offended if you didn't. Lauren's keen to catch up on things." Jim stared at Luke. "See you later."

I hugged Luke and smelled him. "Don't come back without taking a shower, Lukey Boy."

Jim smelled his armpit. "Yeah, mate. She may have a point."

I went to the cafeteria, where I saw Dr. Vachin. I waved to him and ordered toast and cereal. The woman behind the counter asked if I was Colin Chandler's wife. She'd seen me leave the hospital the previous evening on the local television station. She asked how he was and wanted me to convey her best wishes.

"Come up to tell him yourself. He loves to hear from fans. He'd be honored."

"Oh, I couldn't. It's against hospital policy," but she seemed so pleased to receive the invitation. I shrugged.

Dr. Vachin motioned for me to join him. "I think your husband said you are an author, too. Do you have a pen name?"

"My books are light, cozy mysteries. My pen name is Maggie Kincaid. Tell me more about your books."

"I write fiction as you do. I write about someone like me who grows up in India to become a doctor. It's nearly autobiographical, though the protagonist is a woman."

"I see why Colin is interested. It sounds like yours will be a best seller. I hope your father lives long enough to see it published."

"Yes, thank you. According to your husband, your life would make a splendid adventure story for a book. He describes it as an adventure and romance story combined into one."

"An old-lady horse vet who likes to fish and ride horses. I don't think so, but maybe I'll write it someday."

Dr. Vachin stood and picked up his tray. "I'll be back with my family, eating my family's food next week."

"I'll bet your mother is a wonderful cook."

"My mother never cooked a meal in her life. She died several years ago. We have servants who still cook the meals."

"Half your luck." Then I remembered Mrs. Gillard. "We must respect the kitchen goddesses in our lives."

Chapter 52

I returned to Colin's room, and he was awake again. "I will chain you to the bed, Maggot. I hate waking up alone."

"Yeah, so do I. How're you feeling? What do they have you on for pain control?"

"I don't remember, but I certainly know when it's time to have more. Can you get me some water? You know I hate bottled water, but the water here is horrible."

"I think I saw a dispenser downstairs. I'll be back in a jiff."

Several reporters milled about in the lobby. I was surprised they could stay, but maybe it wasn't Colin they were interested in. Maybe it was another performer from the casino shows. I didn't want to ask in case I was wrong. When I spied the water-bottle dispenser, I realized I did not have any money or a credit card. *Damn.*

A woman whom I suspected was a reporter saw me search my pockets. "It's on me." She put the cash into the slot and down came a plastic water bottle.

"Oh, thank you." The bottle was jammed, but I retrieved it after I banged on the front of the dispenser, which attracted the attention of the other reporters.

"Do you mind if I ask you a quick question?" The middle-aged woman wore enough makeup to hide the Grand Canyon.

"Yes, I mean no. Yes, I dye my hair, and no, I've not had any plastic surgery."

She laughed. "How's the patient? I guess you know he's receiving a lot of attention. Everyone's pulling for him."

"He's doing well. I'll pass it on. Thanks again." I turned to go.

"I'm Connie Barret from WFCD in Sacramento. May I take your picture?"

"Connie, I normally wouldn't mind, but it's not a good time right now." I didn't want to elaborate.

"Are you trying to lie low because of the pending court cases with the drug cartel? We heard they're not the fun-loving guys that Charlie McLeod said they are. Are you in fear for your life? I won't report it, and you can trust me. I heard that they've organized a hit on you. I'm surprised you don't have protection. They say you're the one person who can ID the individuals and may have more insight into the various roles of some of the kingpins. Are you afraid?"

"Connie, where did you get this info?" I was alarmed by her knowledge. I stared at her, and she didn't blink. She simply awaited my reply.

When I was about to leave, she admitted, "I have my sources. I heard you received threatening messages on your wedding day. That's why you're up here, and you and your husband are hiding out."

What were her sources? She knew far more than anyone outside the FBI. "I'd better go." While I turned to walk away, Connie said in a loud voice the other reporters could hear. "Thanks again for the exclusive, and happy to hear Colin Chandler will leave the hospital today."

It was bullshit and bravado, but she certainly attracted the attention of everyone in the foyer, and she got mine, too.

If Colin was leaving, it was news to me. He was supposed to leave the following day at the earliest. I didn't respond to either confirm or deny her statement. Was it common knowledge that I might be in danger? When I arrived in the hospital room, Doug Cameron, and Whit Williams stood beside Colin's bed.

"Hey, what's going on?" I was so relieved to see Colin's bodyguards.

"Our plans have changed, darlin'. We're blowing this joint. Remind me not to become involved with someone who is the target of a drug cartel with high-end connections to government institutions."

Doug came around to the other side of the bed as Dr. Vachin entered the room. "Pack your bags, Maggie. We're headed to..." But he stopped, looked around, and put his finger to his lips.

I knew enough not to ask. Alarm bells were ringing in my ears. *Not again.*

"Lead the way, gentlemen. Do we need to get Luke?"

"In due time. We think he's safe. Jim's got it in hand." I was dubious, but these men were professionals. I had to trust them.

"A reporter downstairs said you were leaving today. She asked about a hit the cartel has ordered on me. Do you guys know about this?"

Colin took my hand. "Some women are not worth it." He paused. "Then again."

The men all seemed to have the plan organized. Colin was told to lie flat, and his body was covered.

"Darlin' can you act at all?"

"You know I can't."

"For the sake of us all, I need you to act like a grieving widow. Can you do that?"

"Without laughing? You're asking a lot."

Colin looked at Whit, who shook his head and stared at the ceiling. "I was trying not to tell you. There was an incursion back at our ranch. Someone's shot Digger. We can't take any more chances. Just do your best."

My heart dropped to my pelvis. I was in shock. I nearly collapsed. Whit grabbed me and I sat down. "When? Is he okay?"

Whit looked at everyone. "Maggie, it was yesterday morning. I'm sorry. You were still missing, and Colin wanted me to come to the hospital. I guess the world knows about your resurrection. If the people in the foyer are here for Mr. Chandler, the cartel knows about your location. We need to wait awhile, so the news can get out. We're so sorry. If it's any comfort, it was a direct shot, and he didn't suffer."

Quite a commotion ensued outside the hospital room. I cried. I tried to hold it back, but I couldn't. Colin removed the sheet covering his face and joined me while the other men, including Dr. Vachin, politely looked away.

Dr. Vachin left the room and returned. "The announcement's been made. Colin Chandler is officially dead. It was an unexpected heart attack. You know, at his age.... The room will be guarded until the arrangements for his removal are completed." The medical-monitoring devices were removed from Colin and moved out of the room.

I sat next to Colin's bed and continued to cry. I loved that horse more than life. I hated myself for not being there and for not protecting him more. I hated Charlie McLeod and everything he represented.

After an hour, the sheet was placed back over Colin's head, and the bed was rolled from his room, down the corridor, onto an elevator, and out to a hall where the press was waiting. I was so nervous and searched the crowd. I realized I was a mess and, with little effort, I'm sure I looked the part of a grieving widow.

Colin was transferred onto a stretcher and into a hearse. I rode in the back, where Dr. Vachin joined me. Whit rode in the front seat, and we headed out of the hospital parking lot, where several cars followed us. The driver turned on the radio to find a news station. It wasn't a minute before the announcement of Colin's passing was broadcast. It suggested he was being transported with his grieving wife and grandson back to his ranch for a private burial.

It was apparent the driver was unaware Colin was alive. He drove to the airport and through a security gate, where the rest of the entourage could not follow. Even the driver helped lift Colin's body onto the airplane, waiting next to a private hangar. "I'm so sorry for your loss. He was a wonderful man, and he'll be missed. I never missed an episode of *Comstock*."

Dr. Vachin entered the airplane and, as the doors were closed, announced, "I will take care of Mr. Chandler for a few days. My plans for Chicago have been canceled." He searched under the sheet for Colin's wrist and smiled. He whispered, "A strong pulse. Maybe we should cancel the funeral arrangements."

Even in my grief, I grasped the humor. Jim and Luke sat in the seats next to the stretcher. Luke smiled and proudly said, "I cried my eyes out, Maggie. I can become an actor if I flunk out of vet school."

He obviously hadn't heard about Digger or the hit on me. I'd wait until we were airborne before I'd tell him. "Jim, will you accompany us? Shouldn't you stay with Lauren?"

"No, I want to help you and Collie." Jim took my hand.

Doug and Whit claimed the pilot and copilot seats. It seemed like an hour before we could leave, but when we finally were able to taxi down the runway, Colin leaned over. Luke and his grandfather high-fived each other. They were far too jovial, considering Digger's demise.

Colin turned to me and sat up. "Thank God for those pain pills." He was obviously better than he'd been in days. I gave him the look and tilted my head in Luke's direction. I am certain he realized I was referring to the news about Digger.

"Luke, your grandfather has some bad news."

Colin searched the cabin. "I guess there's no way to escape. Luke, I'd suggest you cover your ears. I have some news that may cause a murder or possibly the foulest language you've ever heard."

Luke sat forward in his seat. "Whose murder, Grandpa?"

"Mine." He turned to me. "Darlin' girl, I hated to do it, but I needed to do some acting coaching. Don't worry. It's all good news. Digger's not dead. I said that to make sure you looked like a grieving widow." I tried to hit him, but Jim caught my arm.

"You bastard. You charming, sneaky bastard. No back tickling for either of you. You'll be lucky if you're even allowed in the matrimonial bed, in the unlikely event you live another day. God damn you all."

Jim raised his hands. "Hey, Luke and I are innocent. Don't blame us."

Doug and Whit high-fived each other. "Don't ya love it when a plan comes together?"

The plane made a sharp turn, and we were soon on the ground in a remote area of the Sierras. "Anyone want to tell me what's going on?"

Chapter 53

The plane descended to a rough landing strip in a small valley north of Reno. The plane taxied only a few yards and turned at the end of the runway, where Doug turned off the engine. Everyone seemed to know what was happening. They all exited the plane, which left only Colin and me.

"Maggie, Margaret, Magpie, Maggot, darlin', we need to talk." Colin strained to sit up. I tried to help him, but he decided to just give up. This journey had taken its toll on him. "When I was brought to the hospital, I was less than discreet. I was worried sick about you. They sent out an alert, and I offered a reward for your return. I figure this alerted the bad guys, and it certainly caught the FBI's attention. An agent was at my bedside in a flash. She explained credible sources said a hit had been organized on you, and you were in extreme danger.

"When Lauren called to say Jim had located you and you were on your way to the hospital, she told me the truth about where they thought you'd been. They felt I knew about this from Alex Conrad. They didn't know I was unaware of the time travel bullshit."

Bullshit? It wasn't like Colin to swear, but this was a desperate situation.

"I pretended to not know anything about the transportation through the water in the creek. I think you can understand."

"And then some." I took a towel, wet it, and wiped Colin's brow. "Who else knows? Does Luke understand?"

"No, and I don't want him to know. The only people who are aware of where you've been are Lauren, Jim, you, and me."

"Will you tell Luke? Why are we stopping?"

Colin took my hand. "I must ask you to be brave. The FBI wants to put you in witness protection. The trial isn't until September. I have doubts about their ability to keep you safe. I talked to Jim at length, and we both decided the best place for you isn't here. You know, I'm not in any shape to travel, but if you go back to the past, as soon as I'm able, I'll join you. Will you do that for me, darlin' girl?"

I considered it for a few seconds. "No. How can we protect Luke and you? We all stay together, or not at all."

"If I promise to join you within the month, will you go?"

"Luke will return here next week after we get you sorted. He'll stay with Jim and Lauren, but for now, he's coming back with me. After all, we have a pending funeral. When I get back, I'll contact the kids. They'll wonder where you are, and I'll say you're with me in seclusion. I will stay up at our private cabin. No one, not even Mrs. Gillard, will know. We both realize Luke will carry secrets to his grave. He's already aware of the plan. He wants to know where you'll be, but he's agreed to do what I tell him. We'll be separated for a few weeks until I'm able to join you. Please?"

It was so painful to even think of a separation. "You know life is perilous in the 1800s. I may be killed, anyway. I haven't told you about all that happened."

"So, it's a yes?" I could tell Colin was on the verge of tears. I wiped his eyes.

"How do I know if those are actual tears or acting?"

"You don't, and you never will. But you must understand what a sacrifice this is for me and how much I love you. If I was sure I could protect you, I'd never suggest this plan, but these men are powerful, and they have people in high places. Thank you, darlin', thank you. The tears are real. It will kill me to be apart. Don't fall in love with that old geezer, Sam Buchanan, before I get there."

"It's not him you have to worry about. I always had a thing for the sheriff."

I leaned out the door of the plane. "I think we're ready." I went to Luke. "See you in a few weeks. Take care of your grandfather for me, and be kind to Mrs. G. If she's not there when I get back, you'd better learn to cook."

"I love you, too, Grandma." Luke had tears, and he hugged me.

"I'll let the 'Grandma' thing go this time. Be safe. Take care of Baxter and Digger. Love you, Lukey Boy."

"Can we have back tickling when you return?"

"Will you behave, do what everyone says, and protect your grandfather for me?"

"Yep."

"Okay."

Luke turned to Colin and held out his hand.

"Again?" I smiled.

Colin shrugged. Dr. Vachin administered something in his intravenous catheter. I mouthed 'thank you' and turned to Jim, who remained by my side. Doug and Whit returned to their seats. I saw a cloud of dust approaching us. I recognized Jim's truck with Lauren in the driver's seat.

We watched the plane rise from the runway. Lauren jumped out of the driver's seat and put her arm around me. "Ready?"

"Yeah, I guess. Want me to take anything back?"

"An ultrasound picture of the baby, and I have some flies for Mom and Sam. I hope they match the hatch."

***

Four hours later, I emerged from the creek. I searched but found no heavy equipment. I was on the other side of time.

It took me a few hours to get to the ranch. The chaos I'd left a few days earlier was reduced to a well-organized throng of men already building a new and larger barn. I noticed two burned horses in a small paddock next to the metal remnants of the old barn. I guessed the other one had been shot.

Merv Little waved and greeted me. "Glad you're back, Mrs. Chandler. Becky will be so pleased to see you." The boss is in the house.

I knocked on the door. Gee Ling answered and greeted me like a family member. "Gee Ling so glad to see Missy again. Come in, come in." He turned to announce my arrival. Both Sam and Hannah greeted me with hugs.

"Becky's out at her infirmary. She's attending to the men burned in the fire. She should be back," but before Sam could finish his words, Becky rushed into the house.

She blinked and stood while she studied me. With no other welcoming hugs, she grinned and hummed the *Comstock* theme music. I joined her.

Sam cocked his head, but knowing Hannah was not aware of the time travel concept, he just shook his head. "What's the world coming to?"

I stared at Hannah, remembering her story about the future. *You would not believe me if I told you.*

The next chapter in the life of Dr. Maggie Kincaid Chandler will be featured in The Travels of Dr. Rebecca Harper. Book 5. This will be the marriage of the two book series.

Acknowledgements

Once again, I have my core beta readers to thank. They include Dr. Sharon Spier, Candace Fox, Mimi Schrumpf. I would like to thank Jasmine Centenera and her family for their permission to use the story of their dear pony in the book. The input of so many peripheral people in my life that help with the production of this and other books includes April Cox for help in marketing, Aubery Clark for my amazing webpage, and especially Fiona Heysen for her cover art.

Elizabeth Woolsey DVM

Elizabeth Woolsey DVM grew up in postwar California. Sure she was the daughter of Roy Rogers, she spent her youth emulating him. Sadly, DNA evidence has proved her wrong. Thus, she followed in her other father's footsteps into equine veterinary medicine. 

She subsequently migrated to Australia, where she practiced near Adelaide, South Australia, until her retirement in December 2020. She began writing about her experiences as a horse vet and published her first book, Horse Doctor An American Vet's Life Down Under in 2005. A few years before her father's death, she discovered a treasure trove of personal and historically significant letters. She knew this would make a great book not only for her family but also for WWII enthusiasts. She published Jack's War, Letters to Home from an American WII Navigator in 2015. While veterinary medicine has been her passion, fly-fishing, horseback riding, and writing occupy her leisure time. Her new books include fictional stories about veterinarians in various aspects of practice and their personal lives. She now resides in North Georgia, where she follows her passions.

She loves to hear from readers! **ewoolseydvm@gmail.com**

You can read more about Elizabeth https://elizabethwoolsey.com/ https://amzn.to/3dPAoGc

Find me on Facebook https://www.facebook.com/woolseyelizabeth/

Preview

A Man's Worth

One more ring, and I knew my call would go to voice mail. My sister finally answered. "What?"

"Hey, it's me, your favorite sister." Crap, I didn't think of the time zone. "Sorry, did I wake you up?"

"No. Oh hell, who am I kidding? Of course you did. Unless Mom or Dad lied, you're my only sister. Call back in an hour."

She's pissed. Not a great way to ask for a favor. "Okay, but I need a ride from the airport tomorrow. I'll text you the details later."

"Is it over? Are you finally coming back?" I heard the disdain in her voice.

"Yeah, go back to bed. We can talk later."

"I'll call you when I'm awake." Control was my sister's weapon of choice. I accepted it and her need to one-up me on every occasion.

I packed my bags and prepared to leave his house. His children will arrive tomorrow for the funeral, and I will be gone before they come. The funeral will only be for his children. I wasn't invited. It didn't matter. We said our goodbyes days ago before he slipped into a coma.

I knew my sister was calling when the phone rang three hours later. No one else would call me at this hour. "What time?"

"Ten-thirty. I'll call you when the plane lands."

"Two years, Hayles. I hope he was worth it."

Two years earlier: "Hayley? Is that you?" There was no mistaking the voice. It was my boss from over twenty years ago.

"Hey, Doc. How are you? I haven't heard from you in how many years?"

"I called you last Christmas. Don't you remember?" Doc's voice was as strong as ever.

"Uh, no. Must have been one of your other girlfriends."

He laughed. "I have a proposition for you. How would you like to come and work for me?"

"Gee, I'm honored, but I've retired. I thought you had as well."

Doc hired me straight out of school to work in his equine vet clinic. I worked for him for ten years until I met my husband and moved to

Georgia, where I lived and worked until I retired. Doc was fifteen years older than me and had retired only a few years ago.

"Are you still married to that idiot?" Typical and to the point, my former boss is laying it on the line.

"No, I divorced the idiot twenty years ago. How about you? How's Myrna?"

"Off with the fairies. I've got her in a home. I tried to keep her here, but the damn kids took her away. It got to be a bit much. I'll tell you about it when you get here."

"I'm sorry, I had no idea." I felt profound sorrow for the man. I knew how much he loved her. Still, what was my role in his plan?

"Life goes on, Hayley. I've adjusted."

I wasn't convinced. "Doc, I can't just come out at the drop of a hat. I have a life. I have kids and grandkids."

"Hayley, don't lie to me. Your kids are no more family than mine. I talked to Ted the other day. He says you're sitting on your ass all day. I need help with a project. You're the one who can help me. Do you need money for a plane ticket?"

"You talked to Ted? How is he? The last time I saw Ted was at his funeral. You do know he died a few years ago, don't you?"

Doc snorted. "Bullshit. Are you sure about Ted Gregory? Damn, no one told me. Now, get your sorry ass and your typewriter out here. We can't waste any time."

"Doc, let me think about it. What kind of help?" *Was this man losing his marbles?* Ted worked with me when I began my career at Doc's clinic. We had a brief fling, and then he left the practice and started a vet clinic in Arizona.

Doc didn't wait for a reply. The phone went dead. What did he want? Maybe he's writing something and needs help? Why was I even considering this? I loved my life. I wrote articles for veterinary journals and novels, fished, and... But what was the "and" these days? The kids had moved to Texas to join one of the many burgeoning tech companies. We talked once a week. My dog, Little Miss Bossy Boots, died three months ago. I hadn't even contemplated replacing her. I wanted some time to travel without worrying about a dog.

I texted him. *How long and how soon?*

Now, and I don't know but not long, he responded.

I called the vacation rental company I had used before and arranged to lease my house for a month. I'd done it many times. It was easy. My personal possessions could be put into one room which I could lock. I called the airline and made reservations.

I made my final text for the day. *Arrival ten-forty-five, Thursday.*

I sat down and made a list of what I needed to do before I left and went down to the creek to fish one more time. The water was getting hot, and fishing in my stream would end soon. It was too stressful on my trout when the oxygen levels dropped in the heat. At least I could fish in Doc's lake.

***

I opened my phone as I landed. Doc had sent a text message.

Look for a red Ford F-250 and a very handsome driver. I'll be behind it in the next red truck.

I laughed. He still had a great sense of humor. I hadn't seen him in twenty years, but he was good-looking in his youth. *Weren't we all?*

I saw a red F-250 and waved. The driver signaled back and then proceeded to drive on past. It wasn't him, and I felt foolish. This was like high school when I had a crush on Darren McMasters and waved to him when he smiled at me. Thankfully, Darren didn't notice me as he smiled at Candy Petersen standing behind me.

Several minutes later, a second older red truck pulled up. Doc appeared pale and thin. I held out my thumb, hoisted my bag into the back seat of the dual cab, and climbed in. He reached over and kissed me. He smelled the same—Old Spice and cigars. There was a cigar butt in the ashtray.

I couldn't help myself. "You know those things will kill you."

"Too late. I'm on my way out but not from smoking." He stared straight ahead, as many elderly drivers do.

Shocked, I glanced at him and then looked away. "I'm guessing you aren't joking."

"You guessed right—lymphoma. But that's not public knowledge. Only my doctor knows. You hungry?"

I was starving. "No, I can wait. Do we need to stop at the store before heading out?"

"That depends. You still a gin drinker and meat-eater?" He gripped the steering wheel like an older driver. Doc had aged.

"I don't eat as much meat as I used to, but I'm easy with whatever you want to eat." I glanced at him again. He was eighty-two by my reckoning and still appeared vigorous, but his hair had thinned, and his tan had faded. "You want to tell me why I'm here?"

"Can you wait until we get to the house? We're stopping at *the home,* so I can see the inmates. You'll have to stay in the truck. I can leave the AC on if you like. I'll only be a minute. I like to check up on her and make sure she's getting what she needs. You can't trust these people."

An hour later and an elevation rise enough to give me a nosebleed, we were in my old stomping grounds. The town was twice the size of what I remembered. The aged care home, Greenbriar, needed paint but appeared to be in reasonable shape. People came and went through the glass doors, and they seemed happy. *How could you tell, though?*

I rolled down the window. "I'm good. Stay as long as you want."

"It's the 'want' that's the killer. I never want to come here. They need to change the wedding vows. Till death or dementia do us part. I'll be quick. There's more. I'll explain later."

He stepped out of the truck, and I could see his unsure stride. We'd both aged, but we weren't ready for *the home*. I wasn't the young girl when we met over how many years ago? As he emerged from the facility, he shook his head. He climbed into the truck and, without a word, drove to a small diner.

"Last chance for a decent meal, kid." He smiled and placed his hand on the small of my back as he guided me through the restaurant's door.

"Hi, Doc." The greeter knew him and pointed to a booth. "Coffee?"

"Yes, please, Sal. This is Hayley. She's one of my former employees. She's here to help me with a project."

Sal acknowledged me. She cocked her head, waiting for me to give her my drink order.

Knowing I needed to maintain hydration at this elevation, I replied, "Just water, thanks."

We sat at a booth, and Doc folded his hands and leaned forward. "I usually get the breakfast special, but it's almost lunch, so have what you want. By the way, you look great."

"Thanks, and one small detail—why the hell am I here?"

The waitress arrived with coffee and water and asked if we were ready to order. "I'll have what Doc is having."

She smiled. "Easy done. It'll just be a sec." She turned to the counter and held up two fingers.

"I liked the book you wrote." He smiled and placed his hand on mine.

"Which one? I thought you were a classics kind of guy."

"The one about fishing. We can fish when we get to the house. I want to explain what I have in mind, and I need to show you something first. Do you mind waiting until after dinner?"

I was dubious. I felt there must be something he wasn't telling me. "All right. Have you fished lately?"

"No. That's part of the reason you're here. My kids don't like me fishing alone, and I promised Myrna that I would outlive her. It's a bit of a race to the end." He sighed and searched for Sal. "What's taking them so long?"

Our food came, we ate, Doc paid the bill and tip, and we drove into the hills and went in through a private gated entrance to his house. The gate was open and appeared to have been disabled.

"Jesus, it's magnificent. How long have you lived here?" The house was a single story with many-windowed rooms facing the lakeshore. The structure stood several feet above the waterline with a large veranda skirting the entire house. The modern and light theme carried from the living room into the kitchen. The clear, expansive view from the living room peered over the lake and the small floating dock anchored to the sandy shoreline. A separate three-bay garage sat behind the home.

He insisted on carrying my bag to my room. After placing it on the bed, he pointed to the dresser. "Yes, some have confused me with Jesus, but since I retired, I don't confuse anyone anymore. I built it shortly after you left. Myrna announced that if she was going to be a vet's widow, she wanted to live in a place where she was happy living alone. Get your fishing gear on, sweetheart. I have needs."

A kayak sat tethered to a nearby tree stump. Doc told me to get in, then he pushed it out over the water and joined me. He appeared to be strong, and I could see his mood lift. He indicated we were going to a cove down the way. A few other homes were along the lake, and a woman waved from her deck as we passed their house. Why did his family ask him not to fish alone?

We entered the cove, and Doc used his paddle to nudge me in the back. He had already selected flies for us to use. "You first, Hayles." I let out some line, and after two false casts, I let the fly land near the bank. The strike was immediate. That was how the afternoon went. After catching two fish, I watched Doc cast and land another good-sized trout.

"This lake is stocked. How about a trout dinner?"

"I won't say no." I glanced around. "Yep, the coast is clear. No purists around to admonish us for not releasing the little buggers."

We returned to the house, and Doc cleaned and placed the fish in the fridge.

"Power nap, old man. The time zone change is killing me."

Doc pointed to the recliner. "Knock yourself out."

"Pun intended and accepted. I'll only be a few minutes."

But I wasn't. An hour later, Doc gently shook my shoulder. "Rise and shine, sleeping beauty. Dinner is on the table. Red or white?"

"White, but don't open a bottle for me. You still a whiskey man?"

"Sit down and let an old man spoil you. You can start working it off tomorrow."

The dinner was delicious and actually appeared to be healthy. I knew the reason for my summons was coming. "Want to tell me why I'm here? I know you've always wanted to get me into the sack, but my guess is I'm here for another reason." *Oops, too much wine.* He never indicated he was anything but faithful to Myrna.

"Funny, but I did want to." He sighed. "You never showed me any indication. Well, that's in the past. I've asked you here for far more than..." Another pause. "I want you to write a book about me." We both knew he never had any interest in me or anyone other than Myrna. I sat up.

"The books I write are fiction. You want a biographer." This was a mistake. He brought me all the way here for something I could not do. *Damn!* My house had been rented for a month. Where the heck was I going to go? I had been so lucky to get a quick renter, but now I regretted that decision.

"You can write it. I read all your books. You talk my talk, and you've walked my walk. You're a vet, and you know what it's really like. You feel like I feel, and you've agonized just like I have over your life choices and decisions. Just write the damn book and stop making excuses. I should have given you more wine before I started this conversation."

"But you're famous. I'll bet several authors could write your story and would pay for the privilege. I think you need a man anyway."

"Hayles, we're a dying breed. We're the last of the old-school vets. The young ones don't understand. In ten years, we'll be gone, and those that follow will not know why we did what we did, and someone will write about us as they write about native Americans with their personal slant on the *whats* and *whys*. Nope, I want you to write it. You're the one person who I can trust. You talk like I talk, and you think Iike I think."

He picked up a cigar and studied it for a minute. "I'm not long for this world, and I want to leave a legacy. How about if I promise not to smoke a cigar ever again?"

"Do you promise to wear the Old Spice, though?"

"Scouts honor, and I'll pay you. Name your price."

"I'll let you know tomorrow. I want to walk down to the lake before I retire. Is it safe?"

He handed me a can of bear spray.

"Thanks." I opened the front door leading to the veranda.

"Lock the door when you return, sweetheart. There are worse things than bears around these days."

"Doc, how much time have we got?" He knew what I was asking.

"Piece of string, but my oncologist says a few months at best. I finished the last of the chemo two weeks ago."

"Sweet dreams, Doc."